T0306276

LEAH on the OFFBEAT

by Becky Albertalli

BALZER + BRAY

An Imprint of HarperCollins*Publishers*

For the readers who knew something was up, even when I didn't

Balzer + Bray is an imprint of HarperCollins Publishers.

Leah on the Offbeat

www.epicreads.com

Library of Congress Control Number: 2017934758

ISBN 978-0-06-264381-0

Typography by Torborg Davern

19 20 21 22 23 PC/LSCH 10 9 8 7 6 5 4 3

❖

First paperback edition, 2019

ALSO BY BECKY ALBERTALLI

Simon vs. the Homo Sapiens Agenda

William C. Morris YA Debut Award Winner

National Book Award Longlist

"Worthy of *Fault in Our Stars*–level obsession."—*Entertainment Weekly*

"The love child of John Green and Rainbow Rowell."—*Teen Vogue*

★ "Funny, moving, and emotionally wise."
—*Kirkus Reviews* (starred review)

★ "Readers will fall madly in love with Simon."
—*Publishers Weekly* (starred review)

"I am so in love with this book."—Nina LaCour, Printz Award–winning author of *We Are Okay*

The Upside of Unrequited

Seventeen Magazine Best Book

"While first kisses, first loves, and even first sexual experiences have all been dealt with in some form or another, she tackles these big milestones head-on and with aplomb. This, coupled with her exploration of Molly's worries about her own weight, results in a character that is not only immensely relatable but also feels real—whether you've had 26 crushes or not."—*Entertainment Weekly*

"I have such a crush on this book! Not only is this one a must-read, but it's a must-reread."—Julie Murphy, *New York Times* bestselling author of *Dumplin'*

"Heart-fluttering, honest, and hilarious. I can't stop hugging this book."
—Stephanie Perkins, *New York Times* bestselling author of *Anna and the French Kiss*

★ "A fresh, honest, inclusive look at dating, families, and friendship."
—*SLJ* (starred review)

Also by Becky Albertalli

Simon vs. the Homo Sapiens Agenda

The Upside of Unrequited

What If It's Us (with Adam Silvera)

1

I DON'T MEAN TO BE dramatic, but God save me from Morgan picking our set list. That girl is a suburban dad's midlife crisis in a high school senior's body.

Case in point: she's kneeling on the floor, using the keyboard stool as a desk, and every title on her list is a mediocre classic rock song. I'm a very tolerant person, but as an American, a musician, and a self-respecting human being, it is both my duty and my privilege to blanket veto that shit.

I lean forward on my stool to peer over her shoulder. "No Bon Jovi. No Journey."

"Wait, seriously?" says Morgan. "People love 'Don't Stop Believin'.'"

"People love meth. Should we start doing meth?"

Anna raises her eyebrows. "Leah, did you just—"

"Did I just compare 'Don't Stop Believin'' to meth?" I shrug. "Why, yes. Yes I did."

Anna and Morgan exchange a capital-L Look. It's a Look that says *here we go, she's about to dig her heels in.*

"I'm just saying. The song is a mess. The lyrics are bullshit." I give a little tap on the snare for emphasis.

"I like the lyrics," Anna says. "They're hopeful."

"It's not about whether they're hopeful. It's about the gross implausibility of a midnight train going, quote unquote, *anywhere.*"

They exchange another Look, this time with tiny shrugs. Translation: *she has a point.*

Translation of the translation: *Leah Catherine Burke is an actual genius, and we should never ever doubt her music taste.*

"I guess we shouldn't add anything new until Taylor and Nora are back," Morgan concedes. And she's right. School musical rehearsals have kept Taylor and Nora out of commission since January. And even though the rest of us have been meeting a few times a week, it sucks rehearsing without your singer and lead guitarist.

"Okay," Anna says. "Then I guess we're done here?"

"Done with rehearsal?"

Welp. I guess I should have shut up about Journey. Like, I get it. I'm white. I'm supposed to love shitty classic rock. But I kind of thought we were all enjoying this lively debate about music and meth. Maybe it went off the rails somewhere, though, because now Morgan's putting the keyboard away and Anna's texting her mom to pick her up. I guess that's game over.

My mom won't be here for another twenty minutes, so I hang around the music room even after they leave. I don't really mind. It's actually nice to drum alone. I let my sticks take the lead, from the bass to the snare and again and again. Some fills on the toms. Some *chhh chhh chhh* on the hi-hat, and then the crash.

Crash.

Crash.

And another.

I don't even hear my phone buzzing until it pings with a voice mail. It's obviously my mom. She always calls, only texts as a last resort. You'd think she was fifty or a million years old, but she's thirty-five. I'm eighteen. Go ahead and do the math. I'm basically your resident fat Slytherin Rory Gilmore.

I don't listen to the voice mail, because Mom always texts me after—and sure enough, a moment later: So sorry to do this, sweetie. I'm swamped here—can you catch the bus today?

Sure, I write back.

You're the best. Kissy emoji.

Mom's boss is an unstoppable robot workaholic lawyer, so this happens a lot. It's either that, or she's on a date. It's not even funny, having a mom who gets more action than I do. Right now, she's seeing some guy named Wells. Like the plural of *well.*

He's bald and rich, with tiny little ears, and I think he's almost fifty. I met him once for thirty minutes, and he made six puns and said "oh, fudge" twice.

Anyway, I used to have a car, so it didn't matter as much—if I beat Mom home, I'd just let myself in through the garage. But Mom's car died last summer, so my car became her car, which means I get to ride home with thirty-five freshmen. Not that I'm bitter.

We're supposed to clear out of the music room by five, so I take apart the kit and carry it into the storage closet, drum by drum. I'm the only one who uses the school kit. Everyone else who plays has their own set in the finished basements of their personal mansions. My friend Nick has a customizable Yamaha DTX450K e-kit, and he *doesn't even drum*. I could never afford that in a billion years. But that's Shady Creek.

The late bus doesn't leave for another half hour, so I guess I'll be a theater groupie. No one ever cares if I wander into rehearsal, even though the show opens on Friday. Honestly, I crash rehearsal so often, I think people forget I'm not in the play. Most of my friends are—even Nick, who'd never auditioned for anything in his life until this. I'm pretty sure he only did it to spend time with his sickeningly adorable girlfriend. But since he's a true legend, he managed to snag the lead role.

I take the side hallway that leads directly backstage, and slip through the door. Naturally, the first person I see is the peanut himself, my number one bro, demolisher of Oreos: Simon Spier.

"Leah!" He's standing in the wings, half in costume, surrounded by dudes. No clue how Ms. Albright talked so many guys into auditioning this year. Simon shrugs away from them. "You're just in time for my song."

"I planned that."

"You did?"

"No."

"I hate you." He elbows me, and then hugs me. "No, I love you."

"I don't blame you."

"I can't believe you're about to hear me sing."

I grin. "The hype is real."

Then there's a whispered command I can't quite hear, and the boys line up in the wings, amped and ready. Honestly, I can't even look at them without laughing. The play is *Joseph and the Amazing Technicolor Dreamcoat*, and all of Joseph's brothers are wearing these fluffy fake beards. I don't know, maybe it's in the costume notes of the Bible or something.

"Don't wish me luck," Simon says. "Tell me to break a leg."

"Simon, you should probably get out there."

"Okay, but listen, don't take the bus. We're going to Waffle House after this."

"Noted."

The boys shuffle onstage, and I step deeper into the wings. Now that the flock has cleared, I can see Cal Price, the stage manager, stationed at a desk between the curtains. "Hey, Red."

That's what he calls me, even though I'm barely a redhead. It's fine—Cal's a cinnamon roll—but every time he does it, there's this hiccup in my chest.

My dad used to call me Red. Back when he used to call me.

"Have you seen this one?" Cal asks, and I shake my head. He nudges his chin toward the stage, smiling, so I take a few steps forward.

The boys are lurching. I don't know any other way to describe it. The choir teacher bangs out some French-sounding song on the piano, and Simon steps forward, hand on his heart.

"Do you remember the good years in Canaan . . ."

His voice is shaking, just a little, and his French accent's a disaster. But he's funny as hell up there—sinking to his knees, grasping his head, moaning—and I don't want to oversell it or anything, but this just may be the most iconic performance of all time.

Nora sidles up to me. "Guess how many times I've heard him sing this in his bedroom."

"Please tell me he has no idea you can hear him."

"He has no idea I can hear him."

Sorry, Simon, but you're too precious. If you weren't gay and taken, I'd totally marry you. And let's be honest, marrying Simon would be amazing—and not just because I had a sad, secret crush on him for most of middle school. It's more than that. For one thing, I'm totally up for being a Spier, because that family is literally perfect. I'd get Nora as my sister-in-law, plus an awesome older sister in college. And the Spiers live in this huge, gorgeous house that doesn't have clothes and clutter on every surface. I even love their dog.

The song ends, and I slip out and around to the back row of the auditorium, known among the theater kids—aspirationally—as Makeout Alley. But I'm all alone back here, and only halfway participating. Surveying the action from across the room. I've never been in a play, even though Mom's always trying to get me to audition. But here's the thing. You can spend years drawing shitty fan art in sketchpads, and no one has to see it. You can drum alone in the music room until you're decent enough for live shows. But with acting, you don't really get to spend years stumbling along in private. You have an audience even before there's an audience.

A swell of music. Abby Suso steps forward, wearing a giant beaded collar and an Elvis wig. And she's singing.

She's amazing, of course. She doesn't have one of those limitless voices like Nick or Taylor, but she can carry a tune, and she's funny. That's the thing. She's a straight-up goofball onstage. At one point, Ms. Albright actually guffaws. Which is saying something—not just because who knew guffawing was an actual thing people did, but because you know Ms. Albright has seen this thing a thousand times already. Abby's just that good. Even I can't take my eyes off her.

When the show ends, Ms. Albright herds the cast onstage for notes. Everyone drapes themselves all over the platforms, but Simon and Nick scoot to the end of the stage, next to Abby. Of course.

Nick slides his arm around her shoulders, and she tucks up closer to him. Also of course.

There's no Wi-Fi in here, so I'm stuck listening to Ms. Albright's notes, followed by an unsolicited ten-minute monologue from Taylor Metternich about *losing yourself* and *becoming your character.* I have a theory that Taylor literally gets off on the sound of her own voice. I'm pretty sure she's having tiny secret orgasms right before our eyes.

Ms. Albright finally shuts it down, and everyone streams out of the auditorium, grabbing backpacks on the way—but Simon, Nick, and Abby wait in a cluster near the orchestra pit. I stand and stretch and head down the aisle to meet them. And a part of me wants to spew praise all over them, but something stops me. Maybe it's just too painfully sincere, a little too fifth-grade Leah. Not to mention that the thought of fangirling over Abby Suso makes me want to vomit.

I high-five Simon. "You killed it."

"I didn't even know you were here," Abby says.

Hard to know what she means by that. Maybe it's a secret diss. Like, *why are you even here, Leah?* Or maybe: *I didn't even notice you, you're so irrelevant.* But maybe I'm overthinking this. I've been known to do that when it comes to Abby.

I nod. "I heard you guys were going to Waffle House?"

"Yeah, I think we're just waiting for Nora."

Martin Addison walks by. "Hey, Simeon," he says.

"Hey, Reuben," says Simon, looking up from his phone. Those are their characters' names. And yes, Simon plays a guy named Simeon, because I guess Ms. Albright couldn't resist. Reuben and Simeon are two of Joseph's brothers, and I'm sure this would all be adorable if it didn't involve Martin Addison.

Martin keeps walking, and Abby's eyes flash. Honestly, it's pretty hard to piss Abby off, but Martin does it just by existing. And by going out of his way to talk to Simon, like last year didn't happen. It's so fucking audacious. Simon doesn't even talk to Martin that much, but I hate that he does at all. Not that I get to dictate who Simon talks to. But I know—I can just tell—that it bugs Abby as much as it bugs me.

Simon turns back to his phone, clearly texting Bram. They've been dating for a little over a year, and they're one of those vomitously happy couples. I don't mean that in the PDA sense. They actually barely touch each other in school, probably because people are prehistoric dickwads about gay stuff. But Simon and Bram text and eyefuck all day long, like they can't even go five minutes without contact. To be totally honest, it's hard not to be jealous. It's not even just about the true-love-heart-eyes-get-a-room-dudes fairy-tale magic. It's the fact that they went for it. They had the balls to say *fuck this, fuck Georgia, fuck all of you homophobic assholes.*

"Are Bram and Garrett meeting us there?" Abby asks.

"Yup. They just got out of soccer." Simon smiles.

I end up in Simon's passenger seat, with Nora in the back, digging through her backpack. She's wearing rolled-up jeans, covered in paint, and her curls are tied back in a messy knot. One ear is pierced all the way to the top, and she has a tiny blue nose stud she got last summer. That girl is honestly too adorable. I love how much she looks like Simon, and I love that they both look like their older sister. They're a total copy-paste family.

Finally, Nora's hand emerges from her backpack, holding a giant unopened bag of M&M's. "I'm starving."

"We're literally driving to Waffle House. Right now," Simon says, but he stretches his hand back to take some. I take a handful, and they're perfectly melted—which is to say, they're not quite melted. Just a little soft on the inside.

"So, it wasn't too much of a shitshow, right?" Simon asks.

"The play?"

He nods.

"Not at all. It was awesome."

"Yeah, but people are still messing up their lines, and we open on Friday. And freaking Potiphar screwed up a whole song today. God, I need a waffle."

I pull out my phone and check Snapchat. Abby's posted this epically long story from rehearsal, and it's like a montage from a rom-com. A snap of Nick and Taylor singing onstage. A mega close-up selfie of Abby and Simon. An even closer one of Simon's face where his nostrils look so big, Abby stuck a panda graphic inside one of them. And Abby and Nick, over and over.

I stick my phone back in my pocket. Simon turns onto Mount Vernon Highway. I feel antsy and strange—like I'm bothered by something, but I can't remember what. It's like a tiny pinprick in the back of my mind.

"I can't figure out what song you're doing," Nora says.

It takes me a moment to realize she's talking to me, and a moment after that to realize I've been drumming on the glove compartment.

"Huh. I have no idea."

"It's like this," Nora says, tapping a straight one-two beat on the back of my seat. *Boom-tap-boom-tap.* All eighth notes, quick and even. My mind fills in the rest of it immediately.

It's "Don't Stop Believin'." My brain is an asshole.

THERE ARE A TON OF cars I recognize from school in the Waffle House parking lot. Simon turns off the ignition and glances at his phone.

The first thing I see when I step outside the car is Taylor's bright blond head. "Leah! I had no idea you were coming. I totally thought it was just theater people, but yay!" She presses her key, and her car beeps twice. Kind of funny—I don't remember Taylor having a Jeep. Especially not one with testicles dangling from the bumper.

"Your car has very realistic balls, Taylor."

"So embarrassing, right?" She falls into step beside me. "My brother's home for spring break, and he blocked my car in. I had to take his."

"Oh, nuts. That's the worst."

"Yeah, he's really testicling my patience," she replies. And, okay. I'll be the first to admit: sometimes I fucking love Taylor.

She holds the door open, and I follow Simon and Nora inside. I really love the smell of Waffle House. It's this perfect combination of butter, maple syrup, bacon, and maybe onions? Whatever it is, they should bottle it up and pour it into a scented marker, so I can draw hot manga characters who smell like WaHo. Right away, I spot a bunch of theater people sitting in the corner. Including Martin Addison.

"I'm not sitting there." I turn to Nora.

She nods shortly. "Agreed."

"Because of Martin?" Taylor asks.

"Let's just sit over here," I say, pressing my lips together. I mean, the stuff with Martin happened a long time ago, and maybe I should let it go. But I can't. I honestly can't. This kid literally outed Simon last year. Actually, he found out Simon was gay, *blackmailed* him, and *then* fucking outed him. I've barely said a word to him since, and neither has Nora. Or Bram. Or Abby.

I settle in next to Nora in a booth near the entrance, and Taylor scoots into the seat Simon was clearly saving for Bram. When the waitress shows up for a first round of orders, everyone but me orders waffles. All I want is a Coke.

"Are you on a diet?" Taylor asks.

"Excuse me?"

Seriously, who says that? First of all, I just ate twenty

shit-tons of M&M's. Second of all, shut the fuck up. I swear, people can't wrap their minds around the concept of a fat girl who doesn't diet. Is it that hard to believe I might actually like my body?

Nora nudges me and asks if I'm okay. Maybe I look kind of surly.

"Oh my God, are you sick?" asks Taylor.

"No."

"I'm like super paranoid I'm going to catch something. I've been drinking so much tea, and I'm resting my voice whenever I'm not in rehearsal, obviously. Can you imagine if I lost my voice this week? I don't even know what Ms. Albright would do."

"Right."

"Like, I'm in almost every song." She does this weird, high-pitched laugh. I can't tell if she's nervous and pretending not to be, or the other way around.

"Maybe you should rest your voice," I suggest.

I swear she's more manageable when we're rehearsing with the band. Also, I have really good isolation headphones.

Taylor opens her mouth to reply to me, but then Abby and the guys arrive all at once. Garrett scoots in beside me, and Bram slides next to Taylor, with Abby and Nick on the ends. And it's funny, because Taylor's been sitting here with her usual runway-in-Paris posture, but now she's leaning so hard toward Nick, she's practically sprawled over the table. "Hey, I hear you and Simon will be in Boston for spring break."

Taylor. You've been mashed up against Simon's body in a booth for twenty minutes. But, of course, you couldn't ask that question until Nick got here.

"Yup," Nick says. "We're doing the last set of school visits—Tufts and BU first, and then Wesleyan, NYU, Haverford, and Swarthmore. So we're flying into Boston, renting a car, and then flying out of Philly."

"Road trip," says Simon, leaning forward for a high five.

"With your moms," says Abby.

I can't even get my head around how much people are willing to spend on this stuff. There are the plane tickets, hotels, car rentals, everything—and they don't even know if they've gotten into these schools yet. Not to mention the fact that Simon spent hundreds of dollars on application fees alone, even though he's dead set on NYU. Which I'm sure has nothing to do with Bram's early acceptance to Columbia.

"That is so awesome!" Taylor beams. "I'll be in Cambridge, visiting Harvard. We should meet up!"

"Yeah, maybe," Nick says. Simon almost chokes on his water.

"Abby, are you looking at the northeast, too?" Taylor asks.

"Nope." Abby smiles. "I'm going to Georgia."

"You're not trying to be near Nick?"

"Can't afford to be near Nick."

Kind of weird to hear her say that out loud. Especially

because I'm going to the exact same school for the exact same reason. The University of Georgia is the only place I applied. They accepted me months ago. I qualify for the Zell Miller Scholarship. It's a done deal.

But I never know how to feel when I have a thing in common with Abby Suso. I especially don't know how to feel about the fact that we're going to the same school. I bet she'll pretend she doesn't know me.

So then Garrett gets going about Georgia Tech's superiority to Georgia. I don't even care, but I guess it's good that Morgan's not here. It's funny—Morgan's such a little social justice geek that you wouldn't expect this, but she's actually from one of those hardcore UGA families. All football, all the time. The whole house is decorated red and black, with bulldog faces on everything, and the Hirsches always tailgate before games. I'll never understand the whole football scene. Like, no shade on football, but I'm kind of more focused on the school part of college.

I want to zone out, but Garrett keeps baiting me. "Okay, here's one. Leah, what are the longest three years of a UGA student's life?"

"I give up."

"Her freshman year."

"Haha."

Garrett Laughlin. Every day.

Eventually, everyone starts talking about Bram and Garrett's soccer game last weekend. Nick looks a little wistful, and I really do get it. It's not that he'll never play soccer again. He'll be back on the field as soon as the play wraps up next week. But it sucks when life moves along without you. Sometimes I feel left out even when life's moving along with me.

The waitress swings by again to take the second round of orders, and within twenty minutes, we've got a mountain of food. Simon's gone off on a rant about the play, so I steal a piece of bacon from his plate when he's distracted.

"And I just have this sinking feeling it's all going to fall apart, now that we finally have the orchestra and the sets. Like, sorry, but the sets should have been done a week ago."

Nora gives Simon the stink-eye. "Maybe they would be, if anyone actually worked on them other than Cal and me."

"Burn," says Garrett.

"But at the end of the day," says Taylor, "the sets don't even matter. It's all about the acting."

Nora sighs, smiling tightly.

We linger over our plates for a bit, and then the waitress brings us all separate checks. Pretty awesome of her. I hate combined checks, because someone always wants to split the bill evenly—and I don't want to be a jerk, but there's a reason I didn't order that twenty-dollar sandwich. We take turns walking up to the cashier to pay, and then we stack our tips in a pile on the table. And of course, Garrett, who ordered scattered, smothered, and covered waffles with sausage and hash browns, leaves literally a dollar. I don't get that. Leave a fucking real tip. I throw an extra couple of dollars down myself to make up for it.

"Pretty big tip for a Coke," Abby says, and I bite back a smile. The others are making their way to the door, but she hangs back, buttoning her peacoat.

"My mom used to be a waitress."

"Well, it's just really nice of you."

I shrug and smile, but my lips feel stretchy. I'm always weird around Abby. I guess I just have issues with her. For one thing, I can't stand people who are that pretty. She's got these Disney eyes and dark brown skin and wavy dark hair and actual cheekbones. And she has the opposite of a resting bitch face. Basically, Abby is human candy corn. She's fine in small doses—but too much, and you'll puke from the sweetness.

She gives me this half smile, and we both step outside. Taylor and her ball sack are gone, and Garrett's already left for a piano lesson. Everyone else is just standing around. Simon and Bram are holding hands, sort of, but only the tips of their fingers are laced together. Which is about as hot as it gets for the two of them in public.

Nick, on the other hand, wraps his arms around Abby, like he has to make up for the hour spent on opposite sides of a booth. Typical. So, I guess we're doing the whole lovesick-couples-in-front-of-Waffle-House thing. Maybe Nora and I should make out now, just to stay relevant.

But Abby disentangles from Nick and walks toward me.

"That's really beautiful," she says, pointing at my phone case. It's actually one of my manga sketches—Anna surprised me with it for my birthday this year. "You drew that, right?"

"Yeah." I swallow. "Thanks, Abby."

Her eyes widen, just barely, like I threw her off somehow just by saying her name. I guess we don't talk a lot. Not outside of group stuff. Not anymore.

She blinks and then nods. "So, hey. The University of Georgia."

"Is a school."

"Yes." She laughs—and suddenly, she's all doe eyes and hesitation. "I kind of wanted to ask you—"

A horn honks, and we both look up. I recognize Abby's car—or Abby's mom's car, I guess, but today, the driver is a boy with the most gorgeous cheekbones I've ever seen—wide eyes, brown skin, maybe early twenties.

"Oh my God, my brother's home! He wasn't supposed to get in until tonight." Abby grins, touching my arm briefly. "Okay, hold that thought. We'll touch base tomorrow."

A moment later, she's kissing Nick good-bye. I look away quickly, squinting up at the sun.

3

I TEXT MOM, WHO SAYS she'll pick me up at Waffle House on her way home. Soon, everyone's gone but Bram, who scoots in beside me on the curb.

I smile at him. "You don't have to wait with me."

"Oh, I'm not. My dad's in town, so he's picking me up."

Bram's parents are divorced, which I find weirdly comforting. I don't mean that in a bitchy way. I don't want Bram to have a shitty home life or anything. It's just that most of my friends have these storybook-perfect families. Sitcom families—married parents in giant houses, with framed family portraits lining the staircases. I guess it's nice not being the only one missing that.

"Just for a visit?"

Bram nods. "He and my stepmom came up for the week

with Caleb. We're getting ice cream after this."

"I can't believe Caleb's big enough for ice cream. Wasn't he just born?"

"I know, right? He'll be one in June."

"Unreal."

Bram smiles. "Want to see him? He's my lock screen."

He hands me his phone, and I tap the screen on. "Okay, this is too adorable."

It's a selfie of Bram and Caleb, smiling with their faces smooshed together, and it's the cutest photo ever taken. Bram's dad is white, and I guess his stepmom must be, too, because Caleb's the palest little white baby I've ever seen. Somehow, it surprises me every time I see a picture of him. He's totally bald, too, with giant brown eyes. But it's funny, because Bram and Caleb look weirdly alike. Even though Bram's skin is brown and he has hair and doesn't drool. It's kind of wild.

Bram sticks his phone in his pocket and leans back on his hands, and I feel this wave of unexpected shyness. It occurs to me, suddenly, that this may actually be the first time Bram and I have hung out one-on-one, even though he moved here after freshman year. He was always in the background for me until he started dating Simon. To be honest, I kind of lumped him together with Garrett.

I try to beat back the awkwardness. "Want to see something?" I ask.

"Sure." He sits up.

"Okay. Brace yourself." I tap into my photos and scroll back through my albums. Then, I pass Bram the phone.

His hand flies to his mouth.

"Amazing, right?"

Bram nods slowly. "Oh my God."

"So, this is seventh grade."

"I'm just."

"I know. Simon was too cute, right?"

Bram stares at the photo, eyes crinkling around the edges, and something about his expression makes my heart twist.

I mean, he's so far gone. This kid is in it with his whole entire heart.

The picture is actually of all three of us—Simon, Nick, and me. I think we were at Morgan's bat mitzvah. I'm wearing this light blue dress, kind of an Eliza Hamilton vibe. I'm holding an inflatable saxophone, smiling, and Nick's wearing oversized sunglasses. But the star of the picture is Simon. My God.

For one thing, there's that glow-in-the-dark tie Simon used to wear to every bar mitzvah and dance. But this time, he's wearing it around his head like Rambo, cheesing for the camera. Also, he's fucking tiny. I don't know how I forgot that. He grew a few inches in eighth grade, and that's about when he started listening to good music and not wearing those giant wolf face T-shirts. Like, I'm pretty sure he stripped off that final wolf shirt one day, and then Bram moved to Shady Creek two hours later.

"You've never seen his baby pictures?" I ask.

"I've seen the little kid ones, but he's got middle school locked down."

"What you're telling me is that Simon should never have left us alone together."

"Exactly." He grins, tapping into his text messages.

Moments later, our phones buzz simultaneously. You showed him the tie? LEAH, WHAT HAVE YOU DONE?

It was a dapper tie, Bram writes.

Well I was a dapper young man, BUT STILL

Should I tell Bram about the night-light? I type.

Bram smiles. "The night-light?"

IT WAS AN ALARM CLOCK. It just happened to have a light.

"It was a night-light." I grin at Bram. "It had a little crescent moon and a mouse on it. He probably still has it."

"That is really cute and not at all surprising."

"Right? He kept it by his bed until eighth grade."

Bram laughs. Then he types something, taps send, and scoots his feet back to the curb.

Except the message never appears. So, it's a private text to Simon. To his boyfriend. Totally allowed. And I probably shouldn't feel like I've been voted off some island.

Mom pulls up to the curb a few minutes later, rolling down the window and waving.

"That's your mom?" Bram asks. "Wow. She's really pretty."

"Yeah, I hear that a lot." No joke: Simon once called her *the quintessential sexy mom*. "Are you sure you don't want us to wait with you?" I ask.

"Oh no. My dad will be here any second."

My mom leans out the window. "Hi! You're Bram, right? The soccer player?"

Bram looks taken aback. "Oh. Yes."

"And you're going to Columbia."

God. She always does this. She whips out these little snippets of random information, just to show off what an Involved Mom she is. My friends probably think I go home and quiz her about them with flash cards.

I mean, I do sort of tell my mom everything, to a degree that's almost pathological. I keep her posted on all the Tumblr gossip, and I tell her about most of my crushes. And of course I told my mom I'm bisexual, even though none of my friends know. I came out to her when I was eleven, during a commercial break for *Celebrity Rehab*.

Anyway, either Bram is a saint, or he's hardcore sucking up to Mom. He calls her Ms. Keane, which is actually pretty impressive. No one ever remembers that my mom and I have different last names.

My mom laughs. "You are so sweet. Seriously, call me Jessica." I can already predict our conversation for the ride home. *Oh God, Lee! He's totally adorable. Simon must be head over heels.*

What a cutie pie. Blah blah blah.

I know I'm lucky. You always hear about parents who disapprove of their kids' friends, and my mom's the exact opposite. She adores every single friend I've ever introduced. She even loved Martin Addison the few times she met him. And, of course, my friends are totally charmed by her. Case in point: by the time I click my seat belt, Bram's already invited Mom to opening night of the play. Because that's not weird.

"I still think you should have auditioned, Lee," Mom says as we pull onto the main road. "*Joseph* is the bomb."

"Don't say *the bomb.*"

"*Joseph* is the blizz."

I won't even dignify it with a response.

"THIS CAME FOR YOU," MOM says, handing me an envelope as soon I come down for breakfast on Thursday.

It's from the University of Georgia—the return address is printed with their logo. It's not a big envelope like my admissions packet. Just a random letter-sized envelope, the perfect size for a letter from the dean retracting my scholarship and reversing my acceptance. *We are writing to notify you that your acceptance to the University of Georgia Honors Program was, in fact, a clerical error. Our records show that our department intended to admit some other Leah Burke who isn't a steaming hot mess. We apologize for any inconvenience.*

"Are you going to open it?" Mom asks, leaning against the counter. She's wearing eye makeup, like she does for work sometimes, and she looks obnoxiously beautiful. Her eyes look electric green. I should say, for the record, that having a mother who's hotter than you sucks balls.

I take a deep breath and open it. Mom peers at me while I read. "Everything okay?"

"Yeah, totally." I feel myself relax. "It's just a bunch of info about tours and accepted students day."

"We should probably do that, huh?"

"It doesn't matter."

I mean, it can't matter. Because my mom isn't Simon's mom or Nick's mom. She can't randomly take off work for a campus visit. I can't even picture my mom on one of those tours. I've never actually been on one, but Simon says it's just a flock of mortified kids cringing while their parents ask questions. Apparently, Simon's dad asked the tour guide at Duke to "please elaborate on the campus gay scene."

"I wanted to fucking die," Simon told me.

Pretty sure if my mom were on that tour, she'd be snickering in the back, rolling her eyes at all the other parents. She'd probably get hit on by frat dudes, too.

"Seriously, it's fine."

She smiles. "I really do think you should sign up for this, though. Let me just sort things out with work, and we can make a whole day of it. And actually, Wells has family in Athens, so—"

I laugh incredulously. "I'm not doing my college tour with Wells."

She flicks my arm. "We can discuss this later. Do you want a yogurt?"

"Yeah." I scrape my hair back. "Anyway, I'll just see when Morgan's going. I can pretend to be a Hirsch."

"That's an idea," Mom says. "And you could wear a Tech jersey to mess with them."

"Totally, Mom. I'll be so popular on campus."

My phone buzzes with a text from Simon. Fuck. My. Life. Leah. Oh God.

"Okay, I better go," Mom says, setting my yogurt down. "Have fun today."

I say good-bye to her and turn back to my phone. I can't fuck your life, I'm monogamously fucking my own life.

Okay, that's funny, Simon writes, but seriously.

What happened?

Three dots.

And then: My voice keeps cracking!

What?

When I sing.

That's really cute. Emoji with heart eyes. I take a bite of yogurt.

LEAH, IT'S NOT CUTE. IT'S ALMOST OPENING NIGHT. THE SCHOOL PERFORMANCES ARE LIKE RIGHT NOW.

I think you're nervous

YOUR nervous.

*You're. Holy shit I can't believe I just did that. And I

capitalized it, ugh, don't tell Bram AHHHHHHHHHHHH FUCK I'M DONE

Simon. You're okay. I throw away my yogurt cup and toss my spoon into the sink. Eight fifteen. Time to get to the bus stop. Even though it's mega cold. Even though my texting fingers are going to hate me.

Also he's never heard me sing and he's going to break up with me.

I laugh. Bram's going to break up with you when he hears you sing?

Yes, Simon writes. I can picture him: pacing backstage, costume half assembled. The school performances are technically dress rehearsals, but everyone misses class to watch them. Seniors don't even have to check into first period. I want to get there early to claim a seat in the front, where I can heckle Simon and Nick. But naturally, my bus is late. It happens every time it's cold out.

He really hasn't heard you sing? I write.

I DON'T SING. And, without missing a beat, he adds, But seriously, what if my voice cracks and everyone throws tomatoes and then they pull me off the stage with an old-timey hook??

If that happens, I write, I will film it.

Nora's waiting for me when I step off the bus.

"Thank God you're here. What are you doing right now?"

She rakes a hand through her curls. I've honestly never seen her look so freaked out. And that includes the time classy eleven-year-old Simon molded brownies to look like actual shit and then proudly ate them in front of us.

I look at her. "What's going on?"

"Martin Addison has a cold," she says slowly, blinking like she can't quite believe it.

"Noted. I won't make out with him."

I don't even think she hears me. "So he's staying home to rest his voice for tomorrow, but now we don't have a Reuben, and we're supposed to start, like, now. So I was wondering . . ."

"I can't play Reuben."

"Right." She presses her lips together.

"I'm the worst singer, Nora. You know that."

"Yeah, I know. I'm not . . . ugh." She laughs nervously. "Cal's filling in for Martin, so now I'm Cal, and I need you to be me."

"To be you?"

"Assistant stage manager."

"Oh." I pause. "What does that mean?"

She starts walking, briskly, which is so unlike her. I have to hop to catch up. "Okay, well, I'm going to be on headset calling the cues," she says. "So I need you to keep track of the actors and make sure everyone's where they need to be, and help flip the sets, and just basically put out fires. You can do that, right? Just yell at people. You'll be good at it."

"What's that supposed to mean?"

"But." She stops short, appraising me. "Crap. Do you have anything black to wear? Or navy? Like a hoodie or something."

"I . . . not with me." I look down, taking in my outfit. Mint-green sundress, dark green cardigan, gray tights, and my gold combat boots. I mean, what else was I going to wear on Saint Patrick's Day?

"Okay." Nora rubs her cheek. "Okay, I'll find something. Just head backstage for now, and somebody will set you up. Thank you so much for agreeing to do this."

I'm not sure I did agree to do this. But Nora shoots off down the hallway again, and suddenly I'm standing outside the backstage door. So. Assistant stage manager. I guess this is happening.

I slip backstage, and it's total chaos. I don't know, maybe Cal's secretly a hardcore strict mega bitch, because apparently shit falls apart when he's off duty. There are freshmen battling with shepherds' crooks from the prop table, which—I'm not going to lie—look exactly like the old-timey hooks from Simon's nightmares. Two Hairy Ishmaelites are making out between the curtains, and Taylor's sitting on the floor with her eyes closed. I think she might be meditating.

I peek through the curtains, and it's a sea of bleary-eyed freshmen and seniors. Right away, I see my squad in the front row: Bram, Garrett, Morgan, and Anna. And an empty seat in the middle—clearly mine. I feel weirdly touched by that.

"Hey." Nora appears, handing me an armload of fabric. "This is Garrett's, so it should cover most of your dress. Sorry if it smells."

I unbunch it slowly, holding it at arm's length. It's a navy hoodie with a tiny embroidered yellow jacket on the chest. A Georgia fucking Tech hoodie. But Garrett's tall and bulky, so it actually fits me, and Nora's right—it smells. But not badly. It just smells like Old Spice deodorant, which is how Garrett smells. And now I feel like some 1950s cheerleader wearing her boyfriend's letter jacket. Like I've been claimed.

I try not to think about it. Instead, I weave through the backstage shitshow behind Nora, who has somehow become Badass Take-No-Prisoners Nora right before my eyes. This girl is normally such a little peanut, but wow. She's throwing down the stink-eye and calling actors out, and people are actually starting to pull their shit together. Finally, Nora settles in at Cal's usual desk in the wings, securing her headset and flipping through his binder. I watch her for a moment, and then I wander over to the prop table, where literally everything is out of place. There are sunglasses and handcuffs and all kinds of things on the floor, so I scoop them up and set them on the table.

"Five minutes, everyone," Ms. Albright calls, poking her head around the curtain.

Simon appears beside me in the wings. "Leah, why are you wearing a Tech sweatshirt?"

"It's Garrett's." His eyes get huge. "Yeah. Wow. Not what you're thinking. Your sister's making me wear it."

"I'm so confused."

"Don't worry about it." I smile at him. "Feeling any better?"

He shakes his head. "Nope."

"Hey."

He looks up.

"You're going to be amazing, okay?"

For a minute, he just looks at me, like he doesn't believe I just said that. God, am I that big of an asshole? He has to know I love him to pieces, right? But maybe I don't say it enough. I don't exactly walk around giving little earnest speeches about how deeply and sincerely I appreciate my friends. I'm not Abby. But I figured Simon knows how awesome I think he is. How could he not? I mean, I was half in love with that kid for most of middle school. True story. Those wolf T-shirts? Weirdly sexy.

He blinks and adjusts his glasses, and then he breaks into one of those face-lighting Simon grins. "I love you, Leah."

"Yeah, yeah."

"I love you, too, Simon," he adds in a high voice.

"I love you, too, Simon," I echo, rolling my eyes.

"*Simeon*," he corrects. And the overture starts to rise.

Cal Price can't act for shit.

Thankfully, he has the whole play memorized, but he plays the part of Reuben like a soft-spoken elderly accountant. And he's a terrible singer—just cringingly, comically bad. But he's so sweet and self-conscious out there, you just want to poke him in the face. He's the personification of a preschool dance recital. D-minus for talent, but A-plus for adorableness.

In any case, it's not the cast's best performance, but it's not a total mess. Taylor sounds amazing, and Simon's voice doesn't crack, and I'm not going to lie: Nick is hot as fuck in that dreamcoat.

When it's over, I catch Simon by the edge of his robe and surprise him with a hug. "You were perfect," I say, and he actually blushes. Then he takes both my hands and claps them together. For a minute, he just looks at me, smiling.

"You're a really awesome friend," he says finally.

It's so soft and sincere that it catches me off guard.

The actors trail back to the dressing rooms to change—they're not allowed to have lunch in their costumes. But Cal walks straight to Nora, and she slides off her headset to hug him. And it's quite a hug: full body, no space between them, Cal whispering something in her ear the whole time. I don't think they see me watching. But when he finally leaves for the dressing room, I lean my elbows on her desk.

"So." I grin. "You and Cal."

"Shut up."

"That is so fucking cute."

"There's no *that.* Nothing's happening."

"Okay, but I just got a boner watching you hug, so."

"Leah!"

"I'm just saying."

She groans and buries her face in her arms, but she's smiling.

"Hey." I feel a soft kick on the heel of my shoe. I peek behind me, and it's Bram. "We're grabbing lunch off campus somewhere. Do y'all want to come?"

Nora shakes her head. "I'm not supposed to leave. We have another performance in forty-five minutes."

"Ah, okay."

"Who's going?"

"Just Garrett, Morgan, Anna, and me."

"Leah, you should go," Nora says.

"I don't want to ditch you guys."

She smiles. "You can ditch us. Cal's getting demoted back to stage manager."

"Oh man. Who's playing Reuben?"

"Ms. Albright."

"I bet she looks great in a beard."

Bram just looks at us, smiling faintly. "So, you're coming?"

"I guess so." I shrug and clasp my hands, feeling suddenly small in Garrett's hoodie. It's that *girlfriend* feeling again, not that I've ever been anyone's girlfriend. But I imagine it feels like this. Like I'm this tiny precious wanted thing. I can't decide if I feel gross about that, or if I only *think* I should feel gross about it.

By now, Simon and the rest of the cast are holed up in the dressing rooms, so I say good-bye to Nora and follow Bram out through the atrium. Anna's sitting on the ledge by the carpool circle, and Garrett's gesturing emphatically to Morgan. But he catches my eye and grins, and when Bram and I walk over, he tugs my sleeve. "So, I see you're a Tech fan."

"Fuck you." I grin back at him. And then it occurs to me that there's absolutely no reason for me to still be wearing Garrett Laughlin's hoodie. "Guess you probably want this back."

"But you look so comfy," he says.

"Um."

His cheeks flush softly. "Not comfy." He swallows. "It looks nice on you."

I narrow my eyes. "It looks nice?"

"Yes."

I tug the sweatshirt over my head and bunch it up in my arms, handing it back to him. "You are so full of shit, Garrett."

He takes it and smiles at me, scrunching up his nose. And I have to admit, he's not terrible-looking. He's got blond hair, bright blue eyes, and a sprinkling of freckles on his nose. Just a few, not like me. I've got freckles all across my cheekbones. But it's cute and surprising and weirdly endearing, and now I'm thinking about the fact that Garrett plays piano. It's funny—his fingers don't look like piano fingers. They're long, but kind of meaty, and now they're wrapped around his sweatshirt like he's trying to choke it.

"What are you looking at?" he says nervously.

I look up. "Nothing. I'm not."

Bram clears his throat. "Okay, so do we want to go to Rio Bravo?"

"Fuck yes," says Garrett. But then he pauses, glancing at me. "Is that where you want to go?"

"Sure."

"Let's just go. Come on. I'll drive." Morgan links her arm through mine, and I link mine through Anna's, and I have to admit, I feel pretty lucky. I love Simon and Nick and all the other guys to pieces, but there's something about Morgan and Anna. They just get it. I'm not saying we agree on everything. Morgan likes dubbed anime, which is basically blasphemy, and Anna once described Chiba Mamoru as "barely attractive." But other times, it's as if we read each other's minds. Like, if Taylor's being a diva at a rehearsal, we don't even have to look at each other. It's as if this secret cosmic eye roll passes among our three brains. One week in seventh grade, we tried to convince people we were sisters, even though Anna's half Chinese, Morgan's Jewish, and I'm basically the size of both of them combined.

But what it really comes down to is that they always have my back. And vice versa. Like, when Anna got the norovirus last year, Morgan and I reenacted the fight she missed in the lunchroom. In seventh grade, I drew fifty-six posters to help Morgan protest the school's racist Thanksgiving play. And when Simon and Nick disappear into boyfriend- and girlfriend-land, Morgan and Anna are there to be cynical assholes with me. I don't even care if they like Journey. They're the best squad in the world.

"Leah, where's your backpack?" Morgan asks suddenly.

"In my locker?"

"Do you need to go grab it?"

I look at her. "Are we . . . not coming back?"

Here's a confession: I've never actually skipped school. I mean, there was a week last year where I was pissed at Simon and Nick, and I might have spent a few class periods in the music room storage closet. But I've never left campus. Don't get me wrong, people do it all the time. But I'm sort of squeamish about the idea of getting in trouble. Partially because I don't want to jeopardize my scholarship, but also—I don't know. Maybe I'm just a giant nerd.

"Leah, it's fine, okay?" says Morgan. "I've done this before. Even Bram has done this before."

I glance back at Bram, and he smiles sheepishly.

I mean, if I'm going to skip school, today's the day. My teachers will assume I'm missing third and fourth period for the play. Come to think of it, I actually *would* be missing class for the play if Nora still needed me—if Cal hadn't been such an adorable disaster onstage.

"You okay?" Morgan asks.

I nod.

"Good. Let's roll."

Morgan drives a shiny, fancy Jetta with seats that smell brand-new. Her parents bought it for her eighteenth birthday and had it equipped with GPS, satellite radio, and a little video screen that shows when you're about to hit something in reverse. Already, there's a UGA cling sticker on the back windshield.

I take shotgun, even though Garrett's six foot two, and I'm pretty sure that makes me an asshole. But he's totally unfazed. He sits in the middle of the backseat, leaning forward, a hand on each of the headrests. My hair is basically draped over his arm. Sometimes I think Garrett calculates the exact most awkward way to position his body in any given moment, and then he just goes for it.

"Okay, you just have to smile and wave at the security guard," he says. "Act like you're allowed to leave."

"Garrett, seniors *are* allowed to leave."

"Wait, really?" He looks amazed.

Morgan inches toward the exit. She's always driven like a terrified alien dropped on a new planet. She moves so slowly she's practically rolling, and every traffic light and stop sign seem to surprise her. I turn up the music—a moody folk song I don't recognize. I think I like it. I think I really like it. It's somehow both sweet and wrenching, and the singer sings it like she *means* it.

"Who is this?" I ask after a moment.

Ahead, the light turns red, and Morgan crawls to a stop. "Rebecca Loebe. My new fave." Considering yesterday's fave was "Don't Stop Believin'," I'd call this the biggest level-up in the history of music.

"Morgan, you have officially redeemed yourself."

We pull into Rio Bravo and pile out of the car, and I stand a little straighter when we step into the restaurant. Not that anyone cares. But I don't want to look like some high school kid skipping third period—even though that's totally, 100 percent exactly what I am. The hostess leads us to a big booth in the back, and a waiter stops by right away to drop off tortilla chips and take our drink orders. Garrett leans toward me. "Let me guess. Coke."

"Maybe." I smile. Bram and Anna exchange glances.

"She'll have a Coke," Garrett says.

"Excuse me, I can order for myself." I smile brightly at the waiter. "I'll have a Coke, please." I don't mean it as a joke—not at all—but everyone laughs, even Garrett.

"You're funny, Burke," he says.

I blush and turn to Morgan. "Hey, I was wondering—are you doing the campus tour and info session thing?"

Morgan grins. "I was just going to ask you. So, Abby and I were discussing it, and we were thinking maybe all three of us could go together over spring break. Did she talk to you about it yet?"

Ah. So, Abby's question. The thing she kind of wanted to

ask me. I swallow. "Pretty sure your parents will want to go to that, Morgan."

"I know. But I'll go twice. I don't care."

"You guys and Abby?" asks Anna. "Since when are you friends with Abby?"

Morgan looks confused. "We've always been friends with Abby."

"Yeah, but not like that. Not like spring break road trip besties," Anna says, pursing her lips. I shift slightly in my seat. Anna gets weird when we talk about college, and I never know what to say. On one hand, I get it. She's the odd woman out. But on the other hand, I don't even think she ended up applying to Georgia. She's been obsessed with Duke since sophomore year.

"Anna Banana, we're not replacing you," I say.

She wrinkles her nose. "You just had to pick the girl with a four-letter *A* name."

"Yeah, but she's not you." Morgan hugs her around the shoulders.

And it's true. Abby could never be inner circle. Maybe once upon a time, I thought she could be. Here's the thing: right after Abby moved here, she and I hung out a lot. Like, *a lot* a lot. To the point where my mom started getting twinkly-eyed and asking lots of questions. And obviously, it wasn't like that. For one thing, Abby's embarrassingly hetero. She's the type who'd watch all of *Sailor Moon* and come away thinking Haruka and

Michiru were just good friends. She probably thinks Troye Sivan's songs are about girls.

Not that I need to be thinking about Abby right now. I stare at the chip bowl. "So what are we doing after this?"

"Well, I have a project," says Bram.

"What kind of project?"

Bram blushes, mouth quirking upward. "I'm kind of working on a promposal."

Ninety minutes later, Morgan, Anna, and Garrett are watching anime in Morgan's living room, and I'm eating microwave s'mores at the kitchen table with Bram. "So you inspired me," he says.

"Me?"

He nods toward my phone. "With the picture you showed me."

"Are you doing a Morgan's bat mitzvah–themed promposal? Because that would be epic."

"Good guess." He grins. "But no. I mean, I don't know. I think I need to pick your brain for a minute."

"About what?"

"I need all your embarrassing Simon stories." He takes a bite of s'more and smiles. There's a tiny blob of marshmallow stuck to his lip.

"You realize this could take all day, right?" I say.

He laughs. "I'm here for it."

"Also, totally unrelated, but I have to know. Did Baby Bram call graham crackers—"

"Bram crackers?" He smiles. "Maybe. Definitely."

"That's amazing."

"I'm making another. You want one?" He stands.

"Obviously." I tuck my chin into my hand. "Okay, so Simon."

"Simon."

There's this tug in my chest. Because when Bram says Simon's name, he pronounces every part of it. Like it's worth being careful over. It's really sweet and everything, but wow. I get so jealous sometimes. It's obviously not just Simon and Bram. It's couples in general. And it's not about the kissing stuff. It's just—imagine being Simon. Imagine going about your day knowing someone's carrying you in their mind. That has to be the best part of being in love—the feeling of having a home in someone else's brain.

I push away the thought. "All right. So I assume you've seen the jean shorts picture?"

"The one on their mantel?" He grins back at me from across the kitchen.

"Yup. Okay, what about when he puked in the wax hand?"

"He actually told me that himself."

"Yeah, he's probably proud of that one." I bite my lip. "Huh. Like, it really shouldn't be this hard to think of embarrassing Simon stories."

"You would think," Bram says. The microwave beeps, and I watch for a minute as he carefully presses the s'mores together. Only Bram could wrangle a giant puffed-up marshmallow so neatly. He carries the s'mores back to the table and slides the plate in front of me. And I'm just about to grab one, but I'm suddenly inspired.

"Wait, do you know about his thing with *Love Actually*?"

"I know his parents make him watch it every Christmas, and he hates it."

"Yeah. He doesn't hate it." I take a giant bite of s'more, peeking up at him with my widest, most innocent eyes.

Bram grins. "It sounds like there's a story here."

"Oh, there's a story. Simon wrote the story."

Bram opens his mouth to reply, but then Garrett pops his head up over the back of the couch. "Hey, Burke. Question. So, I'm trying to figure out the plan for tomorrow."

"Tomorrow?"

"The play," calls Morgan from the armchair.

"Oh, I knew that."

"Are you going?" Garrett asks.

"I was planning on it."

Bram and Garrett glance at each other quickly, whatever that means. "Want to come with us?" Bram asks. "We want to get there early and get good seats."

"In other words, Greenfeld wants an unobstructed view of his boyfriend's ass."

Bram shakes his head, smiling.

"Maybe we can grab dinner or something beforehand," Garrett adds.

"I guess so."

"You guess so? Leah. *Leah.*" Garrett shakes his head.

I force a giant, cheesy smile. "Oh. My. God. I can't wait!"

"Better," he says, sinking back into the couch.

But all night, at home, I'm not thinking about the play. I collapse onto the couch with a Coke, feeling edgy and restless. My mind keeps drifting back to what Morgan said at Rio Bravo. Abby wants to tour UGA with us. It's not like it's totally out of left field. We're technically friends. But probably a hundred people from our grade applied to Georgia, and Abby's friends with all of them. She's friends with everyone. So it's a little bit surprising that she'd want to go with us.

My phone buzzes on the table, and my heart just swoops.

But it's Garrett.

Hey I'm glad you're coming to the play tomorrow, should be really fun.

I curl back onto the couch, staring at it. Garrett does this sometimes. He sends me these texts out of nowhere with no real opening for a conversation. Just a statement. And I never know how to respond. To be honest, I get this vibe sometimes that Garrett likes me. I mean, I'm probably imagining it, and Garrett's probably just really awkward. But sometimes I wonder.

Me too! I start to type. But it reads a little too much like OMG GARRETT I LOVE YOU PLS KISS ME. So I delete it, and then stare at my phone, and then retype it without the exclamation point, and then delete it again, until I finally give up and turn on *Fruits Basket*. This is what a mess I am. I can't write a two-word text without losing my shit. And I'm not even particularly attracted to this boy. If I were, I'd be dead. *RIP Leah Burke. She died of acute awkwardosis.*

I need a distraction. God knows TV isn't enough. I pull up some random fanfic on my phone, and then I take it down the hall. I can't read Drarry in the living room, even when my mom's not home. Drarry belongs in my bedroom. I don't care if that sounds dirty.

But I can't focus. It isn't the fic's fault. It's well written, and Draco has some bite to him, which is refreshing. I hate when writers make Draco sweet. Sorry, but Draco's a bitch. Own it. I mean, yeah, he's a ball of mush underneath, but you have to *earn* it with him.

I guess that speaks to me, somehow.

But the distraction's not working, so I shut it down. I stick my phone into its charger and then wiggle it around for a minute to trick it into actually charging. My phone's a piece of shit. I crank up Spotify and log onto my art Tumblr, scrolling through my archives. I should upload something new. Or even one of my more decent older pieces. I have a whole bunch I've photographed and saved on my phone. All my ships, straight-up kissing: Inej and Nina, Percabeth, a few original characters. Plus a few random portraits of my friends, not that I ever plan on showing those to anyone. I did that once. Huge fucking mistake.

I scroll quickly past them, landing instead on a pencil sketch of Bellatrix Lestrange. It's not the most polished thing I've drawn, but I sort of love her facial expression. And I don't mind it being a little sloppy, since my Tumblr page is anonymous. If people think I'm a shitty artist, so be it. As least they don't know I'm me.

5

MORGAN'S NOT AT SCHOOL ON Friday, and she's not replying to my texts.

"That's sort of weird, right?" I say to Anna at lunch. We're the first two at the table. "Is something up with her?"

"With Morgan?" She bites her lip. I have the distinct impression that she's avoiding my eyes.

"What, is she mad at me or something?"

"No, it's not that." Anna pauses. "I think she's processing things."

"What are you talking about?"

She looks up at me, finally. "She didn't tell you?"

"Uh, she's not returning my texts, so."

"Yeah." Anna leans back in her chair. "Well. She heard from Georgia last night."

"The school?"

Anna nods, and something in her expression makes my heart sink.

"She didn't get in," I say quietly.

"Nope."

"Was she wait-listed?"

"No."

"You're kidding me."

Anna shakes her head.

"But she's a legacy."

"I know."

"She must be devastated." I blink. "How could she not get in?"

"I don't know. It's messed up." Anna sighs and tugs the ends of her hair. "Maybe her SAT scores? I know she retook it a few times. I feel so awful. I think she's in shock. And her parents just lost it. Like, they're calling the school, withdrawing their donations. I don't even know."

"Jesus."

"I'm going over there after school," Anna says.

I nod. "I'll go with you."

"Yeah." She pauses. "I don't know if that's . . ."

"She doesn't want to see me?"

Anna doesn't respond.

I flush. "Did she say that?"

She shrugs. "I don't know. I'm so sorry, Leah. Ugh. This is so awkward."

"Whatever. It's fine." I stand abruptly. "I'm gonna eat in the courtyard."

"She's just upset right now. You can't take this personally."

Okay, I hate when people say that. *You can't take this personally. It's not personal, Leah.* Morgan's skipping school to avoid me, but it's *totally* not personal. God. I know I should be sympathetic, and I know I'm a jerk, but it just hurts.

"Leah, it's not about you. She's just disappointed," Anna says. "And probably embarrassed."

"I know that." It comes out louder than I mean it to, and a couple of freshmen turn to stare at us. I lower my voice. "I know it's not about me."

"Well, good. It's not."

"I just want to be there for her, you know? I want to make it better."

Anna leans forward. "Yeah, I just don't think you can make it better. You know? It's obviously not your fault that you got in and she didn't, and she knows that, but it's still going to feel like you're rubbing it in her face."

"I'm not going to rub it in her face."

"I know you're not," Anna says slowly. "Not intentionally. But don't you see how it would feel like that?"

My cheeks burn. "It's fine. I'll give her space."

Anna taps her toe against mine. "I know you're worried

about her. I'll make sure she's okay."

I shrug. "Do whatever you want."

So, now everything's off-kilter. I feel heartless, not texting Morgan—though Anna made it pretty clear that I shouldn't. But all through class, I can't stop picturing Morgan holed up in her house, surrounded by pictures of bulldogs. Red and black everywhere. She must be losing her mind. I think I know how she's feeling. I mean, I've never been rejected from a school. But I know what it's like to not be good enough, in some bone-deep fundamental way.

Not that I'm making this about me. For example, I haven't given a shred of attention to the upcoming campus tour and whether Abby might still want to go with me.

"Leah," Simon hisses, poking me.

I snap back to earth. Ms. Livingstone is giving me a Look. "I assume you're deep in thought about the French Revolution, Ms. Burke. Care to weigh in?"

My cheeks burn. "Yes. I'm. Um."

Oh God. Ms. Livingstone can smell the bullshit. *Why yes, I'd like to weigh in. About the French Revolution. Not about road tripping to Athens with Abby Suso. Not that I'm considering road tripping to Athens with Abby Suso.*

"Thomas Jefferson helped the Marquis de Lafayette draft a declaration," Simon blurts.

"Mr. Spier, memorizing the *Hamilton* soundtrack is not going to save you on the AP Euro exam."

A bunch of people snicker. Ms. Livingstone shakes her head and calls on someone else. So, I kick Simon's foot, and when he looks up, I smile. "Thanks."

"No prob." He smiles back.

6

"SO, LET'S TALK *LOVE ACTUALLY*," Bram says, leaning toward me. Garrett's finally out of earshot, scoping out the dessert counter. Which is actually the only counter, because we're at Henri's, and Henri's is a bakery. Sorry, but cupcakes are a dinner food—fight me.

I glance back to make sure Garrett's fully absorbed in pastries and iced doughnuts before turning back to Bram. "Okay, so, Simon may kill me for telling you this."

"Of course. He's very secretive," Bram says, and we grin at each other. Simon Spier may be the least secretive person on the planet.

"Anyway, I didn't know about this until last year, but *apparently*—" I pause to bite into my cupcake. "Apparently, our very own Simon Spier has written a single work of *Love Actually* fanfiction."

Bram's eyes light up. "Okay."

"And I have reason to believe it's on fanfiction.net."

"Are you serious?" He presses his fist to his mouth.

"But he won't tell us his pen name."

"I bet we can figure it out." Bram's already pulling his phone out. "Fanfiction dot org?"

"Dot net."

"Okay." He's quiet for a moment, scrolling.

"I think there are like a hundred stories in the whole fandom. Abby and I were able to narrow it down to fifteen possibilities."

"Oh, so you've already been working on this."

"I tried for weeks, Bram. *Weeks.*"

Junior year, right after Abby moved here.

We were all spending the night at Morgan's, and her mom had exiled the boys to the guest room after an illuminating game of Truth or Dare. Morgan and Anna fell asleep pretty quickly, but Abby scooted all her blankets next to mine on the floor—on our stomachs, side by side. "Leah, we have to find it," she whispered. She was still a little tipsy from Truth or Dare, and I was somehow tipsy by association. I had the full list of *Love Actually* stories pulled up on my phone.

"Do we start at the top?"

"Or we could start with the Keira Knightley self-insert sex erotica," said Abby.

I giggled. "Sex erotica?"

"Yes."

"As opposed to sex-free erotica?"

"I mean, I'd read that, too," she said. "Okay, this one."

And so we started. Right away, we could rule out a few grammatical shitstorms, along with anything that seemed too technically knowledgeable about sex. "There's no way," I'd insisted. "I guarantee you—I would literally bet you a million dollars that Simon Spier has never heard of the perineum."

"I concur," Abby said, tapping the back arrow. I've always thought that was such an intimate thing to do: touching the screen of another person's phone. She opened the next story. It was weird. Once we knew Simon had written one of them, it started to feel like he could have written *any* of them. Or all of them. Under ninety different pen names. Maybe all those times he said he was checking his email, he was actually writing sex erotica.

Then she shifted slightly under her blankets, and her whole body pressed against mine. My right side to her left. And I forgot how to speak.

"It's this one," Bram says, jolting me back to the present. He slides his phone toward me on the table.

"No, you did not just find Simon Spier's secret fanfiction in five minutes."

"I did." He smiles. "I'm a hundred percent sure."

I read it aloud. "'All I Want for Christmas Is You,' by youwontbutyoumight. How do you know this is him?"

"Well, first of all, the pen name."

"I don't get it."

Bram leans forward on his elbows. "*You won't, but you might*. It's an Elliott Smith lyric. That's the first giveaway."

I tilt Bram's phone closer, reading the summary. "'Sam/Joaquin (semi-original character).' Okay . . ."

"Read the rest of the summary."

"'Original male character based closely on Joanna. Just a fluffy m/m retelling of the school concert scene. Smiley face.'" I look up at Bram, grinning. "Oh my God. Simon was such a sweet baby gay, writing the gayest fanfiction. I love it."

Bram smiles. "It's perfect."

"How did Abby and I miss this?"

"Did you even know he was gay, back then?"

"No. Okay, wow. That was even before the whole Martin thing. I guess we weren't looking for the gayest fic in the bunch."

"This isn't even the gayest," Bram says.

"Ladies and gentledudes, I'm back," Garrett announces, and we both look up with a start. Garrett slides into his seat, setting a cardboard cake box on the table in front of us. "Check it out."

Bram nudges the box open, revealing an extravagantly decorated buttercream cake with polka dots and rosette flowers. And a message, carefully piped onto the center:

EISNE
SPIER

"You bought Simon and Nick a cake?" Bram asks slowly.

"Fuck yeah. I love those dudes."

"Well done, Garrett," I say.

"Thank you, Burke. I appreciate that."

"So, no *congratulations* or anything. Just, like . . . their names."

"Yeah, but look at the R," Garrett says, glancing back and forth between Bram and me. "That's badass, right? Totally my idea."

"It's very badass," I assure him.

Bram just raises his eyebrows and smiles.

Add this to the list of things I'm never doing again: sitting in the front row of a play.

Eye contact. So much eye contact.

Simon once said that when the stage lights are on, the

audience looks like a giant dark blob. But maybe the front row is the exception, because I swear Taylor just spent forty-five minutes gazing directly into my face.

But the show was amazing, even with Martin Addison back in commission. Or maybe it's because Martin was back in commission, as much as it kills me to admit that. I hate when assholes have talent. I want to live in a world where good people rule at everything and shitty people suck at everything. In short: I want Martin Addison's voice to crack like an earthquake.

After curtain call, we linger in the lobby, waiting for the actors to come out. Garrett sidles up to me, holding the cake box, his blond hair winging out from under a baseball cap. "So, Eisner can really sing, huh?"

I feel strangely shy. "Yeah."

There are hordes of parents out here, holding flowers. I spot Simon's family near the dramaturgy display, doubled up on bouquets. "Alice is here?" I say to Bram.

He nods. "It's her spring break."

Alice Spier is exactly who I want to be when I'm in college. She is nerd-cute perfection—effortlessly smart, hipster glasses, and zero tolerance for Simon and Nora's bullshit. I *may* have had a low-key crush on her in sixth grade, until I fell hard for her adorable dumbass little brother.

"So, Burke." Garrett nudges me. "I'm guessing you need a ride home."

"Oh. I guess."

"Cool." He nods. "I've got you covered."

I feel awkward all of a sudden—heavy-limbed and tongue-tied. "Thanks," I manage. Yesterday it was Garrett's sweatshirt. Today he's giving me a ride home. It's like the universe is trying to make him my boyfriend, which is messed up. Even if a tiny weird part of me wonders what it would be like to kiss him. It probably wouldn't be awful. Technically, he's cute. He has very blue eyes. And everyone thinks athletes are hot. Is Garrett hot?

He could be.

Though the idea of objective hotness fucks me up a little. The idea that certain arrangements of facial features are automatically superior. It's like someone woke up one day with a boner for big-eyed, soft-lipped, tight-bodied cheekbone people, and we all just decided to go along with that.

The doors to the back hallway swing open, and the cast and crew start to trickle into the lobby. But Garrett rests his hand on my arm.

"Okay, what does the average University of Georgia student get on the SAT?" Garrett asks.

"I don't know."

"Drool."

"Haha."

He pokes my arm. "You're smiling."

I snort and look away, my eyes drifting toward the Spiers. Nick's parents are there, too—Abby's mom is chatting with them while her dad and brother check their phones. And even though I've never met Abby's dad, there's no question: he's a middle-aged male version of Abby, eyelashes and all. Which is super disorienting. I turn quickly away, and my eyes fall on Mom.

Mom, as in *my* mom, dressed in work clothes and looking slightly out of place. I had no idea she was coming. I guess she snuck in through the back. She's standing a few feet away from the other adults. To be honest, she's always been weird around my friends' parents. Maybe because she's the youngest, by over a decade. I think she's paranoid that they secretly disapprove of her.

She shoots me an awkward wave, and I start walking toward her—but I'm intercepted by Alice Spier.

"Leah! I love your boots."

I look down and shrug, smiling. "How long are you in town?" I ask.

"Not much longer. I'm actually driving up, so I'm leaving tomorrow and picking up my boyfriend in New Jersey." She checks her watch. "Okay, Simon, where are you?"

"He just texted me. They're coming out now," Bram says.

Moments later, Simon, Nick, and Abby slip in through the side door, out of costume but still in makeup. For once, Nick and Abby aren't holding hands. Actually, Abby's holding Simon's hand, with Nick trailing behind them. People keep stopping him to talk, and every single time, he looks sheepish and uncomfortable. Nick Eisner is truly an awkward cinnamon roll of a leading man.

Simon spots the cake box immediately. "Is this cake? You got me a cake?" Garrett nods and starts to pop the box open, but Simon's beaming too hard at Bram to notice.

"Actually," Bram starts to say, but Simon kisses him on the cheek before he can get the word out.

"Dude, it's from me. Where's my kiss?" Garrett says.

I look at him. "Wow."

"Okay, Burke." He grins and digs for his keys. "You ready to roll?"

I point out my mom, and Garrett's entire face falls.

"I guess you don't need a ride anymore."

"I guess not."

He lingers, holding his car keys, and he doesn't say a word for what feels like an hour. I sense my mom watching us with interest.

"So . . . ," I say finally.

"Right. Hey." He clears his throat. "So, I was wondering. Do you want to come to the game tomorrow?"

"The game?" I glance at him.

"Have you ever seen us play?"

I nod. It's funny—soccer's the one Creekwood sport I've actually watched. I even used to enjoy it, back in sophomore year, when I had a crush on Nick. And it wasn't just about staring at his ass. It was weird. I started caring about the game, to the point that Simon used to call me an undercover jock.

"It's against North Creek," Garrett adds. "It should be a pretty sweet game."

"Oh. Um." I glance back over my shoulder. I *really* don't want to talk to Garrett in front of my mom right now.

He's still talking. "I'm sure you're busy, though. That's totally cool. You're probably going to the Saturday matinee of the play, right? Seriously, no worries."

"No, I'll come," I say quickly.

He looks startled. "To the game?"

"Yeah."

"Oh. Okay. Sweet." He grins, and my stomach twists weakly.

"So, what was that about?" Mom asks, voice lilting, as we walk to the car. Even in the darkness, I can see that she's smiling.

"Nothing."

"Nothing? Are we sure?"

"Mom. Stop." I sink into the passenger seat, turning quickly toward the window.

For a moment, we're both quiet. The parking lot is clogged with traffic and pedestrians, and Mom drums her hands on the steering wheel. "That was such an awesome play."

I grin. "It was the blizz."

"I still can't believe Nick's voice. And you know who's adorable?"

"Who?"

"Abby Suso."

I almost choke.

"That girl is pure charisma," Mom barrels on. "And she just seems like a total sweetheart. Like, I'd honestly love to see you with someone like her."

"Mom."

"You don't think she's cute?"

"She's Nick's girlfriend."

"I *know* that. I'm just saying. Hypothetically."

"I'm not talking about this."

Mom raises her eyebrows.

"Oh, hey." Her tone is suddenly cautious. "Question for you."

"Okay."

"So, Wells's birthday is tomorrow."

"Is that the question?"

"No." Mom laughs. "Okay. So, I was thinking the three of us could grab brunch together? He has a golf thing in the afternoon, so maybe late morning."

I gape at her. Birthday brunch. With Mom's boyfriend. I don't know, maybe this is normal for some families, but Mom never makes me get brunch with the boyfriends. And yet, here she is, just casually presenting it as if it's just another fun family Saturday. With *Wells*, of all people.

"Um. I'm going to Bram and Garrett's soccer game, so . . ." I shrug. "Sorry."

I stare out the window, eyes tracing the curve of the sidewalk. There's hardly anyone on the road tonight. You wouldn't think that would make a car feel smaller, but it does. And even though we aren't looking at each other, I feel Mom's eyes on me.

"I wish you'd give him a shot."

"Who, Garrett?" I ask, my voice jumping half an octave.

"Wells."

My face burns. "Oh."

I glance at Mom, who's sitting rigidly straight, chewing on her lip. She looks vaguely distraught. I don't entirely know what to make of it.

She sighs. "Okay, what if—"

"I'm not getting brunch with your boyfriend."

"Leah, don't be like this."

"Don't be like what?" I narrow my eyes. "How are we at the family brunch stage? You've been dating him for, what, three months?"

"Six months."

"Okay, you've literally been dating him for a shorter time than Simon and Bram. I know people who had longer relationships than that in middle school. Simon and *Anna* dated longer than that."

Mom shakes her head slowly. "You know, you'd never talk to one of your friends the way you talk to me. Can you imagine if you went up to Simon and said stuff like this about Bram?"

"Okay, that's—"

"You wouldn't. You would never do that. So why do you think it's okay to talk like that to me?"

I roll my eyes so hard my eyebrows hurt. "Oh, okay, now you're going to make this about Simon and Bram?"

"You're the one who brought them up!"

"Yeah, well." I throw my hands up. "Simon and Bram are actually legit. They are literally so in love. How could you even compare that to Wells?"

"You know what? Just stop talking," she snaps.

For a minute, it throws me. My mom's normally so mellow. I sputter, "Yeah, well—"

"No. Just stop. Okay? I don't want to hear it."

For a minute, it's silent. Then Mom turns on NPR and pulls onto Roswell Road. I lean back against the headrest and tilt my head toward the window. Then I squeeze my eyes shut.

7

I WAKE UP TO A blast of overhead lights. Mom pries the pillow off my face.

"What day is it?" I mumble.

"Saturday. Come on. Wells is on his way."

"What?" I sit up straight, pillow sliding to the floor. "I said no to that."

"I know. But I looked up the soccer schedule, and we'll be back by then anyway. Wells has tee time at two."

"What the fuck is tee time?" I rub my face and tug my phone out of the charger. "It's not even ten a.m."

Mom sits on the edge of my bed, and I tuck my legs up instantly, hugging them.

"I'm not going," I tell her.

"Leah, this isn't a question. I want you to do this. It would mean a lot to him."

"I don't care."

"Well, it would mean a lot to me, too."

I glare up at her.

She puts her hands up. "Look, okay. I don't know what to tell you. He's coming over. It's his birthday, and I already made the reservation. So you can start by putting on a bra."

I flop backward on my bed, yanking the pillow back over my face.

An hour later, I'm tucked into a booth at a steakhouse in Buckhead, next to Mom and across from Wells. A *steakhouse*. It's not even noon.

We put in our drink order, and Wells jumps right into the forced small talk. "So, your mom tells me you're in a band."

"Yup."

"Nice. I used to play the clarinet." He nods eagerly. "Good times, good times."

I don't even know how to respond to that. Like, I'm in an actual band, Wells. I'm not saying we're the Beatles, but we're not exactly honking our way through "Hot Cross Buns" in the school auditorium.

"Wells is a huge music fan," Mom says, patting his arm. I cringe every time she touches him. "What's the name of that singer you like?" Mom asks him. "The one from *American Idol*?"

"Oh, you mean Daughtry?"

Daughtry. I'm not even surprised. But wow—Mom should know better. If she wants me to respect this guy, she should have kept that detail under wraps.

"Have you heard of Oh Wonder?" I ask, even though I know he hasn't. It is physically, chemically impossible for a person who likes Daughtry to have heard of Oh Wonder. But I want to see if he'll admit it. Maybe I'm a dick, but this is how I test people. I never judge someone for not knowing a band. I only judge the ones who try to fake it.

"No, I haven't. Is that a band or a singer?" He pulls out his phone. "I'll write that down. Oh Wonder—two words?"

So he's honest. I guess that's something.

"They're a band."

"Are they anything like Stevie Wonder?"

I bite back a laugh. "Not really." I glance up at Mom and catch her smiling.

Confession: I think Stevie Wonder rules. That's probably not cool to admit, but whatever. Apparently, my parents used to play me "Signed, Sealed, Delivered (I'm Yours)" on their old-timey CD player, even before I was born. I think my mom read somewhere that I'd be able to hear it in utero. And I guess it worked, because I used to sing it around the house and in the grocery store. And even now, that song makes me calm in a way I can't explain. My mom said they picked it because it was the one song she and my dad agreed they'd be willing to listen to over and over, every day, for the rest of their lives.

The rest of their lives. Look how quickly that blew up in their faces. Just thinking about it hurts in a way I can't quite pinpoint.

We split a massive pile of designer tortilla chips with spinach and queso, and everything's sort of okay for a minute. Mom and Wells are talking about work, so I pull out my phone. I've missed a few texts.

From Anna: Ugh, so Morgan's REALLY upset.

From Garrett: You should totally wear this today. Laughing-crying emoji. He's attached a picture of a girl wearing what appears to be a helmet cut out of a soccer ball. With holes on the sides. And pigtails. Through the holes.

Obviously happening, I reply.

Then I turn back to Anna's text. I guess I'm kind of at a loss. Like, I don't want to be a negligent friend, but I don't know how to help Morgan if I can't even talk to her. I think I hate the concept of *needing space.* What it really means is that the person's mad at you, or hates you, or doesn't give a shit about you. They just don't want to admit it. Like my dad. That's just how he put it. He *needed space* from my mom. And now here we are, almost seven years later, at a steakhouse with fucking Wells.

Show her the video where the dog's owner dresses like Gumby, I write finally.

GENIUS, Anna replies.

"Sweetie, put your phone away, please. We're in a restaurant."

"Seriously?" I point my chin toward Wells. "He's literally on his phone right now."

Mom narrows her eyes. "He's confirming his tee time."

"Oh, right. So it's like a golf emergency."

"Leah."

"I mean, clearly, it's so urgent, or he wouldn't be—*gasp*—on his phone in a restaurant."

"Don't be an asshole," she hisses, leaning toward me. "It's his birthday."

I shrug and press my lips together like I don't give any shits at all, but there's this tug in my chest. Because birthdays are sort of sacred, and maybe I really am an asshole. I'd been thinking of Wells as the interloper, busting in on my Mom brunch with his tiny ears and his Daughtry love. But maybe I'm the one crashing the party.

Wells ends the call, turns to Mom, and starts babbling about handicaps on the birdie par or some other golfy bullshit. I let my eyes drift shut.

I mean, parents sometimes date people. I know this. Moms are technically human beings, and human beings are allowed to have romantic lives. But I have this feeling, suddenly, that I'm on a too-fast treadmill—like things are moving so quickly, I might slide off the back end. I never imagined I could be bumped out of my own family. I feel knocked down.

I feel *demoted.*

And the thought makes me so tired, I can barely sit upright. Like, even the thought of walking to the car feels like prepping for a marathon. And it's barely past noon. All I want is to collapse on my bed. Possibly with music. Definitely not with real pants on.

I can't go to the game. Not feeling the way I feel right now. I can't deal with Garrett and his try-hard, dudebro act. Like, we all know you're secretly a dreamy-eyed piano kid, so stop pretending to be a douchebag. And stop messing with my head. Either flirt with me or don't. Either be cute or not.

I don't know. I don't have the energy for Garrett. That probably makes me a jerk, and I should clearly text him an excuse, but I don't even know what I'd say. *Sorry to miss the game, Garrett. Turns out, you're confusing and annoying and I kind of can't deal with your face.* I just can't. Not today.

Mom asks me, hours later, if I need a ride to the game.

I say no.

Then I ignore six texts in a row, all from Garrett.

I DESTROY THINGS IN MY dreams.

I scream and argue until everyone hates me, then I wake up in tears from how real it feels. Sunday morning is like that. I sit up in bed, feeling battered and alone. And the first thing I see are those six missed texts from Garrett.

Hey, you up there somewhere? I don't see you!

Yo, are you in the parking lot or something

Where are you?

Ok Greenfeld and I are heading to WaHo with Spier and everyone. You should come!

Oh man, I don't know how I missed you today. I feel bad.

Oh well, I hope you enjoyed the game anyway. Next time, stick around okay lol. Are you going to the play tomorrow?

Holy shit. I'm the worst.

Garrett thinks I was there. At the game, in the bleachers, probably wearing a homemade soccer ball helmet. As opposed to moping around my bedroom, ignoring his texts.

I am such a dick. Like, I'm an actual flaccid penis of a person.

And now I want to lock myself in my room all over again, but I can't miss the last performance of the play. I'm not that big of an asshole. I don't even mind the idea of hanging out with Garrett, in theory. But I don't want to face him. If there's one thing I hate, it's apologies. I don't like getting them. I *really* don't like making them.

I think it's unavoidable.

I dress myself carefully, like I'm going into battle. I feel stronger when I look cute. I zip into my universe dress—the greatest thrift store find of my entire life. It's cotton, blue and black, sprinkled with stars and galaxies across my chest. My boobs are literally out of this world. Then I muss up my hair so it's just a little wavy and spend twenty minutes giving myself flawless winged eyeliner. It makes my eyes look super green in a way that almost catches me off guard.

Mom needs the car, so she drops me off at school. I'm early. Early is good. I pick a seat near the front, but I can't stop turning toward the entrance—and every time the auditorium door opens, my heart jumps into my throat. I have this feeling that as soon as Garrett sees me, he'll know I was lying. And then he and the guys will be pissed, and it will be this whole big thing, and our whole friend group will implode. Because of me.

There's a tap on my shoulder, and I almost fall out of my seat.

But it's just Anna. "Can we sit here?"

"We?"

"Morgan's in the bathroom."

Another conversation I'm not ready for. *Oh, hey, Morgan! Sorry you didn't get into your dream school. Hope it's cool that I'm totally going there.* Panic must be written all over my face, because Anna purses her lips. "You know she's not mad at you, right?"

"Right."

"I think she's worried you'll be awkward."

"I haven't even talked to her."

"I know, I know. She's just paranoid. It's fine. I'm texting her where we are." But before Anna can hit send, Morgan trails in behind a pack of giggling middle schoolers. She looks miserable. She looks like she just got dumped. She's in sweatpants and glasses, her blue-streaked hair scraped back into a messy bun. Anna catches her eye and waves, and she cuts down the aisle and across a row of seats.

"Hey," she says quietly.

"How are you doing?" My voice sounds so painfully gentle that I cringe.

"Fine. I'm fine."

I nod, and Morgan shrugs, and Anna's eyes shift back and forth between us.

"Sorry about UGA," I say finally. "That really sucks."

"Yeah." She sounds defeated.

"Sorry," I say again.

She sinks into her seat. "Whatever. I'm not mad at you or anything."

I perch on the edge of the seat beside her.

She leans back, covering her face with her hands. "It's just . . . ugh. It's just so unfair."

"Yeah . . ."

"Not you. You totally deserved to get in. You're like a genius. But other people . . ."

I swallow. "I don't know how they make their decisions."

Morgan smiles humorlessly. "Well, I know how they make some of them."

"What do you mean?"

"I'm just saying. I'm ranked eleventh in the class. And some of the people who *did* get into Georgia . . . aren't." She shrugs. Beside me, Anna shifts uncomfortably.

I blink. "You think someone lied on their application?"

"I think I'm white," Morgan replies.

The whole world seems to stop. The blood rushes to my cheeks.

"Are you talking about Abby?" I say quietly.

Morgan shrugs.

My mouth falls open. “I can’t believe you.”

“Well, sorry.” Her cheeks flush.

“That’s really fucking gross, Morgan.”

“Oh, so you’re sticking up for Abby now. Awesome.”

I lean forward, chest tight. “I’m not sticking up for anyone. You’re being racist.”

I can’t believe this—and coming from *Morgan*. Morgan, who read *All American Boys* three times and drove all the way to Decatur to get it signed. Morgan, who once shouted down a stranger in a grocery store for wearing a Trump hat.

“I’m being honest,” says Morgan.

“No, I’m pretty sure you’re being racist.”

“Who’s racist?” Garrett asks, sidling up. I glance up at him, and Bram’s there, too. Morgan sinks into her seat, like she’s trying to disappear.

I stare her down. “Well, according to Morgan, Abby only got into Georgia because she’s black.”

Bram winces.

Morgan’s face is blotchy red. “That’s not what I meant.” She grips the armrest, eyes flashing.

“Well, you said it.” I stand, abruptly, my jaw clenched and sore. I’m furious, down to my bones, in a way I can’t even articulate. I push past the boys and storm up the aisle. Random people tilt their heads toward me as I pass. They know I’m pissed. I always wear it on my face. I slide into an empty row near the back and squeeze my eyes shut.

"Hey," Garrett says, plopping down next to me. Bram sits beside him.

"I'm so angry," I say.

"Because of Morgan?" asks Garrett.

I shrug, lips pressed tightly.

Garrett and Bram exchange glances. "She thinks Abby took her spot at Georgia?" Garrett asks.

"I don't know. But she thinks Abby only got in because she's black, and that's bullshit."

"People think that a lot," Bram says softly.

"That's messed up," Garrett says.

"Uh, yeah."

"You know, I didn't realize you and Suso were such good friends."

I feel the heat rise in my cheeks. "We're not. It doesn't matter. Jesus. I'm just saying it's racist."

He props his hands up defensively. "Okay."

"Okay," I huff back at him.

Bram just watches us, not saying a word, which makes me even more self-conscious. I tug my dress down and stare at my knees. Maybe I could send a telepathic message backstage to the powers that be. *Dear God and/or Cal Price: please start this show now. Dim the lights so I can disappear.*

Garrett nudges me. "So, did you get my texts?"

And . . . fuck my life.

"Yeah. Oh. Yeah, I'm sorry. My phone just . . ." I trail off uselessly.

"No worries. Just wanted to hear what you thought of the game!"

God, I can't. I'm sorry. I should tell him, but I can't. I'm like an actual fuse. Overload me, and I shut down. I guess Garrett's the hair dryer who pushes me over the limit.

I lie. "It was cool."

"Yeah. Ha. If you forget about the first half."

"Mmhmm." I nod vaguely.

"Where'd you run off to afterward?" Bram pipes up. "We missed you."

"Oh. Um. My mom needed the car, so . . ." I swallow.

"That sucks."

"Yup."

The houselights dim. Thank God thank God thank God.

The overture begins, and my whole body sighs.

9

HOURS LATER, I'M IN SIMON'S backseat, driving to Martin Addison's house, of all places.

"Who let him host this?" I ask. I can't help but growl a little when I talk about Martin. Abby, sitting next to me, shrugs and shakes her head.

"I don't know," says Simon. "He offered."

"We should have had our own party," Abby says.

"Can we just suck it up? Please? It's the last cast party." Simon's voice skids on the word *last*. He's never been good at endings.

"You okay?" Bram asks softly.

Simon pauses. "Yeah."

The light turns green, and Simon makes a left. Martin lives at the end of a cul-de-sac in one of those leafy neighborhoods off Creekside Drive. I've only been there once. It was freshman year for a history project. Me, Martin, and Morgan. And we chose one another, too. What a joke.

No one talks for the rest of the ride. Bram fiddles with the music, and Abby stares out the window, lips tightly pursed. I can't remember the last time I've seen her look so upset. And I know she hates Martin, but I can't help but wonder if it's more than that. Maybe Morgan said something to her.

Martin's whole street is lined with cars, and it's almost dark when we get there. We pull in behind Garrett's minivan, which is parked but still running. He drove here with Nick—they turn off the car and step out when they see us. And wow. It's ridiculously cold out, especially in a cotton dress and a cardigan. I'll just say my out-of-this-world boobs are extra out of this world tonight.

We end up walking in twosomes. Nick and Garrett, Abby and Bram, Simon and me. It's weird that Abby and Nick aren't walking together. I lean toward Simon, close enough that our arms touch. "Hey, is something up with Nick and Abby?"

Simon grimaces and shrugs. "Yeah. I don't know. I talked to Nick for a minute earlier. I think they're fighting."

"About what?"

"Well, Nick got into Tufts yesterday."

"Oh, wow."

"I know, he's psyched," Simon says, "but then I guess he and Abby had the talk."

"The talk?"

"The are-we-doing-long-distance-or-what talk."

"Oh." Something tugs in my chest. "Okay."

"Yeah. It didn't go well."

I glance up at Abby, paces ahead of me, thoroughly bundled in an oversized cardigan. She's walking so close to Bram, you'd think they were conjoined.

"Okay, so translate that," I say quickly.

"Translate what?"

"*Didn't go well.* What does that mean?"

Simon frowns. "I don't know. Nick wants to stay together, but Abby doesn't want to do long distance."

"Oh shit."

"Yeah."

We walk in silence for a minute, almost at Martin's house. There's music coming from the basement—the soundtrack to *Joseph.* A little too on the nose for the *Joseph* cast party, in my opinion, but what do I know?

"I'm scared they'll break up," Simon says finally, his voice barely audible. "I think it could ruin us."

"You and Bram?"

"No. God. No. We're good." Simon smiles. "No, I mean *us.*" He waves his hands around vaguely. "Our group. Our posse."

I snort. "Our posse."

"I'm serious. What if there's drama and it gets weird and we have to go to prom in separate limos?"

"Oh no. Not separate limos." I try not to smile.

"Shut up. It would be sad and you know it."

"Aww, Spier. Why are you sad?" Garrett bursts between us, hooking his arms around our shoulders. "Don't be sad. We're about to walk into a partaaaay."

"Are you already drunk?" I ask.

"No." He scoffs. "I'm naturally like this."

"I actually believe that."

"You kidder," he says. He nudges Simon, hard. "She's *such* a kidder. She loves me. Did you know she came to the game on Saturday?"

My stomach drops.

"That's right, Spier. Leah Andromeda Burke picked my game over your play. And she wasn't there to see Greenfeld. I'm just saying."

"Andromeda?"

"That's not your middle name?"

"No."

"Now it is." He squeezes my shoulder. "Leah. Andromeda. Burke."

Yeah, he's already drunk. I don't know how he managed to do that walking from his car to Martin's house, but he did. It's in his voice, in his grin, on his breath. I tug his hand off my shoulder and walk straight to the doorstep, where Abby and Bram are waiting.

"Buuuuuurke. Wait up!"

"How did he get drunk already?" I ask Bram.

"He brought a flask in the car."

"He drove drunk?"

"Oh no. He wouldn't do that. Apparently, he and Nick drank it while they were parked."

"Of course they did." Abby rolls her eyes.

"That's so stupid. How are they getting home?"

Bram sighs. "Probably me."

There's a note taped to the door, written in loopy handwriting. *Welcome, Egyptians and Canaanites! Venture down to the basement!* Abby catches my eye and smiles faintly. I look quickly down at my feet. When I look up again, Simon, Garrett, and Nick have caught up to us on the stoop. Abby pushes the door open and walks straight inside.

Martin's basement is huge. These Shady Creek houses are unreal. The Addisons aren't even rich. Not like Jeeves-shall-show-you-into-our-parlor rich. They're just the usual Shady Creek rich: three floors and flat-screen TVs and a pinball machine in the basement.

I'm guessing from the tiny sandwiches and ceramic plates that Martin's parents had a hand in setting this up. There are sophomores draped over the couches, legs over hands over laps. A couple of people are singing and dancing along with the *Joseph* soundtrack. Cal and Nora are tucked into an armchair, scrolling through his phone. I think Bram, Garrett, and I are the only non-theater people here.

"You guys came!" Martin bounds over to us. Kind of like a golden retriever, as insulting as that is to Bieber Spier. "Okay, so, people are just hanging out, and, uh. Let me know if there's anything you want. My mom can run to Publix." He pokes his elbow nervously and lowers his voice. "And there's vodka. In the bathroom."

"In the bathroom?" Simon raises his eyebrows.

"Yeah. It's, uh. Don't tell my parents. It's under the sink behind the toilet bowl cleaner. It's the one in the vodka bottle. Don't drink the toilet bowl cleaner."

"The vodka is the one in the vodka bottle. Got it."

"Cool," Martin says. And for a minute, he just stands there nodding. "Okay, so, I'm gonna . . . yeah." He walks away backward, almost knocking over a freshman. Then he turns back around, makes finger guns at Simon, and almost bumps into someone else. I swear to God, that kid should wear a protective rubber bumper and possibly water wings.

I turn back to find Simon, but he's already settled onto a corner of the couch with Bram. Abby turns to me. "You don't drink, do you?"

"Nope."

"Right. Okay. But you'll come with me, right? To the bathroom? So I don't drink the toilet bowl cleaner?"

Out of the corner of my eye, I catch Garrett dropping it like it's hot to "Go, Go, Go Joseph." Nick's leaning against the wall nearby, flushed and smiling. He's talking to Taylor Metternich.

Abby rolls her eyes. "What an asshole. Come on." She grabs my hand and tugs it. *Abby.* This is weird. "I don't even care, you know?" she says as I follow her down the hallway. "Like, I'm not even upset. He can do whatever he wants. Is this the bathroom?"

"I think so?"

She tries the door, but it's locked. "Someone's in there. Only Martin would put the booze in the bathroom. Let's just sit." She slides against the wall, landing cross-legged, and I settle in beside her. Legs straight ahead, pressed together. I should have worn jeans.

She sighs, shifting toward me. "I can't believe he's talking to her. Seriously, Taylor?"

God, what do I even say to that? *Sorry you and Nick aren't as perfect as everyone thinks you are.*

"Taylor's annoying," I say finally.

"Yeah." She folds her legs up, hugs her knees, and tilts her head to look at me. "Anyway, I heard you stood up for me today."

"The Morgan thing?"

"Mmhmm. Bram told me what happened." She smiles. "You didn't have to do that."

"I mean, Morgan was being racist."

"Yup. But not everyone would have called her out, so." Abby shrugs. "Thanks."

There's this flutter in my stomach. I don't exactly feel like puking. But I don't *not* feel like puking. This is why I don't get close to Abby Suso. It always ends in nausea. I shift slightly to the right, putting an inch of space between us.

"Did she ever mention the tour thing?" Abby asks, after a moment.

"Yeah." I smile wryly. "Guess that's not happening."

"Well, you and I could still go."

Suddenly, the bathroom door bursts open, and out stumble two juniors. They're flushed and draped all over each other, and something tells me vodka and toilet bowl cleaner aren't the only liquids we'll find in this bathroom.

"They have sex hair," Abby whispers.

"I know."

"Like, you can't do that in Martin Addison's bathroom. I am perturbed. Aggrieved. Disquieted. Hey, Morgan, guess who got an 800 on the SAT critical reading section." Abby locks the bathroom door behind us and kneels in front of the sink.

I perch on top of the toilet seat. "Did you really?"

Her mouth quirks. "Yeah. Ugh. Sorry, I feel like I'm bragging."

"No, it's cool."

She smiles up at me and shrugs. "I don't know. Anyway, here's the vodka, and there's Coke. Is vodka and Coke a thing?"

"I have no idea."

"Clearly, Martin has no idea either." She rolls her eyes. "You sure you don't want any?"

"I'm sure."

"Okay. I'm just gonna . . ." Abby tips some vodka into a red plastic cup, and then she fills the rest with Coke. She takes a sip and grimaces. "Wow. This is gross."

"I'm sorry."

She shrugs. "Am I allowed to bring the cup out? I don't have to drink this in here, right?"

"I mean, that would be weird."

"Yeah, but it's Martin."

I laugh. "Right."

I tap the toes of my flats on the tiles, staring down. I feel awkward and strange. This is so unexpected. Alone with Abby Suso in Martin Addison's bathroom. I sneak a peek at her through my lashes. She's leaning against the bathtub now, back straight, pretzeled legs. Every time she sips her drink, her nose wrinkles. I've never understood the appeal of drinking. It's not like liquor tastes good. I mean, I know it's not about that. It's about feeling loose and light and unstoppable. Simon described it to me once. He said drinking lets you say and do things without filtering or overthinking. But I don't get how that's a good thing.

Abby yawns. "It's like—okay. He didn't apply anywhere in Georgia. That's fine. But that's where I'll be, and the closest he could be is North Carolina. And I'm sorry, but I don't want to stay home from parties because I'm expecting a call from my boyfriend. I don't want to miss out on *college*, you know?"

Sure, Abby. I totally know. My boyfriends are *always* trying to call me during parties. So many parties. Which I totally go to, because I love sitting in bathrooms watching other people drink.

I should hate this.

Why don't I hate this?

Someone bangs on the door, and Abby hops to her feet. "Just a minute!" She chugs her drink. "Oh my God, this is so gross. I'm literally going to vomit."

I stand abruptly, pushing up the toilet lid.

"Not *literally* literally. Come on, let's go." She takes my hand.

We step out of the bathroom, and there's Garrett, blue eyes shining. He's acquired a party hat somehow, which he's wearing cocked to the side. He stares at our hands and his mouth falls open.

"Oh my God. What. OH MY GOD."

"Not what you're thinking, Garrett."

"Ladies, wow. Okay. Hear me out. I have an idea. Let's just *all* go back into the bathroom, and whatever happens . . ."

"Nope," I say flatly.

Abby releases me and twines both of her hands through Garrett's, peering up at him with doe eyes. "Garrett, sweetie," she says, "I will never, ever do that." Then she tugs her hands away and pats him firmly on his bicep. "In front of you," she adds quietly, nudging him toward the bathroom.

My stomach swoops.

"WHAT?" Garrett shrieks, eyes darting back and forth between us. "You should. Do that in front of me. Okay? Please. Good. I have to pee."

"So go pee."

I think my brain's made of Jell-O. My thoughts won't stay in one place. *She'd never do that.* In front of Garrett. But maybe otherwise?

How am I supposed to interpret that?

We leave around eleven. Garrett's a drunk mess, so Bram drives him home in the minivan, with Simon following behind. Then we all pile into Simon's car for a shitshow of a ride. Simon and Bram take the front. Nora and I are basically on top of each other, squished between Nick and Abby, who aren't talking. It's the kind of silence that has its own gravity. Black hole silence. Simon tries to fight it with a steady stream of Simon-babble, but after a few minutes, even he stops speaking.

We pull into Bram's driveway, and Simon leans over the gearshift. They kiss softly and quickly, and Bram mouths something to Simon. Simon shakes his head, grinning. Abby calls shotgun as soon as Bram unbuckles his seat belt.

"You sure you don't want to spend the night?" Simon asks for the fifth time tonight. And normally I would. I don't care that it's Sunday. Simon lives so close to school that it would actually make my morning easier.

But Abby's sleeping at Simon's tonight. And I've had enough Abby weirdness for one night.

My mind reels through the last few hours. Morgan's blotchy red anger. Lying to Garrett. Abby kneeling in front of the bathroom sink. Abby taking Garrett's hands. Abby saying *never.* But only never *in front of Garrett.*

And I have no idea if she's kidding.

10

THE SECOND I STEP OFF the bus on Monday, Abby's in my face. "Hey," she says casually, falling into step beside me. "So, last night was weird."

"Uh, yeah." I wince as soon as I say it. I have this problem sometimes where I sound bitchier than I mean to, and it's a thousand times worse when it comes to Abby. Simon once asked me point-blank why I dislike her so much. But here's the thing: I don't even dislike Abby. It's just that my brain doesn't work right around her.

It doesn't help that she looks obnoxiously cute—striped shirt tucked into a red skirt over tights, hair clipped back with bobby pins. She covers her mouth, yawning, and then catches my eye and grins.

"Okay, so I have a proposition for you," she says.

"Oh yeah?"

"Mmhmm." She tilts her head sideways and her eyes glint like she's about to make a joke. She's an inch or two shorter than me, and probably half my weight. Or not. I don't know. She's not actually that thin. Just kind of trim and muscular. *Mesomorph.* That's the word I know from the magazines Mom leaves in the bathroom.

"So, this campus tour," she says when we get to my locker. "I'm not going with my parents. Not doing it."

"Everyone brings their parents."

She shakes her head. "Not me."

"You sound very certain about that." I feel myself smiling.

"Do you want to come with me?" she asks. "Spring break. Any day. I can borrow my mom's car and drive us up there, and we can stay with my cousin's friend. It could be like a whole road trip."

"Like Simon and Nick?"

"Uh, they *wish* they were coming on our trip. Because we'll get to go to parties and do whatever we want. It'll be amazing. We'll actually get a real idea of what it's like there."

I look at her, speechless. Other than Martin Addison's bathroom, I don't think we've been alone in a room together for over a year. But suddenly Abby's talking like we're the kind of friends who go to parties and take selfies and split French fries at midnight. Am I losing my mind?

"Or not," she adds quickly. "We don't have to go to parties.

I seriously don't care. Totally up to you."

"So, you want me to go with you to Athens," I say slowly. Then I realize my fingers are tapping out a drumbeat. On my locker. I let my hand fall.

"Yes."

"Why?"

"What do you mean?"

I shake my head quickly, staring at my shoes. "We're not . . ." I shut my eyes.

I'm not friends with Abby Suso. I'm not anything with Abby Suso. And to be honest, this whole thing is fucking me up a little.

"Obviously, I know you have to ask your mom and everything."

"I just . . ."

I glance up in time to see Taylor charging toward me, hands clasped together like she means business. "We'll talk," Abby says, the palm of her hand grazing my arm. Then she disappears up the stairs, like she was never here at all.

"So?" Taylor says with a big, expectant smile.

My eyes drift toward the staircase. "What's up?" I say half-heartedly.

"So, what did you think?"

"What did I think?"

"Of the play!"

"Oh," I say. "It was great. Congrats."

"Obviously, a few people could benefit from formal training, but overall, it was good, right? And Nick was just so wonderful." She smiles. "Hey, speaking of Nick . . ."

God, this girl. I don't think she knows the meaning of the word *subtle.* Like, if you're going to bust in talking about Nick and then segue into talking about Nick, it's going to be pretty goddamn clear that you want to talk about Nick.

"I just had this really cool thought," Taylor continues. "So, like, everyone—oh my God, *everyone*—is telling me they love the way my voice and Nick's voice blend together. Like, so many people have told me they just got *chills* listening to us." She laughs. "Isn't that funny?"

"So funny."

"Anyway." She beams. "I was thinking—what if Nick was in our band?"

I pause, narrowing my eyes. "What?"

"Like, we could add a harmony line to the lead vocals, or maybe even rework our set list to include some duets. And, obviously, he could play guitar."

"We have Nora."

"Right, of course! But what if we had two lead guitarists? I just think it would add this extra dimension to the sound, you know? And obviously, having a guy in the band would add so much vocal range."

"Yeah, but we're an all-girl band. That's kind of the point."

Taylor nods eagerly. "Oh, totally. Like, I totally get that.

But I was also thinking maybe it would be sort of cool to have, like, an all-girl band with a guy singer. You never see that. You always see an all-boy band with a girl singer, so this would be like a reversal, you know?"

I mean, holy shit. She's serious. She wants Nick in our girl band. So, now I'm wondering how hard you can side-eye someone before your eyes stick that way. Permanent side-eye. It'll look great with my resting bitch face.

"Anyway, maybe we could discuss it at rehearsal? We're still meeting today, right?"

Fuck. Hadn't remembered that. And I'm *really* not up for an afternoon with Morgan. Really, extremely, wholeheartedly not up for it.

But I'm not a total dick. So at the end of the day, when Anna finds me at my locker, I follow without protest.

Everyone's already in the music room when we get there. There's Nora, cross-legged on the floor, tuning her guitar. Taylor's on the floor, too, in a butterfly yoga pose, and Morgan's planted stiffly in a plastic blue chair. She stares at her knees when I walk into the room.

"Well," Anna says slowly. "We're all here."

I scoot near the piano, scrunching my legs up in front of me. Nora bites her lip, eyes drifting from Morgan to me. No one speaks.

Anna shakes her head. "Okay, y'all want to do the whole

awkward silence thing? Fine. Get it out of your system." She pulls out her phone. "Five minutes. Go."

"What, you're timing us?"

"Four minutes and forty-eight seconds." Anna holds up her phone.

"This is ridiculous," Morgan mutters.

Anna nods shortly. "I agree. You guys are being ridiculous."

"Are you serious?"

"Four minutes and nineteen seconds."

I blink. "Wow. So, Morgan says something blatantly racist, I call her out on it, but somehow we're both equally ridiculous? Just some silly girl drama?"

"Leah, you're overreacting, and you know it. It was one stupid comment," says Anna.

"One racist comment." Out of the corner of my eye, I see Morgan wince.

"Yeah, don't lecture me about racism," Anna says.

My whole body clenches. "You know what? I don't even know if I want to be in the band anymore."

"Oh, come on." Anna rolls her eyes. "Because of Morgan?"

I shrug, cheeks burning.

"So, you're telling me," Anna says, "that you're throwing away a year of work and collaboration and everything, because of one comment?"

Anna's looking at me like I just choked a puppy. Nora and

Taylor are silent, and I don't dare look at Morgan. I stare down at the floor.

"I'm just—"

"Like, you're mad. I get it. But holy shit. Quitting the band?"

"It's not like the band's going to last forever." I laugh, but it comes out flat. "We graduate in less than three months."

And in that moment—for a split second—I *feel* it. How short that is. How soon everything changes. It's strange, because good-byes are a thing I can understand intellectually, but they almost never feel real. Which makes it hard to brace for impact. I don't know how to miss people when they're standing right in front of me.

"Look, we had a good run." A lump rises in my throat. "But you can't force this. I'm not okay making music with—"

Anna's phone alarm rings, making all of us jump.

Then Morgan stands. "You know what? Let's just do it this way. I'm the fuckup. I'm the one who ruined the band." Her voice breaks. "So clearly, I'm the one who should leave."

Anna sighs. "Morgan, come on."

"No, it's cool. I know when I'm not wanted. I'm super used to it." She swipes the corners of her eyes with her fingers. Then she scrunches up her mouth and walks swiftly to the door, slamming it shut behind her.

"Wow. Hope you're happy," says Anna.

"Okay, can you stop?" Nora says, whirling to face her. "This isn't Leah's fault."

Anna opens her mouth to reply, but Taylor cuts her off. "Okay, can someone please explain to me what just happened?"

We all look at her.

Taylor looks perplexed. "Morgan just quit the band?"

"Apparently," Anna says.

"Okay." Taylor pauses, pressing her lips together. You can almost see her mind whirring. "Wow. So, I guess we need a fifth person."

Jesus. "Taylor, we're not letting Nick in the band."

"Okay, but—"

"Nick isn't even a keyboardist," Nora says.

"No, he's not," confirms Nick, and my head whips toward the doorway. He's standing, flanked by Bram and Garrett, all in soccer shorts. And then there's Abby, in gym clothes. I'm a little caught off guard. I didn't even hear them come in.

Taylor beams. "What are you guys doing here?"

"Well," Bram says. "I have a favor to—"

"Wait," Garrett interjects, smiling almost sheepishly. "Did you just say you need a keyboardist?"

"You're a keyboardist?" asks Taylor.

"Well. I'm a pianist."

Nora gapes at him. "Excuse me?"

Garrett laughs. "A pi-a-nist," he enunciates, sauntering into the music room. He sinks down next to me and grins. "A pianist with a—"

"Yeah, we get it," I say.

"We do need a pianist," Taylor says slowly. "Morgan just quit the band."

"What? Really?" says Garrett.

"Yeah, because Leah was being a dick again," Anna mutters.

"Oh." Garrett glances nervously between Anna and me. "This is about the UGA thing?"

"You mean the fact that Morgan thought I got in because I'm black," Abby says.

"She doesn't actually think that." Anna blushes. "No one thinks that."

Abby snorts. "You'd be surprised."

And then no one speaks for what feels like an hour.

Finally, Taylor turns to Bram. "What's your favor?"

"Right." Bram shoots her a tiny smile, shutting the door gently behind him. "So, I think I've got my promposal figured out."

"What? Oh my God!" Taylor exclaims. "You're promposing to Simon?"

He nods slightly, and she emits a joyful squeak.

"But I need you guys—Nora, you especially. He's giving you a ride tomorrow, right?"

"To school?" Nora nods. "Yeah."

"Do you think it would be possible to get him down here at exactly eight fifteen?"

"You're promposing to him in the music room?" I ask.

"Yes. Hopefully. And actually, I have a question for you, too."

"Hit it," I say, peeking over his shoulder, where Nick's settled onto the floor beside Taylor. It's hard to know what to make of that. Maybe it means he hasn't made up with Abby. Not that I care. It's just weird.

Bram bites his lip. "Do you think I could borrow that drum kit?"

11

THE TRICKY PART IS THE timing. Getting Simon to school by 8:15 is easy. Getting him there at *exactly* 8:15 takes a little more finesse. Thank God Nora talked me into spending the night, because who knew Simon Spier was so aggressively punctual in the mornings. It's taking all our combined efforts to stall him.

"You guys," Simon bellows up the stairs at 7:44. "Come on, let's go!"

"Just a minute!" Nora yells back.

"What are you guys even doing up there?"

Nora pokes her head out into the hallway. "Dude. Cool your jets."

"Is he always this excited about school?" I mutter.

Nora rolls her eyes. "Yeah. He likes to do homework in the mornings with Bram."

"Homework," I say, with air quotes.

"Exactly."

Simon clambers up the stairs and hovers in Nora's doorway. "Guys. We're going to be late."

"No we're not." Nora calmly latches her guitar case. "You just want to get there early to see your boyfriend."

Simon huffs. "I have homework. Come on. We're leaving." He grabs Nora's backpack.

"Wait," Nora says. Simon looks exasperated, but Nora just shrugs. "I think I'm wearing two left socks."

"No. No you're not. That's not a thing," says Simon. "Let's go."

Then he hoists the backpack onto his shoulder, already tugging his keys out of his pocket. I swear to God, that clueless little peanut. It's like he's determined to ruin his own promposal.

Nora and I exchange wry glances as soon as he leaves the room. "It's fine. We can stall him in the parking lot." She grabs her guitar case.

The Spiers live five minutes from school—I think they can technically walk there. Simon pulls into the senior lot and checks his phone as soon as the car's off. I check the clock on the dashboard: 7:57.

"Actually, I need advice," I blurt.

It's a foolproof question—Simon loves being needed. And

sure enough, his whole face lights up. "Yeah. Okay, yeah, sure. Let me just text Bram . . . okay. What's up?" He turns all the way around to face me.

"It's about Garrett," I say, leaning forward between the seats.

Ten minutes later, Simon's talking in circles. "So, you just no-showed?" he asks.

I shrug sheepishly. "Yeah."

"But Garrett thinks you went to the game."

I nod.

"Leah!"

"Am I the worst person?"

"Well, no," says Simon. "That would be Voldemort."

"But I'm close, right? Like, Voldemort is here." I level my hand up, almost to the roof of the car. "And I'm here." I drop my hand a few inches. "And then the next worst guy is down here. Like, the dentist who killed that lion. He's right here."

Nora laughs. "Wow."

"You have to tell him," says Simon.

My stomach drops. "You think?"

"Yeah." He nods. "You should be honest. Just explain what happened, you know? Garrett's a really nice guy. He'll totally understand." Simon rubs his cheek, pondering this. "Or . . . you could say you got sick. Okay, that actually sounds more plausible. You could just be like, 'Hey, I was about to leave, but then I got really, really sick, and I couldn't even check my phone.'"

The corners of my mouth tug upward. "So I should be honest . . . but also lie."

"Yes," Simon says.

"Simon."

"I could tell him for you. I could hint that you had really bad diarrhea and were too embarrassed to mention it. Garrett, of all people, would *definitely* understand that." Simon snickers.

"I'm not telling Garrett I had diarrhea!"

"Right, I'll tell him."

"I will hurt you."

"Me too," Nora says.

"Why are girls so violent?" asks Simon.

I don't even respond. I just side-eye him to hell.

"Maybe you shouldn't mention it," Simon says a moment later. "He'll probably just forget about the whole thing."

"So now you're saying she shouldn't say anything?" Nora asks.

"Definitely not." He nods firmly.

So I should definitely tell the truth and definitely lie and also definitely avoid the conversation altogether. Thank you for this classic Simon wisdom.

"Hey, so what do you think of Garrett?" Simon asks slyly.

"Oh, hey! Will you look at that? It's almost eight fifteen," I say. Already, my hand's on the door.

Now I just have to get Simon to the music room. I could ask him to watch me drum. Is that weird? I don't think he'd suspect anything, but what if he's just like *nah*? Then it's basically game over, unless I want to seem pushy and obsessed. But I can't let Bram down, so—

"I have to go the bathroom. Here." Nora shoves her guitar case at Simon, and hurries into school.

"Diarrhea," Simon says, nodding sagely. He glances down at the guitar case. "What do I do with this?"

Nora, you fucking hero.

"We could drop it off in the music room," I say with the most casual shrug I can muster.

The entire music room is lit up with Christmas lights. In March. And Simon doesn't even notice.

"Someone left your drum kit out," he remarks, setting Nora's guitar beside it.

"It's not actually my drum kit." I glance at the storage closet before turning back to Simon. "Anyone can use it."

"Really?" His whole face lights up.

"Totally." I nod. "You should try it."

Simon settles onto the stool, looking like a toddler about to fly an airplane. I bring him some drumsticks and he peers up at me, beaming. "I've seriously always wanted to do this."

"Really?"

He nods. "So, do I just . . . ?"

I glance at the storage closet again, biting back a giggle. "Just go for it. Bang it."

As soon as he does, I hit record on my phone. There's a loud rustle from the storage closet, followed by a soft chime of music.

"What was that?" asks Simon.

Someone cranks up the volume, and the storage closet bursts open, revealing Bram, holding a hairbrush.

"Ohhhh I . . . don't want a lot for Christmas . . ."

I step hurriedly back to catch the reaction shot. Simon's perched on the drum stool, hands over his mouth, eyes saucer-wide. The music speeds up, and Bram takes a step closer—and then Garrett, Nick, and Abby rush up behind him.

And it's a revelation. Abby and the guys wag their fingers and throw their arms up, letting them shimmy down slowly—while Bram flawlessly lip-synchs into the hairbrush, a single word centered boldly on his chest in black stick-on letters.

Joaquin.

Meanwhile, Simon's at the drum kit, quietly losing his shit.

I don't even know where to look. It's too goddamn wonderful. Simon's fanfiction dream come to life. I can't believe Bram thought of this. I can't believe they're pulling it off.

Of course, Abby's the real professional, hitting every cue and grinning like she's on Broadway. Nick plays it tongue in cheek, smiling self-consciously. It's funny—they seem totally normal with each other. Watching them, you'd think they'd never fought in their lives.

Garrett, though. Total hot mess. Limbs everywhere, hopping sideways on one foot. He's definitely almost fallen over twice.

When the song ends, Bram points straight at Simon, smiling breathlessly. "Simon Spier, will you go to prom with me?"

Simon nods and jumps up to hug him, laughing so hard he can barely speak. "I hate you so much. Oh my God. Yes," he says, cupping Bram's face. Then he gives him a giant swoony movie kiss.

Garrett whoops, and Simon flips him off over Bram's shoulder.

"I can't believe you guys," Simon says when he resurfaces. He pokes Bram in the chest, grinning. "Joaquin."

Bram smiles.

"Like, how did you even find that?"

"It was a team effort," Bram says.

"I hate all of you so much."

Abby appears beside me, out of nowhere. "That was so epic," she murmurs.

"I can't even handle it."

She smiles faintly. "I know."

And then my mouth disconnects from my brain. It's the only explanation. Because I'm saying it. I'm just going for it. "So you've probably made other plans or whatever, but . . ." It dies in my throat. Why the hell is this so hard?

"Are you asking me to prom, Leah Burke?"

"Yes," I say flatly. "We're literally standing five feet away from your boyfriend, and I'm asking you to prom."

She raises her eyebrows, like she can't decide if I'm kidding. So that's a twelve out of ten on the awkward scale. Do I really have to clarify that I'm not asking Abby to prom?

"I'm not asking you to prom, Abby."

"Oh well."

My cheeks flush. For a minute, neither of us speaks.

"Okay, but seriously," I say finally. "This road trip thing . . ."

Abby gasps. "Are you saying you want to road trip to Athens?"

I shrug. "I mean, if you're still up for it."

"AM I UP FOR IT?" she yells, flinging her arms around me. And I feel it in my stomach, like a tiny buzzing cell phone.

12

SO, PROM FEVER IS A thing.

Literally all Simon wants to do now is watch the promposal video, over and over. He even texted it to his mom. And Nick and Abby are back to their obnoxiously happy normal, holding hands in English class and discussing corsages over lunch. It's like a looming apocalypse, but with formal wear.

And then there's Garrett, who keeps watching me with this weird, twinkly expression. I catch Bram at his locker on Thursday and make him tell it to me straight. "Is Garrett going to prompose to me?"

"Um," says Bram.

"Please tell me he's not planning something public."

God, I'll die. I just can't. It's not like I have issues with Garrett. Honestly, I wouldn't even mind going to prom with him. But public promposals are my actual worst nightmare. This stuff is awkward enough without the audience. "Seriously, I need to know."

"Well . . ." Bram bites his lip.

"Got it." I grimace. "So, like . . . when is this happening?"

"Lunch," he says. "Um. Do you want me to . . ."

I pat him on the shoulder. "I'll handle it."

I mean, yeah. I'll go to prom with Garrett. I don't care. We'll go as friends. As buds. As bros. It will be fun. We'll take some god-awful staircase pictures, and hopefully I won't stab him with a corsage pin. Accidentally, probably.

I find him camped out in the library. "Hey, can we talk?"

He peers up at me in surprise. "Yeah. What's up?"

"Privately." He follows me over to the magazine racks, and I don't even hesitate. "Okay, here's the thing. I know what you're planning."

His eyebrows shoot up. "What?"

"Listen. I'll go to prom with you, okay?"

His jaw drops.

I blush. "If you want. I mean. We don't—"

"Yeah—Burke. Yeah, I want to," he says slowly. "Let's—but, uh, you're kind of stealing my thunder here."

"Yes." I roll my eyes. "That's kind of the point."

"You don't want my thunder?"

"Literally not even a little bit."

"But." He rubs his forehead, face breaking into a smile.

"You'll go to prom with me? For real?"

"Sure."

"Dude." He beams. Then he wraps me in a bear hug, and it's actually sort of sweet. This kid. This blue-eyed boy who calls me by my last name and never shuts up. My prom date. That actually happened. I just asked a boy out. Or he asked me. I guess we asked each other.

Anyway, it's done, and I did it, and I guess I'm going to prom. With a date. I'm an actual high school cliché. A part of me feels like I should announce this. In fact, people do announce this shit on the creeksecrets Tumblr. There's even a list of prom couples, kept up to date in the notes section. I guess it's to save people from those excruciating Harry-asking-Cho-to-the-Yule-Ball situations. Though, let's be real: if Katie Leung sweetly rejecting Daniel Radcliffe in a Scottish accent wasn't your sexual awakening, I don't even want to know you.

I just wish I knew how to feel about Garrett. This shouldn't be so complicated. It has to be easier for people with penises. Does this person get you hard? Yes? Done. I used to think boners literally pointed in the direction of the person you're attracted to, like a compass. That would be helpful. Mortifying as fuck, but at least it would clarify things.

I'm home before Mom—there's a note on the fridge that says to call her at work when I get there. And out of nowhere, I remember a thing Abby told me right after she moved here. Her dad was still in DC at the time, and I guess he thought Shady Creek was some drug-fueled bacchanalia fuckland, because he didn't want Abby to go *anywhere* after dark. He used to call her on the house phone to make sure she was really there. Foolproof dad-maneuver, except for the part where Abby forwarded all her landline calls to her cell. Not that I'm randomly thinking of Abby Suso again.

I sink onto the couch and dial Mom's office number. She picks up on the first ring.

"How come you didn't tell me there was a promposal video?"

I grin. "Who told you?"

"Alice Spier shared it from Simon's Facebook."

God, you have to love how my mom isn't friends with my friends' parents. She's friends with their siblings.

"I need details," Mom says.

So, I tell her everything. Or I try to. I'm not sure it's possible to put into words what it looks like when Garrett dances.

And—okay. I guess I should tell her about Garrett asking me to prom. I'm almost scared of how happy it will make her. She has a thing about school dances. She went to all of them, even as a freshman—even junior prom, when she was four and a half months pregnant. She has this theory that every teen movie should end in a prom scene.

"I think every teen movie *does* end in a prom scene," I'd told her.

She thinks it's romantic. She explained it to me once. "It's this night where all the usual drama gets suspended. Everyone looks different. And everyone's a little more generous with each other." I remember she paused after she said that, and for one horrible moment, I thought that might be a euphemism. But then Mom added softly, "I remember the feeling like it was okay to *care*. To not be so blasé. There's something really earnest about school dances."

I've never known how to respond to that. *Cool, Mom. Glad that worked out for you.* I don't know. Maybe some of us like being blasé.

I squeeze my eyes shut, already dreading this. "So I asked Garrett to prom."

My mom gasps. "Leah."

"And it's not a big deal, okay? It's just Garrett. It's not a thing. We're just going as friends."

"Uh-huh," she says. I can actually hear her smiling.

"Mom."

"I'm just wondering. Does Garrett know you're going as friends?"

"*Mom.* Yes."

Except—shit. I don't know. I mean, I think we're going as friends. No one said it was a romantic thing. But maybe prom is romantic by default. Is this a thing I have to specify? Can ambiguous social situations kindly go fuck themselves?

Of course, as soon as I hang up, there's a text waiting for

me from Garrett. So I'll talk to Greenfeld and we can figure out limo and dinner and everything! Prom's going to be so baller this year, I can't wait

Garrett saying *baller.* Now my mind can't un-hear it.

By Friday, Creekwood High School's collective prom fever has morphed into college fever. I swear to God, there's nothing more toxic than a suburban high school in March. The halls look like a screenshot from college *Jeopardy!*—humblebrag T-shirts hitting you from every direction. It's like the entire school turned into Taylor overnight.

Anna got into Duke. Morgan got into Georgia Southern. Simon and Nick both got into Wesleyan and Haverford, and both got rejected from the University of Virginia. Abby had looked at them incredulously when she heard that. "Are you literally the same person?"

"They just know we're a package deal," Simon said.

"That's super weird," said Abby.

Also, our lunch table is a war zone—but it's the silent kind of war zone. Morgan and I stake out opposite ends of the table, communicating only in glares. But it's not just us. Abby and Nick are lowkey fighting again, too. And then there's Simon in the middle, glancing back and forth like we're a street he has to cross. I don't think I've ever met a person so nervously attuned to conflict.

Garrett, on the other hand, is perfectly oblivious. He sinks into the chair across from me, next to Abby, and grins. "Okay, ladies, I need your help." He gestures around the table. "I'm in charge of making the dinner reservation for all of these beautiful people on prom night. So now I'm taking requests."

"Maybe something near the venue?" Abby says distantly.

"Something cheap," I add.

Garrett beams at me. "Well, *that* is not something for you to worry about, Burke. I believe your meal is covered."

"Okay." I blush. "Thanks."

Abby turns to face me, suddenly. "Wait, are you guys going to prom together?"

"Yup," Garrett says. I nod, looking down.

"Are you serious? How did I not know this?"

Garrett pretends to gasp. "She didn't tell you?"

"No, she didn't," Abby says. She's still looking at me.

I mean, was I supposed to call her? Did I somehow miss the moment when that became an expectation? I don't get her. I don't. Everyone thinks Abby's so fun and sweet and bubbly, but she's actually the most confusing girl in the universe.

I glance up at her, and she looks right in my eyes. I can't read her expression. "Anyway," she says, "we should figure out spring break."

"What's happening over spring break?" Garrett asks.

Abby's eyes flick sideways. "Oh, nothing. Only the greatest

road trip in the history of road trips." It's weird. Her voice is perfectly calm. But something sparks in her eyes like she's issuing a challenge.

To Garrett. Or me. I have no earthly idea.

"I'm pretty flexible," I say slowly.

"Good, me too. God, I'm so ready for this. I'm so ready for college."

"Oh, you guys are visiting UGA?" asks Garrett.

"Yup," Abby says, sliding her hand across the table, palm up, like she wants me to high-five it. So I do.

And she threads our fingers together.

Right here at the lunch table. I don't even know what's happening.

"You know what they say," Abby murmurs, glancing sideways at Garrett. "What happens in Athens stays in Athens."

Garrett raises his eyebrows, grinning. "Say no more."

And suddenly, I'm pissed. No, actually, I'm furious. I tug my hand away from Abby's and scoot my chair out abruptly.

"Wait, what just happened?" Simon asks.

When I'm mad, I escape. It's what I do. I stalk out of rooms and storm down hallways and disappear into bathroom stalls. Because if I stay, I'll lose my shit at someone. I will. I swear to God. I don't even know who I'm more pissed at. Abby, for teasing me. Garrett, for making it about him every fucking time. Because that's why bi girls exist, Garrett. For your masturbatory fantasies. I want to scream in his face. Dude, if you like me—if you actually like me—then be jealous. Be worried. Be *something.* If this were Nick flirting with me, Garrett would think *whoa: competition*. But because it's Abby, it doesn't mean anything. It's like it doesn't count.

Not that Abby was flirting with me. She probably wasn't. Definitely wasn't. And I definitely don't care.

13

I feel like you're mad at me, Garrett texts me after school. About the Abby thing. I'm sorry Burke, I was honestly joking, but I'll stop for real. I'm sorry.

I stare at the screen. I don't know where to begin. I mean, how do I call him out if he doesn't even know I'm bi?

I sink into the couch, feeling suddenly exhausted. It's fine. Just promise me you'll stop being a dick, okay?

I promise! he responds immediately, smiley face and all. So, we're cool?

We're cool.

Except I'm the opposite of cool. All weekend, I'm uneasy. Because Garrett actually apologized, but Abby didn't. Not that she would. I just don't get her. I don't get what she's doing. And it's not even the *what happens in Athens* comment. That could mean anything. It could mean frat boys and keg stands and hetero trash for days.

But the look on Abby's face when I said I was going to prom with Garrett. How surprised she seemed that I hadn't told her. But why would I tell her? She has a boyfriend. So what if they're fighting? She. Has. A. Boyfriend. Therefore, none of this matters, and prom can go fuck itself.

Of course, my mom is totally high on prom hype. She takes two hours of leave time on Wednesday to pick me up right after school. "Hop in. We're going dress shopping."

I look at her. "Do we have to?"

"Yes, ma'am. Because you're going to pro-om." She gives it a solid two syllables. "I'm so excited right now."

It's like we're from two different planets. Every once in a while, it hits me: if I knew my mom in high school, I don't think we'd have been friends. It's not like she was an asshole in high school. She was kind of like Abby. In every play, at every party, perfect grades. She always had a boyfriend—usually a soccer player with really defined abs. But sometimes she dated nerdy guys, or musicians, like my dad, who apparently used to smoke a lot of pot. I guess it didn't lower his sperm count.

"You know, the last time we went prom dress shopping together, you were on the inside."

"Haha."

"My little prom fetus."

"Gross."

"It's beautiful. You're beautiful." She pulls into the mall parking deck and finds a spot near the elevator. My mom has charmed luck with parking spaces. It's essentially her superpower. "And you have a date!"

"Yeah, with *Garrett*."

"Garrett's so adorable, though." She pauses to grin at me. "Okay, so here we are. Where's formal wear?"

Department stores are like diners. No focus. Too many options. I feel overwhelmed just being here. Mom pauses by an escalator, examining the store map.

"Aha. Upstairs." I follow her onto the escalator. "So, what's typical these days? When I was in high school, everyone wore floor length, but I hear that's not a thing anymore."

"It's not?" I swallow.

"Or maybe I'm thinking of homecoming. I don't know. Oh, here we go."

Racks and racks of dresses. I don't think I've ever seen so much satin in my life. They're all electric-bright and strapless and loaded with sparkles. I don't own anything like this. I have nothing close to prom-appropriate. I've skipped every single dance since we grew out of bar mitzvahs. Which was clearly the right decision, because these dresses are trash, and prom is stupid anyway.

Except it doesn't feel stupid.

It makes me cringe to admit this, but I want the whole prom

thing. The dress, the limo, all of it. It actually hurts, imagining prom happening without me. Me, alone in my pajamas, spending the whole night trolling Instagram and Snapchat. Watching everything unfold virtually. Seeing once and for all how little I'm missed.

Mom starts pushing through hangers, pinching fabric between her fingertips and peeking at size tags. "These are kind of cool, Lee. I'm digging the two-piece."

"Are you joking?"

"It's like a skirt and a top. It's different. I like it." She shakes her head. "Stop making that face."

My hand grazes a dress—intricately beaded bodice, voluminous taffeta skirt. It's the actual worst. But it's also weirdly gorgeous. I can't stop running my hands along the fabric.

Okay, it's silly, but I've always wanted one of those *holy shit* teen-movie moments. Like when the skinny nerd girl walks downstairs in her red dress. Or Hermione at the Yule Ball. Or even Sandy in her tight pants at the end of *Grease.*

I want to surprise everyone. I want everyone I've ever liked to wish they hadn't missed their chance.

"That's cute," Mom says—carefully, without looking at me, like I'm a deer she's trying not to spook. It's extremely annoying.

"Not really," I say.

"Why don't you try it on? Nothing to lose, right?"

Except my dignity. And my flawless eighteen-year streak of not wearing hideous trainwreck ball gowns.

So, here's the thing about me: I'm stubborn. I'll admit that. But I always underestimate how stubborn Mom is, too. She's never a bitch about it like I am, but she can be very persistent. Which is how, twenty minutes later, I'm in a dressing room wearing that taffeta shitshow of a gown. Biggest size on the rack, and it doesn't even zip. My back feels goose-prickled and naked, and when I glance into the mirror, I want to throw up. The skirt balloons around my hips and hangs straight past my ankles. This may be the worst idea Mom's ever had.

"How's it going in there?" Mom's hovering outside the door to my dressing room. "I want to see!"

Yeah, that's not happening.

"This is the ball gown, right? That color's going to look amazing with your hair. Trust me."

"It's hideous."

"I'm sure it's not hideous."

"No. I mean it's an actual Dumpster fire."

"Wow, okay. Tell me how you really feel." She laughs. "On to the next."

I'm already rolling my eyes as I wrestle myself into a purple chiffon nightmare. It's a bigger size, so it actually zips. But it stretches tightly over my hips and almost molds itself around my stomach. I know that sounds awful, but it's not. It's sort of wonderfully unapologetic. But the dress itself is a steaming piece of matronly garbage, and I'm not showing up at prom looking like someone's grandma.

"Any luck?" Mom asks.

I laugh harshly.

Someone gasps in the next dressing room. "Jenna! Oh my God, I love it."

"You don't think it makes my arms look fat?"

"What? Shut up. You're not fat. You look amazing."

My whole body tenses. The only thing worse than trying on dresses is hearing a bunch of skinny girls trying on dresses next door. Listening to them pick at themselves. It's like it doesn't even matter if I like my body, because there's always someone there to remind me I shouldn't.

You're not fat. You look amazing.

Because fat is the opposite of amazing. Got it. Thanks, Jenna's friend!

"Should I try the size four, or will that just be huge?" Jenna asks. Jesus Christ.

But Mom presses onward, and I snap back to earth. "Did you try on the yellow one?"

I mean, it's barely yellow—more like pale yellow-gold. And it's printed with bright multicolored flowers: tiny on the bodice, growing bigger toward the edge of the skirt.

I hate yellow. And florals.

I should hate the crap out of this dress.

But I can't explain it. It's just so badass. No one wears a

floral prom dress. It's sort of fitted, with a sweetheart neckline, and I guess the skirt is really an A-line, but there's a layer of white tulle underneath.

I don't know. I fucking love it. I'm sure it won't fit me. I'm sure it was made for a girl like Jenna, from the next dressing room. Whom I'm definitely picturing as Zoey Deutch. No question: this dress would look amazing on Zoey Deutch. But I guess I'll try it anyway.

I unzip it, stepping carefully into the skirt and tugging it up over my hips. It's strange wearing a dress like this on a Wednesday afternoon, with my TARDIS socks poking out the bottom.

It's strange wearing this dress, period.

It zips. That's a start. Though I'm pretty sure I'm going to look like a douchebag with my bra straps poking out. I stare at my feet. I don't want to look at the mirror. Better just to imagine the dress looks amazing.

"What do you think?" Mom asks.

Deep breath. I look up.

It takes a moment to adjust to the image of me in the dress. Me in yellow. I press my hands to my thighs and just stare.

It's not awful.

The bra straps look ridiculous.

But I kind of like the way the skirt hangs, skimming my hips and grazing the floor. I think I could actually wear this. I don't know if I've achieved *holy shit* levels of boner inspiration, but still. It's the prettiest I've ever felt.

I crack the door open and peek out, and Mom whips her head up. "Do I get to see this one?"

I shrug and step out slowly, feeling like I'm on a stage. Mom doesn't say a word. Maybe she's holding back tears. Maybe she's rocked by the transformation. I think I look different. Maybe older. My hair looks really red. I fidget with the satin of my skirt.

Mom tilts her head to the side.

"Eh," she says finally. "I don't like it."

I deflate. "Oh."

"I think it overpowers you. It's just kind of loud."

"Wow. Okay. I actually liked this one."

"Really?" Mom's brow wrinkles. "I mean, it's not bad, but I don't think it's the one, Lee."

"Of course you don't." My chest feels squeezy-tight.

She looks stricken. "What's that supposed to mean?"

I full-force glare at her, trying not to cry. I don't even have an answer for that. I don't know what I mean. I just know I feel like shit, and I hate everyone in the entire world.

I shake my head. "I'm over this."

"Leah, come on. Where's this coming from?"

I laugh without smiling. I didn't even know that was possible. "I'm just done. And this is stupid." I push back into the dressing room, leaving Mom gaping outside the door.

She sighs loudly. "Seriously?"

I unzip the dress and step out of it, draping it over the hook on the wall. I swear to God, it's staring at me. I tug my jeans up quickly.

Meanwhile, my mom's still trying to talk to me. "Leah, if you love that one, let's get it. I love it, too."

I crack the door open and stare her down. "No you don't."

"Yes I do. It's really pretty. And you know, I actually think it will look perfect once we style your hair. I'm serious."

"It's whatever."

"Can I see it again?"

"I'm already dressed."

"Okay. Then let's just get it. I'll pay for it right now."

And as soon as she says that, I realize I have no idea how much the dress costs. I never thought to look—which *really* isn't like me. I peek at the tag, heat rising in my cheeks. "It's two hundred and fifty dollars."

Mom pauses. "Don't worry about it."

"What?" I inhale sharply. "We can't afford that."

"It's fine, sweetie. It's not a problem."

"What, are you going to rob a bank or something? Or are we using Wells's money?" My stomach coils tightly at the thought.

"Leah, don't you dare give me that look."

"I'm just saying—"

"I don't want to hear it," she snaps. It seems to echo off the ceiling.

There's this pit in my stomach. Neither of us speaks.

"You don't even like the dress," I say finally.

"Leah, I do like the dress." She closes her eyes briefly. "And this is something I'd like to do for you. This doesn't have to be complicated."

"Are you serious?"

"You know, I'm curious, Leah. What was your plan for paying for a prom dress? Enlighten me."

I don't even know what to say. Obviously, I have no clue. I can't afford a two-hundred-and-fifty-dollar dress. I can't afford a fifty-dollar dress. And maybe I could have found something secondhand, but those places never have bigger than size two. Which is just about big enough for one of my legs.

For one excruciating minute, no one speaks. Even Jenna and her friend next door have gone silent.

"I don't care about the dress," I say softly.

Mom rubs her forehead. "Leah."

"I just want to go home."

"Fine."

All the way to the car, we're silent, but my mind's tumbling in every direction. *This doesn't have to be complicated.* Right. Imagine if it weren't. Imagine if I were Jenna—*omg my arms look fat* Jenna. Girls like Jenna step out of dressing rooms, and people gasp and applaud. I'm sure she carries her parents' credit card—her parents, who are married and forty-five and not dating random dudes with plural names.

"Sweetie, I'm sorry." Mom pulls into our driveway, setting

the car in park. "I really like the dress. I had no idea you loved it so much."

"I don't." It comes out shaky.

Mom pauses. "Okay."

"I don't even want to go to prom."

"Leah." Mom shakes her head. "You've got to stop doing this."

"Doing what?"

"Burning everything to the ground whenever something goes wrong."

For a minute, it hangs there. I don't know what to say. I don't do that. I don't *think* I do that.

"You know what I want for you?" Mom says finally. She smiles, almost wistfully. "I want you to let things be imperfect."

"Okay." I frown. "But I do."

"No you don't. You know? You have a sucky time dress shopping, and you're ready to call off prom. You wouldn't try out for the play because you're not the best actress in the universe."

"I'm the worst actress in the universe."

Mom laughs. "But you're not! Not at all. You just want to be the best. And you have to let that go. Embrace the suck. Let your guts hang out a little."

Yeah, that's a fucking joke. *Let your guts hang out.* I don't even get that. Why would anyone want to live like that? Like it isn't bad enough I'm always one breath away from falling apart. I'm supposed to fall apart under a spotlight?

It's too much. And I don't want to embrace the suck. I want things to not suck. And I don't think that's too much to ask.

14

I SPEND THURSDAY FLOATING THROUGH classes in a fog. I barely say a word at lunch, and I don't linger after the bell rings. I don't look for Simon and Nick on Friday morning. I don't lurk by the lockers. I just duck into the library, staking claim to a computer. Typing without thinking.

Simon finds me anyway. "Oh, hey! What are you working on?" He scoots a chair next to me.

"The Treaty of Vienna."

"Amazing," he says, and I can actually hear him grinning.

"Okay, why are you so cheery?" I turn to face him—and my mouth falls open. "Simon."

His shirt. It's crisp and bright purple, totally plain except for three white letters: NYU.

"This isn't an April Fools' thing, right? You got in?"

"I got in!"

"Simon!" I punch his arm. "Why didn't you text me?"

"I wanted to surprise you."

"Does Bram know?"

He beams, nodding.

"Oh my God, Simon. You guys are going to be in New York together."

"I know!"

"You're going to live in New York!"

"That's so weird, right?" He rolls his chair closer. Then he exhales and laughs all at once, eyes bright behind his glasses.

"I mean, you're literally going to be right in Manhattan. I can't even process this."

"I know."

"Do you realize that living in New York is like one step away from being famous?" I say.

"Right."

"I'm serious. You better not forget about me."

"Um, I'm going to stalk you online a thousand times a day."

"That seems like a good way to spend your time."

He laughs. "Whatever. You know we're going to visit you and Abby at Georgia, right?"

"Right."

"I still can't believe you guys are road tripping together. If you guys end up as roommates, I swear to God."

I pause. "You swear to God what?"

"I don't know. I swear to God I will smile approvingly."

"Is that a threat?"

He smiles. "I just really like the idea of you guys being friends."

Something tugs in my chest. I feel strangely offbeat.

I try to shake off the feeling. "So, are you still going on your college tour, or is that kind of moot now?"

The first period bell rings, and Simon stands, tugging the straps of his backpack. "No, I'm going. My mom wants me to visit the last few schools before I make my choice." He shrugs. "But whatever. It'll be fun. Okay, I need to find Abby and switch our phones back."

"You switched phones?" I fall into step beside him. "Why?"

"She's sending herself pictures. See?"

He holds up Abby's phone, with its Rifle floral phone case—and sure enough, there's a massive text thread of photos. Mostly Simon and Abby, but I'm in a few of them, too. To be honest, I didn't know some of these pictures existed. Like one of Abby, Bram, and me, half asleep on Mr. Wise's couch after the AP Lit exam last year. We're all shoeless, in T-shirts and pajama pants. Basically, exams happened, and everyone promptly stopped giving a shit. I kind of like how I look in the picture, though. My hair's loose and rumpled, and I'm literally yawning, but all three of us look soft-eyed and sleepy and happy.

"She's going to make a collage for her future dorm room," Simon says. "I should do that." He taps into her pictures.

I fall into step beside him as he swipes through them. "I look so drunk in this one," he says. And then, a moment later. "Nick needs to learn how to open his eyes in pictures." I peer at the screen, and my stomach twists softly. It's just a random couple selfie—not even a new one, because it's clearly taken at play rehearsal. Classic Nick and Abby picture: Abby smiling sweetly with her head slightly tilted, and Nick looking like he just got punched.

"I'm kind of worried about Nick and Abby," Simon says after a moment.

"Oh yeah?"

"Yeah, they're not . . . wow," he says suddenly, holding up the phone. "Did you draw this?"

I freeze.

"It's beautiful," he adds, and my heart thuds in my chest.

Because—okay. Holy shit.

I can't seem to form words. I just stare at the phone.

Abby still has the picture, a year and a half later. It's in her album of favorites. I don't know what that means. Or if it even means anything. My mind's in a knot.

"When did you draw that?" Simon asks.

I feel my cheeks burn. "Last year."

Junior year. I'd come home from Morgan's sleepover, feeling too big for my skin. And no matter what I tried, I couldn't shake the feeling. So, I pulled out my sketchpad and drew without a plan. Two girls on their stomachs, peering at a cell phone. All soft lines and curves and overlapping limbs. I colored us in with pencils—the brown of Abby's skin, the pink of my cheeks, the dark red of my hair. I drew like I was in a trance. It felt like I'd pinned my heart to the page.

I should have tucked it away, but I guess I felt brave. We were in the courtyard when I showed her. I used to wait with her there after school when her bus was late. It was September 19—a Friday, the day before my birthday—and the air felt crisp and new. I hadn't even brought my sketchbook that day, but I'd taken a photo of the drawing on my phone.

"You can't laugh," I'd told her. She laughed as soon as I said that. I could barely sit still, my heart was beating so fast. I passed her my phone, and then stared at my knees. She was quiet for a few excruciating moments, and then she turned to me at last.

"Leah."

I looked up to find her staring at me, silent. Her mouth was twisted up at the corners.

"It's really rough, obviously."

"I can't believe you drew that," she said. "It's—wow."

"It's nothing."

But it didn't feel like nothing. It felt like a love letter. It felt like a question.

"I'm just." She sighed. "I love it so much. Leah. I'm going to cry."

"Don't cry," I said. I was like an overinflated balloon. Full of air and tension, both anchored and floating. "I'm glad you like it."

"I love it." She scooted closer. No one else was in the courtyard. She smelled like vanilla, and her eyelashes were like thick black parentheses. That was it. My brain only had room for those two facts.

Abby's waiting outside Ms. Livingstone's classroom, Simon's phone in hand. I can't look at her without blushing.

She still has my drawing. She kept it.

"So here's what I want to know," Abby says. "How do you find time to take literally three hundred and sixteen selfies with Bieber?"

Simon scoffs. "I make the time."

"Apparently."

He makes a face at her. "How do you have time to count my selfies?"

"I don't even know." She grins, eyes cutting toward me. "Oh, and Leah."

She touches my elbow.

"Yup?"

"We need to figure out road trip stuff. Were you going to ride the bus home today?"

I nod carefully.

"Okay, cool." She smiles. "So, I've got my mom's car, and

I was wondering if maybe we could do WaHo after school? Then we can hammer out the plans, and I can drive you home afterward."

"Um. Yeah." I swallow. "Sure."

"Yay! All right, I have to get to calc, but okay—great! I'll meet you outside the atrium?"

I nod, feeling dazed. I feel Simon studying my face, lips pursed like he's about to ask me something. God. I don't want to talk about the drawing. Or Abby. Or the most pointless crush I've ever had. I mean, Simon doesn't even know I'm bisexual. But he keeps looking at me with his *Thinker* face, nose wrinkled like a bunny's.

The weird part is, it should be easy to tell him this. Simon, of all people. It's just that my heart and lungs and pulse don't seem to realize this.

"Leah?" he says softly.

I swallow the lump in my throat.

He's quiet for a moment. And then he looks me straight in the eye. "Do I take too many dog selfies?"

See, now I don't know whether to laugh or choke.

Seven hours later, I'm in Abby Suso's car.

Her mom's car. Whatever. I'm in a tiny, enclosed space with Abby, who's wearing a fucking sundress and tiny moonstone earrings. She hums as she backs out of her parking space.

I feel breathless and unsteady.

“So we’re good to go on the apartment. We can have it whenever we want. My friend will just stay with her boyfriend.”

“Wow. That’s really nice of her.”

“Right? I’ve actually only met her once. She’s actually my cousin’s girlfriend’s friend’s sister.”

I laugh. “What?”

“I know. It’s ridiculous.” She pauses, adjusting the air-conditioning. “She’s my cousin Cassie’s . . . girlfriend Mina’s . . . friend Max’s . . . older sister. Caitlin.”

“And she’s just giving us her apartment next week.”

Abby nods, turning right on Mount Vernon Highway. “We can literally drive up tomorrow if we want.”

“Wow.”

“But I think we should do like Monday through Wednesday, or something, so it won’t be so crazy there. Unless you want to see what campus is like on a Saturday night.”

“Yeah, I’m good.” I lean back against the headrest. “And Monday works. That’s the fourth, right? Today’s the first . . .”

My phone buzzes with a text from Simon. Oh! My inner goddess has a question for you

I stare at the screen. He’s still typing.

WAIT

He types again. We aim to please, Miss Steele

And again. *w-t-f WHAT’S HAPPENING???

I glance sideways at Abby. “I think Simon’s texting me quotes from *Fifty Shades of Grey.*”

"Hmm," Abby says. She gets these crinkles by her eyes sometimes—like old people get, but she makes them look young. Abby Suso is singlehandedly reclaiming eye crinkles for our generation.

Simon texts me again. I think someone hacked my virginity

*p-h-o-n-e not my virginity!!!

Why does it say virginity when I type virginity??????

I mean p-h-o-n-e

"Wait." I stare Abby down. "Does this have something to do with you using Simon's phone this morning?"

Abby shrugs, eyes wide. "I don't know. Does it?"

Holy. Shit.

"You're a fucking genius, Suso."

My phone buzzes insistently. LEAH WHY IS THIS HAPPENING??? I swear this isn't me, it's my subconscious

WHAT NO STOP, he adds. It's my a-u-t-o-c-o-r-r-e-c-t We aim to please, Miss Steele HOW DO I FIX THIS

I burst out laughing. "I'm screenshotting this."

Abby's lips tug upward. "This is why you don't lend your phone out on April Fools' Day, Simon."

Abby Suso. Who knew she was so evil?

I shake my head. "I'm legit so impressed right now."

"Thank you."

"Sent you a screenshot," I say as we pull into Waffle House.

"YES." She turns off the car and taps into her texts. "And . . . someone hacked his virginity. I'm dead."

I rub my cheek, smiling. "I don't even know how to respond to him."

"Because it's too perfect."

"I want to frame these texts and put them in a museum."

Abby smiles.

I smile back. It's like my facial muscles have gone rogue. And now my heart's banging around my rib cage like a drunk, blindfolded bird.

Yeah. I don't know why I decided a road trip was reasonable, because I can't even handle the Waffle House parking lot with this girl. I should have gotten a doctor's exemption. *To Whom It May Concern: In my professional opinion, Leah Catherine Burke should be barred from any and all prolonged interactions with Abigail Nicole Suso, whose middle name she has absolutely no reason to know, but knows anyway.*

Of course I fucking know it.

I trail a few steps behind her in the parking lot, feeling foggy. Thank God this girl could converse with a rock, because my brain isn't working. It just stopped out of nowhere, like a car stalled on the highway.

She's searching for something on her phone. Abby gestures so much when she talks. Even now, even while actively Googling, she keeps waving her phone emphatically.

"Ah. Okay, here we go," she says, tilting the screen toward me. "I'm so excited about these." I think she's talking about prom shoes.

I peer at the screen. "Are these jellies?" I ask finally.

She beams. "Yes!"

They're the classiest jellies I've ever seen—crosshatched, clear ballet flats, infused with silver glitter. Kind of like what Cinderella would wear if she were a six-year-old sucking a rocket pop by the neighborhood pool.

"They're really awesome," I say.

"I hate wearing heels. I'm not doing it. I need to be able to dance."

A waiter stops by and is instantly spellbound by Abby. Like, she smiles, and he's done for. It's kind of gross how fast that tends to happen. We both order waffles, but I'm 50 percent sure he'll only bring hers. I guess I should be used to this.

The funny thing is, Abby doesn't even seem to notice. She looks at me, mouth quirked at the corners. "So, you and Garrett . . ."

"That's not a thing."

"Why not?" Her eyes narrow. "He definitely likes you."

God. What do I even say to that? Maybe he does like me. Maybe Garrett and I should be a thing. I'd probably like kissing him. And I like being wanted. I like being the crushee for once.

I mean, he's sweet. He's cute. And yes, he's annoying, but

he's not a bad guy. I should like him. I want to like him.

I change the subject. "So, you and Nick."

"Me and Nick." She exhales. It comes out like a sigh.

I wait for her to elaborate, but she doesn't. She just sits there. Then, a minute later, she smiles brightly and seems to snap back into herself. "Anyway, I'm excited for our trip."

"I need to give you gas money."

She shakes her head. "Nope. My parents want to cover that."

"They don't have to do that."

"I'm telling you, they want to."

My cheeks feel warm. "I should pay for something."

I mean, I hate not being able to pay for my shit. I'm already getting a ride and a free place to stay. I should cover gas. I know how this works. Of course, I can't actually afford to cover gas. Because I can't make money without a job. And I can't get a job around here without a car. Which is why I need a ride in the first place.

I hate money stuff. I hate it.

"You're in charge of music," Abby says. "Just make the most epic road trip playlist of all time."

"Okay, but I was going to make the second most epic playlist."

"I don't want the second most epic. That's not good enough, Leah."

It's like someone's squeezing my heart, just a little. One tiny pinch. It's the way she says my name. I'm Lee-uh. And maybe strangers call me Leia, like Star Wars. But when Abby says it, it falls halfway between.

It catches me off guard every single time.

15

THEY LOCK THE MUSIC ROOM on school vacations. Which would have been fine. I'm not dying to revisit the Morgan and Anna shitshow anytime soon. But then I made the mistake of telling Taylor about Nick's drum kit—the one he can't even play—which made Taylor realize that rehearsing in Nick's basement was her life's great purpose.

So, now it's Saturday, and I'm waiting for my ride to Nick's house. From Garrett, our brand-new keyboardist. Apparently, that's a thing that's happening. I'm actually nervous, waiting for him to get here. For one thing, Garrett and I haven't been alone together since I asked him to prom, but he's texted me a lot. Definitely more than usual. I guess it's starting to feel like Garrett's a question I'll eventually have to answer. Like there's an asterisk by his name.

It's sunny and cool out, so I wait for him on my stoop. I feel pretty antsy. I mean, part of it's just knowing that Morgan quit the band. Because of me. God knows Anna won't let me forget that. But how am I supposed to even talk to Morgan, let alone make music with her? What would Abby think of me then?

Before long, Garrett pulls up in his mom's minivan. He parks and then immediately hops out to open the passenger door.

"Do you not know how to turn off the child locks, or something?" I ask, because I have to give him shit. I have to. He's Garrett.

"What? Dude. I'm being a gentleman."

A gentleman. Who calls me *dude*. I should definitely not be charmed by this. I click my seat belt into place.

"What's in the envelope?" He glances at my lap.

"It's a drawing, for Taylor's birthday."

"I didn't know it was Taylor's birthday," he says.

I mean, you have to admire Taylor. She knows exactly what she wants, and she just makes it happen. I don't know what her deal is with Nick, but clearly, his house is where she wants to spend her birthday. And boom. Here we are.

"So, Morgan really quit the band, huh?" Garrett asks after a moment.

"Yup."

"Weird. I wonder why."

"I know why. It's because she doesn't want to deal with me."

"How could anyone not want to deal with you, Burke?" He pokes my arm, and my stomach sort of lurches. Like, how do I even respond to that?

"She didn't like being called out," I say finally.

He stops at a red. "You mean about the Abby thing?"

"It's not about Abby. It's about Morgan being racist."

"You think she's racist?"

"You were there."

"I mean, she shouldn't have said that, but don't you think she's just bitter? She'd just gotten rejected."

I whip my head toward him. "Yeah, you don't even get it."

"Okay." He tilts his hands up. "Explain it to me."

"I mean, Morgan one hundred percent implied that Abby got into Georgia because she's black."

"Right. And obviously she's wrong about that."

"She's super wrong." I clasp my hands. "You know Abby got a perfect score on the SAT reading, right? And she makes straight As."

"Really?"

"Yup, the only reason she's not in the top ten is because she transferred, and the classes from her old school aren't weighted the same."

"That's fucked up."

"And look at what she does for extracurriculars. God. But Morgan's going to say she didn't deserve Georgia? Fuck that."

For a moment, Garrett doesn't speak—he just turns onto Nick's street. Simon and Nick's neighborhood looks like a storybook illustration, with its carefully mowed lawns, painted shutters, and buds on all the dogwoods. He pulls up along the curb by Nick's house and turns off the ignition.

"So, has anyone ever told you that you cuss a lot?" he says finally.

"Oh, fuck you." But the corners of my lips twitch upward.

"Look. You're right. Morgan was an asshole," he says. Then he turns to face me, head-on. "How do you know so much about Suso?"

"What? I don't." My heart leaps into my throat.

Garrett looks at me strangely. "Okay."

We hop out of the car, and there's Taylor, sitting on the stoop next to two guitar cases. "Hey, birthday girl," I call out, walking toward her. She flashes me an electric-bright smile that doesn't reach her eyes.

I settle in beside her, punching her softly in the arm. "You okay?"

"Of course!" She nods. "Hey, have y'all heard from Nick?"

"Well, no, but, uh. We're at his house."

"Right." Taylor nods. "But, like . . . no one's home?"

"Maybe his parents are at a workshop?" I mean, they're doctors. It happens.

"Oh, totally," Taylor says, looking unconvinced. "But Nick should be here. We just texted this morning."

"Weird," Garrett says.

"Do you think he's okay?"

"I'm sure he's in the basement playing video games." I shrug. "He probably didn't hear you knock."

"Maybe." Taylor tilts her head. "Anna and Nora are checking down there now."

"Or he's passed out, asleep. He's fine."

Taylor nods and twists a strand of hair around her finger. Moments later, Nora and Anna tromp up the path from the backyard. "Basement's locked," Anna says. "What do you want to do? Should we just take a rain check?" She looks from Garrett to Taylor to me.

"I don't know," Taylor says.

"I could text him," Garrett adds.

Taylor sighs. "We've been texting him all morning, and we've called. He's not answering. It's just so weird."

"He's fine. I'm sure he'll text us later," Garrett says. "Burke, why don't we grab some lunch?"

"Let's just wait another few minutes," Taylor begins, but then her voice falls away. Because, suddenly, Nick's car is in the driveway, the garage door rumbling open. Taylor's whole face lights up. But he doesn't drive in or get out or anything. He just sits there, frozen, like he's in a trance.

So I stand. "I'll go talk to him."

I jog over to his car. It's like he doesn't even see me approach. I knock on the window, and he slowly rolls it down. "Hey," he says dully. His eyes are red-rimmed and wet.

"Holy shit. Are you okay?"

He shrugs, staring straight ahead.

"Nick?"

"I don't want to talk about it."

Okay, I'm slightly freaked out. Maybe a little more than slightly. I don't think I've ever seen Nick like this. I mean, I've definitely never seen him cry. Truthfully, I never know how to act in these moments. I don't have the instincts for it. Like, I literally can't tell if he wants me to go away or if he wants me to bust into his car with a bear hug. So I split the difference and just sort of . . . hover. "You don't have to talk about it."

He sighs and buries his face in his hands. "Why are they all here?" he asks, voice muffled.

"For rehearsal . . ."

He doesn't respond.

"For Emoji? The band?"

"Fuck," he says finally.

"Bad time?"

He peeks up at me. "Yeah."

"I'll deal with everyone. Just head inside." I swallow. "Seriously, are you okay?"

"I don't know. I just . . . want to be alone." He sighs. "Anyway. Thanks."

"No problem." I pause. Then, before I can overthink it, I stick my hand into the open window and ruffle Nick's hair.

Because I'm that awkward. But he smiles a little, so it's worth it.

He slides the window up again as soon as I step back. Then he drives straight into the garage, turns his car off, and shuts the garage door without looking back.

I walk back to the stoop, and Taylor leaps up right away. "What happened? Is he okay?"

"He'll be fine." I bite my lip. "He said he wants to be alone, though."

"Oh." Taylor looks crestfallen.

Anna shrugs. "Works for me."

Garrett jangles his car keys. "You ready, Burke?"

But Nora presses a hand to my arm. "Wait. Simon says he'll kill me if I don't bring you back to our house." She holds her phone up. "He says it's an emergency."

I freeze. "An emergency?"

"I'm sure it's not an *emergency* emergency. He's just being Simon."

I nod—but now I'm thinking about Nick's shiny red eyes. There's this clammy feeling in my chest—which is just how it felt when my dad left, right before my mom broke the news. It's like my body knew first. So maybe it really is an emergency. Maybe something really bad happened.

I follow Nora up the road, leaving Garrett visibly deflated. But I can't worry about Garrett right now. I almost ask Nora if I should run back, just for a minute. Just to check on Nick. But then I think of how quickly he shut that garage door. And he did say he wanted to be alone. I don't want to bust in on his alone time.

God. This whole friendship thing. You'd think I'd have a handle on it by now.

Simon's in his driveway waiting for us, perched on the hood of his car. He slides down as soon as he sees me. "Thank God you're here." He hugs me tightly. "Ugh. Leah. Everything's the worst."

My heart thuds. "What happened?"

"Hop in." Already, he's opening the driver side door. Nora lingers, looking concerned.

Simon waves her off. "I'll fill you in later." Nora rolls her eyes.

I slide into the passenger seat. "What's going on?" My stomach twists nervously as I turn toward Simon. "Si, you look like you're going to cry."

"I might." He sighs and turns the car on. "Did Nick tell you?"

"Tell me what?"

"Abby broke up with him."

The whole world seems to pause.

"Abby broke up with Nick?"

He nods, slowly, and backs out of the driveway.

"When?"

"This morning. Like thirty minutes ago. I just got off the phone with her."

"Holy shit."

"Yeah." He sighs faintly.

And for a moment, I'm silent. Sometimes, I swear there's a little knob beside my heart. It's as if someone reached in and dialed it ever so slightly to the right, one notch faster.

"Okay," I say finally. "Wow. Do you know why?"

"I mean, sort of," says Simon. "I haven't talked to Nick yet, but going by what Abby said, she just didn't want to be in a long-distance relationship."

I pause. "Right."

"Which—I'm sorry, but that's ridiculous, right?" Simon says hoarsely. "Like, seriously? You're not even going to give it a shot? It's like, hey, look, I've got this amazing relationship, but it's a tiny bit inconvenient, so let's just end it." He turns onto Mount Vernon Highway, lips pressed tightly together.

I turn toward the window, my heart in my throat. "Maybe it's not an amazing relationship," I say.

"What? It's Abby and Nick."

"Okay."

"They're like a legend. They're perfect." He sniffs. "They're OTP."

"But they're not," I say softly. And maybe this is out of left field, but I find myself thinking about Taylor. About the way Nick and Taylor were maybe, definitely flirting at Martin's cast party. About Taylor's new obsession with Nick joining the band. Maybe something's actually been going on. Except—I don't know. I don't think Nick would cheat. And especially not on Abby. God. He's so moony-eyed for her. I'll never forget the way he looked the first few weeks they were dating. He had that particular kind of nerdy-boy swagger, that back-and-forth between braggadocio and wonder.

"And of course it's right before prom."

"Yikes."

Simon shakes his head. "What are we going to do?"

"Well, how did they leave things?"

"I mean, Abby's like, oh, it's amicable, we're still friends, et cetera, you know," Simon says. "But Nick? I don't know."

"He . . . uh . . . didn't look happy," I say.

"Do you think I should call him?" Simon exhales. "Actually, maybe I'll just drop you off and head over there."

"That works."

"This is going to be fine." He nods quickly, like he almost believes it. Then he glances at me. "But I need a tiny favor."

"How tiny?"

"Okay, not that tiny. You have to talk to Abby."

My stomach twists. "What?"

"You guys are leaving on Monday, right?"

I nod slowly.

"Leah, you have to talk to her. This is just—I don't know." He shakes his head. "Like, I'm not trying to get in the middle, but this is just unnecessary, right? There's literally no reason for them to break up right now. Abby's just assuming it's not going to work." He turns onto my street, gripping the steering wheel hard. "Why can't they just try it out and see how it goes?"

"Simon, we don't get to decide that for them."

"I *know* that."

"Okay."

Simon pulls into my driveway, and then puts the car in park. "I'm just saying you could talk to her," he says, after a moment. "I bet she'd listen to you."

"Pshh."

"Seriously, she, like, super respects you. Though she's sort of intimidated by you."

I narrow my eyes. "Why?"

"I don't know. Because you're intimidating?" I shove him, and he smiles. "For real, though. She just thinks you're really cool, like with the band and everything. So I think she'd listen to you."

"That's not . . ." I trail off, blushing.

"Just talk to her, okay?" Simon leans back in his seat, rolling his head toward me. "Just—maybe you could remind her how awesome Nick is, and how great they are together. And then I'll work on Nick, and we can keep each other posted?"

"Yeah, I *really* don't think we should be meddling in this."

"This isn't meddling! We're just looking out for our friends. You want them to be together, right?"

The question hits me like a punch—I feel my whole body clench around it. I mean, obviously I want them to be together.

I want them to be happy. I don't want any tables flipped at prom. But the thought of bringing the topic up with Abby makes me gag.

"Please. Just talk to her."

"I'll try," I say softly. I look everywhere but his eyes.

16

"AND YOU'RE SURE YOU'VE GOT your phone charger?"

"Yup."

"And the car charger?"

"Yes."

"And you'll call me when you get there?"

"Mom. Yes."

She's pacing the length of the kitchen, hands scraping against her hairline. I don't know why she's being like this. It's like all of a sudden, she thinks I'm going to the moon.

"Mom, it's an hour and a half. That's like driving down the block at rush hour."

"I know. It's just weird. This is your college tour. I feel like I should be there." She sinks into a chair, resting her chin on her purse. "I don't like missing this stuff."

"But I'll be fine. I'll be with Abby."

"This better not be *Girls Gone Wild*," Mom says sternly. "No hooking up with college kids."

"Mom."

"I'm just looking out for you." She tweaks my nose. "And for Garrett."

"Oh my God. I'm never telling you anything again, ever."

"Okay, but call me at the office." She stands, smoothing down her skirt. "I mean it. As soon as you get there. And have fun, okay?"

I lean back in my chair, head tilted toward the ceiling. Two hours until Abby gets here, and I don't have a clue what to expect. I don't know whether she'll be crying over Nick or wanting to hook up with every guy in sight. And of course, Simon's counting on me to find the magic words that will fix everything. Like I'm somehow going to be able to talk her into reversing the breakup and living happily ever after. With Nick.

I'm starting to think this is the worst idea in the history of bad ideas.

I don't know. I just feel so amped up and wired, and I can't pinpoint why. It's like when a song changes key, or starts on the offbeat, or shifts its meter halfway through. It's that hiccup you get in your chest. That tiny *huh* moment. Like maybe something's kind of wrong.

Or maybe something's about to change.

* * *

Abby's fifteen minutes early. And she doesn't text from the driveway. She knocks on the door.

I *knew* she would do that.

Which is why I spent all weekend clearing piles of clothes and papers out of the living room, piling everything into my closet in one giant, precarious stack. From the doorway, the living room looks almost normal, even though the couch is kind of patchy and faded, and the wallpaper is from the nineties. At least you can see the floor now.

I sneak a glance at her through the window—and she's definitely not crying. She actually looks pretty cheerful. To the point where I'd think she and Nick were back together if I hadn't gotten a mopey update from Simon just this morning. But I guess Abby's the smile-through-anything type. For all I know, she's secretly heartbroken.

I slip out through the door before she can step inside. It's cloudy and cool out, cold enough for my Hogwarts cardigan. "I'm finally reading that," Abby says, pointing to the Slytherin crest. "I was bullied into it."

"By Simon?"

"And my cousin Molly. She spammed me with quotes for a week straight."

"My hero."

Abby smiles. "I like it so far. I'm halfway through the third one."

"You like it?" I almost sputter. Abby *likes* Harry Potter.

That's like saying Mr. Rogers was nice. Reece King is decent-looking. You can't just like Harry Potter. You have to be balls-out obsessed with it.

The breeze catches her hair as she roots for her car keys. She's Casual Abby today—curls and skinny jeans and a loose blue sweater. She pops open the trunk, and I set my duffel bag next to her little rolling suitcase. Her mom's car is kind of old, and the trunk is filled with books and stacks of papers. It's strangely reassuring, seeing the clutter. I always expect everyone else's lives to be immaculate.

"So let me put Caitlin's address into the GPS," she says, "and then we'll cue up the second most epic, bottom-tier bullshit playlist you worked so hard half-assing." She grins up at me.

"Wow. Shots fired, Suso." I climb into the passenger seat.

She does this very animated shrug, palms up and everything.

I side-eye her, but I'm smiling. "Okay, well, I've actually got two playlists. Your choice."

"My choice, huh." She starts the ignition. "This feels like a test."

"Oh, it is. I'll be judging you."

Abby laughs. "I knew it."

"Upbeat music or moody music. Go."

She scoffs. "Like that's even a question."

"I assume that's code for I'm Abby Suso and I want happy."

"As opposed to I'm Leah Burke and I want to cry all the way to Athens."

"Pshh. I don't cry."

"See, now you've just issued a challenge."

I grin at her. "I see."

Wow. So, this is strange. She's certainly not crying over Nick. She's acting like she's never cried in her life. And this teasing. Even when we used to be friends, we were never like this. I've never been able to pull my shit together enough to talk to her like a normal person, and banter wasn't even in the realm of possibility. But it's like a tiny door just opened inside my brain. I feel weirdly clearheaded. For once, I can keep up with her.

This is actually really fucking wonderful.

We fall into a peaceful silence on the highway. I stare out the window, and all I hear is Vampire Weekend, Ezra Koenig's voice decrescendoing. And then the song flips to Rilo Kiley. A moment later, Abby laughs.

I look at her. "What?"

"This breakup song. Wow. The timing on that."

"Oh shit." There's this feeling in my chest like an elevator dropping. "I didn't notice. I'm sorry."

"Why are you sorry?"

"Because." I swallow. "I don't want to make things weird for you."

"You're not."

"Do you want to talk about it?"

"About Nick?" She presses her lips together.

"We don't have to," I say quickly.

"No, it's fine. I'm just . . ." She nods, staring at the road. "Okay, this stays between us, right?"

"Of course." I smile. "Whatever happens in Athens stays in Athens."

"We're not in Athens yet."

I glance up at the exit signs. "Okay, whatever happens in Lawrenceville . . ."

"Promise?" She stretches her hand toward me, pinkie extended.

I hook it with my own. "Promise."

I don't think I've pinkie sworn since I was ten years old.

"I don't know what to do, Leah."

"About Nick?"

She tucks a curl behind her ear and exhales. "Yeah. Kind of. I mean, I talked to Simon, and he obviously thinks I'm making a huge mistake, but . . . I don't know. Like, do I feel shitty right now? Yeah. But it's not because I want him back."

I just look at her. I don't know what I'm supposed to say. I know Simon would want me to challenge this somehow, or at least press for details. But it's like I've been pushed onto a stage to recite lines I've never rehearsed. How would I know how a breakup's supposed to feel? I've never even kissed anyone.

Finally, Abby sighs. "I just feel like such a bitch. We've been dating for over a year. I love him. I do. It's just." She taps the steering wheel. "I don't want to do long distance. Like, at all. But a part of me feels like I owe him that, since I'm not following him to New England or whatever. Which is ridiculous, I know, but I just feel so guilty."

"Because you're not giving up your scholarship to pay student loans for the rest of eternity?"

"Right." Abby sighs. "I mean, yeah. Why is this even a question?"

"Look, if he wanted to simplify this, he could have applied to Georgia."

"Yeah." Abby bites her lip. "Though I'm glad he didn't."

Oh.

"Okay."

"Like, am I the biggest jerk? He's an incredible guy. He's been an incredible boyfriend. I mean, he's Nick. I just can't . . ." She laughs wryly. "You know, I kept wanting to imagine there was something going on with him and Taylor, because then there would have been a reason to break up with him."

"Why do you need a reason?"

"Because it sucks that there wasn't one. I just wasn't feeling it. At least not as much as I should be? Like, I'm sad about it, but it doesn't *wreck* me, and I really feel like it should wreck me."

I glance at her sidelong. "You want it to wreck you?"

"Do I want to love him enough that leaving him would wreck me? Yeah."

And somehow, that single word expands like a balloon. It fills the whole car. *Yeah.*

"Then I think you did the right thing," I say after a moment. I feel strangely charged up. Like if you touched me, I'd zap.

"I know," she says softly.

For a minute, we're both quiet.

"God. I just feel so bad. His birthday's coming up. Prom's in two weeks. Like, I'm pretty sure I just ruined everyone's senior prom." She laughs flatly. "That's going to be a fun limo ride."

"You can't stay in a relationship just so prom won't be awkward."

Abby's lips tug upward. "It sounds so ridiculous when you put it that way."

I shrug.

"It's just such a weird feeling. I've never broken up with anyone before."

"Really?"

"Well, I only had one real boyfriend before Nick, and he dumped me." She rakes a hand through her hair, smiling sadly. "Like, how does this work? Am I even allowed to feel good about this?"

"I mean . . . probably not in front of Nick. Or Simon."

"Yeah." She laughs out loud. "God. Boys are just so . . . ugh. I'm never dating one again."

"Maybe you should date girls," I say.

She grins. "Maybe I should."

I turn quickly toward the window, face burning.

Just. Holy fuck. I said that.

I didn't plan to. I don't know where it came from. But I said it, and it's out there, thickening the air between us. I have this sudden mental image of our car filling with smoke. But maybe it's all in my head, because suddenly Abby's singing along to Wham! like it's nothing.

I'm sure it really is nothing. Just like the drawing was nothing.

Except she kept it, and I can't imagine why. I wonder what she thinks about it—or if she even thinks about it at all. She probably just likes how I colored the background. Or she forgot it's in her phone in the first place.

But here's what Simon doesn't know: the drawing's in my phone, too.

The traffic on Route 29 is suddenly fascinating. There's a minivan in front of us, with a little stick figure family in the corner of the rear windshield. Perfect magic hetero dream family: mom, dad, two girls, and a boy. Now I'm picturing my own family as a sticker tableau. Mom and me hanging tight in the left corner; Dad on the top right, mostly out of frame. And, of course, Wells creeping his way in on the side. Just your basic American love story.

The song changes to Passion Pit. Way too upbeat. I should have picked the moody playlist. We drive and drive, and it's like I'm teetering on the edge of something. Now it's been ten minutes since we've spoken. The music feels too loud and too soft all at once, and underneath its bass line, I can hear Abby breathing.

17

AND THEN WE'RE IN ATHENS. Abby cuts down Prince Avenue, and I take in the colorful jumble of shops and cafés. There's a little indie bookstore with tall, arched windows, a grocery co-op on the corner, and two guys walking down the sidewalk, holding hands. I don't think it's hit me that I'll be living here. Not just visiting. Not just staring out of a car window, driving by. It doesn't feel like real life.

Abby's friend lives in an apartment building near the center of town—understated and modern, with its own covered parking deck. "Caitlin says we just park wherever," says Abby. "She's letting us borrow her parking permit."

"This is wild."

"I know."

I peer out the window as we loop around each row of

the deck. It's a funny mix of cars—some freshly washed and expensive-looking, others dented and battered. Lots of University of Georgia cling stickers. Apparently, almost everyone who lives here is a student.

We find a spot on the third level, ride an elevator to the lobby, and sign our names on a sheet at the front desk. Then we take another elevator to the sixth floor, where Caitlin's apartment sits, halfway down a long, carpeted hall.

When she and Abby see each other, they shriek and hug in the doorway, even though I'm pretty sure they've met literally once. Honestly, how well can you know your cousin's girlfriend's friend's sister? But it's Abby, so who knows.

"And you must be Leah," Caitlin says. "Here, let me grab your bags." We follow her into a sunny open kitchen with marble countertops, chrome appliances, and cheerfully stacked Fiestaware. It looks so perfectly adult. I knew Caitlin lived off campus, so it's not like I expected a dorm room, but this apartment looks like something out of HGTV. I didn't realize college sophomores could live like this.

"So, this is it. Bedroom, bathroom, I've got the Wi-Fi password written down, and you have my number. You guys are going on a tour tomorrow, right?"

Abby nods. "In the afternoon."

"Cool. Well, if you're up for it, my friend Eva is having people over tomorrow night. They live downstairs—it's literally this exact apartment, but on the fifth floor. Leah, you would *love* them. They're a drummer."

That casual singular *they*. It isn't even my pronoun, but it feels like a hug. Because if Caitlin's unfazed by her enby friend's pronouns, she'd probably be unfazed by me being bi.

"Anyway, I can text you the info."

"So, it's a party?" Abby asks.

Caitlin shrugs. "I guess so? Not really, though. I think it's going to be super chill." She twists her hair back and releases it. "You guys should totally stop by. And here's the parking permit. You can just prop it near your windshield."

"I should do that now," Abby says.

"Perfect. I'll walk you to the parking lot. And I guess that's everything."

"Thank you," I say. "Seriously."

"Oh my God, of course!" She hugs me, and it's like hugging a flower. It's like that with skinny people. I'm always terrified I'll crush them.

They leave, and suddenly I'm alone in this stranger's apartment. But I hear Abby's giggle all the way down the hall.

I call Mom at the office.

"There you are! I was starting to worry. How was the drive?"

"Good."

"That all you're giving me? *Good*?"

"It was amazing," I say. "It was unicorns vomiting sunbeams." I push aside two fuzzy white throw pillows and sink onto the couch.

"And Abby's good?"

"Yup."

"Run into any hotties yet?"

"Mom."

"I'm just asking."

"Okay, first of all, we've been here for five minutes. Second of all, don't say *hotties.*" I roll my eyes. "And I'm not hooking up with anyone."

"Okay, but you know the drill. Dental dam! Condom!" Mom's golden rule. Not super relevant, considering I get no action. And even if I did, it sure as hell wouldn't be on this trip. Not in Caitlin's apartment, and definitely not in front of Abby. I can't imagine bringing a girl home. Abby wouldn't even know what was happening. I'm 99 percent sure she thinks I'm straight. Even Simon thinks I'm straight.

I feel weird about that sometimes—the fact that Simon's out to me, but I'm not out to him. It's like when Leia says *I love you*, and Han Solo says *I know.* Like everything's slightly off-balance. It bugs me. But the thought of telling him now makes me want to throw up. I should have told him a year ago. I don't think it would have been a big deal then, but now it feels insurmountable. It's like I missed a beat somewhere, and now the whole song's off tempo.

And that's pretty much how I feel when I end the call with Mom. I tuck up against the armrest of Caitlin's couch, but my limbs feel twitchy and restless. I want to explore the apartment, but something about that feels wrong. Maybe it's the fact that I would die before leaving someone alone in my space. I get sick just imagining it. All my dirty clothes and half-finished fan art. I don't get how people walk through life with all their windows wide open.

I hear the doorknob turn—Abby's back from the parking lot. She flops down beside me. "This place is amazing."

"I know."

"And it's a one bedroom. How does she even afford that?" She kicks off her flats and tucks her feet up onto the couch. "I don't even think I'd want that."

"You mean money?"

"No, I mean a one bedroom. I definitely want a roommate. Or a suite-mate."

"A roommate would be cheaper."

"Cheaper is good," she agrees. She sits up straighter, meeting my eyes. "Have you thought about that at all?"

"Roommates?"

She nods, then pauses. "You and I could be roommates."

"That's what Simon wants."

"Yeah, I know. He mentioned that. But it's not a bad idea, you know?"

She has to be kidding. *Not a bad idea?* Abby living in my

bedroom. I'd lose my mind in a week.

"Or not," she says quickly. "Just a thought. We don't even have to decide now."

I nod wordlessly.

"So, I asked Caitlin about the party."

"Okay." I frown.

"Apparently, it's just a few people hanging out. Like, just a Tuesday-night thing." She bites her lip. "I don't think it's even a real party."

"Let me guess. You want to go."

"Only if you're going."

"Yeah, I don't know."

"Maybe we could just stop by for a second." She scoots closer, hands clasped. "Just to cheer me up after my breakup?"

I scoff. "You dumped him!"

"But I still feel shitty about it."

"And a party will fix that?"

"Definitely."

I pause and then sigh. "See, this is why we can't be roommates."

"What? Why?"

"Because you'd make me go to parties. You'd do doe eyes at me until I agreed."

"Oh." Abby grins. "Yeah, that's probably true."

I look away, smiling. "Whatever. It's tomorrow, right?"

"Right."

I roll my eyes. “All right, but I’m not drinking anything.”

“Ahhhhh!” She presses her hands to her cheeks. “I can’t wait. Leah, we’re going to an actual college party!”

“Mmm.”

“No, I’m serious—this is going to be so awesome. Do you realize this is the beginning?”

“The beginning of what?”

She sinks back, smiling dreamily. “Of real life. Of adulthood.”

“That’s terrifying.”

“It’s amazing.”

I roll my eyes—but when she smiles at me, I can’t help but smile back.

18

WE SPEND THE AFTERNOON WANDERING through downtown Athens—past music venues and into vintage clothing shops, where Abby spends her food money on a pair of faux leather ankle boots. Outside, there are flyers all around, advertising deejay nights and college theater and a band called Motel/Hotel, scheduled to play this weekend. And everywhere we look, there are restaurants. Abby announces that she's starving—and, luckily, she has her parents' debit card, so we stop at an ATM.

"When I was little, every time my mom took out money, I used to think we'd won the jackpot," says Abby. "I was like, Mom *rules* at this game."

"I just loved how crisp the bills were when they came out," I say.

"I still love that."

"I think now I just love it for being money."

Abby smiles. "That's sweet, Leah. You love it for who it is."

We stop at a diner for buttery grilled cheese sandwiches, and then we follow it up with ice cream before returning to Caitlin's. And for the whole walk back, there's this happy buzz in my stomach. Like, maybe this is it. This is what college is like.

Back upstairs, we tuck in on opposite ends of the couch with our phones, Abby texting her cousins while I text Simon.

How's she doing??? he asks.

She seems okay.

Really? Ugh. Well, Nick's a mess.

Abby nudges me. "Want to see a picture of my cousins?" She scoots closer, tilting her screen toward me. I peer at the image: Abby sandwiched between two white girls, all bright-eyed and beaming, with loosely wavy hair. "Molly's the brunette, and Cassie's the blonde," Abby says. "This was from their moms' wedding."

She swipes through a few more pictures, landing on a brightly lit shot of two women grinning at each other under a floral arch. One is honey-blond with kind of a granola vibe, even in a wedding dress. The other woman is wearing pants, and she has Abby's face. I mean, literally, she's an older version of Abby. It's really disorienting.

"I didn't know you had gay aunts," I say finally.

"Yeah, my aunt Nadine is a lesbian. I think Aunt Patty is bi."

I look at the picture again. "Nadine is your dad's sister?"

"Yup. He has two. She's the youngest."

"Is he weird about her being a lesbian?"

"Not at all."

"I'm kind of surprised."

"Really?" She smiles slightly.

My cheeks heat up. "I don't know. You always said your dad was so strict and traditional."

"No, he is. But he's cool about that. I mean, I don't know what he'd say if my brother or I came home and announced we were gay—" She cuts herself off, blushing.

And then neither of us speak. I fiddle with the remote control. Abby stares at it for a moment.

Then her phone starts vibrating, and she snaps back into herself. "It's Simon," she says. She meets my eyes while she answers it. Then she slips back to Caitlin's bedroom, the phone to her ear.

For a minute, I just stare at the ceiling fan. My phone buzzes a few times. Sometimes I think texting is the single worst technological advancement in history. Because yeah, it's convenient. But in moments like this, it's like someone's poking you repeatedly, going *hey hey hey.*

Of course it's Nick, king of casual. Hey how's it going down there? Just wondering if you guys have any cool plans.

Bet there's lots of college guys there, heh. Abby probably won't miss me too much.

Has she mentioned me? lol

I stare at the phone. I don't know what to say. Like, holy shit. I feel bad for Nick. I really do. But this is so far above my pay grade, I don't even know where to begin. So I give up. I set my phone down and dig around for my sketchpad and pencils instead. I need to get into my zone. That happens sometimes when I'm drawing. It's like the world stops existing. Everything disappears, except the point of my pencil. I can never quite explain it to people. Sometimes there's a picture in my head, and all I have to do is translate it into curves and shading. But sometimes I don't know what I'm drawing until I draw it.

I settle back onto the couch and start sketching—and instantly, my body calms. When I draw, it's almost always fandom stuff. People on Tumblr seem to like it.

But today, I draw a box.

Not a box—an ATM.

I draw it like it's an arcade game, surrounded by Skee-Ball and claw machines. I make dollar bills spurt out of the cash dispenser and soar through the air. I draw Abby, gasping joyfully, like she just won the jackpot. Then I draw myself beside her, hands clapped over my mouth.

It's the first time I've drawn Abby in a year and a half. It's the first time I've drawn myself since then, too.

"What the heck are you writing?" Abby says. I look up to

find her smiling expectantly. She sinks back onto the couch and sets her phone on the coffee table. "I love how you're just sitting here giggling to yourself."

"I'm drawing."

"Can I see?" She scoots closer.

I tilt the sketchpad toward her, and she bursts out laughing. "Oh my God. Is that us?"

I nod.

"We're playing the ATM!"

"And we're winning."

"Of course we're winning. We're awesome at this." Her lips tug up in the corners. "God. You're so talented, Leah. I'm jealous."

"Whatever." I stare down at my sketchpad, letting my hair fall forward to hide my smile.

"I'm serious. You could do commissions or something. People would totally pay for your stuff."

"No they wouldn't."

"Why not?"

"Because." I shrug.

Because I'm not good enough. Because there's something *off* about every single drawing. There's always one ear higher than the other, or too-short fingers, or visible eraser marks. It's never perfect.

"I swear, you're so much more talented than you realize. I'd pay for this in a heartbeat."

I blush. "You can have it."

She inhales. "Really?"

"Sure." I tear the page out, carefully, and hand it to her.

She peers at it for a moment, and then hugs it to her chest. "You know, I still have the other picture you drew of us."

Everything freezes: my heart, my lungs, my brain.

She looks up at me. "Can I ask you a question?"

"Okay."

She pauses. Shuts her mouth. Opens it again. And then she says quietly, "Why did we stop being friends?"

My stomach flips. "We are friends."

"Yeah, but last year. I don't know." She bites her lip. "I kept trying to figure out what I did, or if I said something to upset you. It's like, you were my best friend here for a while, but then you just stopped talking to me."

God. There's definitely some tiny invisible asshole punching me in the lungs. And winding up my heart to hyperspeed, and using my stomach like a trampoline. I can't make my thoughts line up. All I know is that I don't want to talk about this. I'd rather talk about literally anything but this.

I pause. "I didn't mean to."

"So what happened? Did I do something?"

"No, it's just," I begin—but it dies on my tongue.

It's just that she was funny. And beautiful. And I felt more awake when I was around her. Everything was amplified. We'd be waiting by the buses, or she'd be talking about her old school, and I'd catch myself smiling, for no reason at all. I had a dream once where she kissed me on the collarbone. Softly and quickly—barely a thing. I woke up aching. I couldn't look at her all day.

And the catch in her voice when I showed her my drawing. *I love it so much. Leah. I'm going to cry.*

She'd looked at me then, her eyes practically liquid. If I'd been just a little braver, I swear to God, I would have kissed her. It would have been easy. Just the tiniest lean forward.

But then she'd tucked her legs up onto the ledge and clasped her hands together. "Can I tell you a secret?" She studied my face for a minute, and then pressed her hands to her cheeks, smiling. "Wow, I'm really nervous."

It was strange. She'd seemed breathless.

"Why are you nervous?"

"Because. I don't know." Then she poked the edge of my drawing. "God. I really love this. I know *exactly* what moment that was."

"Okay," I'd said quietly.

Then her hand brushed close to mine, and my organs rearranged themselves. That's literally how it felt. Like someone stirred me up from the inside. I drew my knees up to my chest, feeling sharp-edged and awkward. Abby glanced at me for a split second, touched her mouth, and blinked.

"You know, my bus is probably here." She swallowed. "I should get down to the loading dock."

"So you're just going to leave me hanging on the secret, Suso?"

She smiled faintly. "Maybe I'll tell you tomorrow."

But she didn't. She texted me once. Happy birthday, with a balloon emoji. I wrote back, thanks, with a smiley face.

And that was it. No reply.

By Monday, everything was painfully normal. No more nervous glances. No weirdness. Abby and Nick spent all of English class jostling and play-fighting on the couch. At lunch, Abby and Simon yammered on about play rehearsal. It was like the secret had evaporated.

And now Abby's staring at my face like I'm a movie in another language. Like she's looking for the subtitles. "It's just what?" she asks finally.

"Sorry?"

"You trailed off, mid-thought."

"Oh." I stare at my hands.

She pauses. "If you don't want to talk about it—"

"Okay," I say quickly.

"Okay what?"

"Okay, I don't want to talk about it."

And Abby rolls her eyes, just barely.

We spend our first evening in Athens eating popchips and watching *Tiny House Hunters*. There's a young, white hipster couple featured today—though I guess that's every day. They're named Alicia and Lyon, and Lyon keeps using words like *repurposed* and *sustainable*.

"This can't be real," Abby says.

"Oh, it's real."

"How does this even work? Where are they keeping their car?"

"They're keeping their old house. They're putting the tiny house in the backyard."

"My God," Abby says, pressing her lips together. She shakes her head at the TV. Then, a beat later: "Hey, we should order those cookies that come in pizza boxes."

"Dude."

"Right?" Abby says.

And in this moment, it's easy to imagine this working. This friendship. Maybe we really could be roommates. We could hang around in pajamas and Skype with Simon and eat cookies every night and make straight As all the time. She can have a boyfriend, I can hopelessly pine for some sophomore, and we'll be legit best friends. At least I wouldn't have to live with a stranger.

But then sometime around eleven, Abby yawns and stretches. "I think I'm ready to go to sleep."

And suddenly, I'm very aware that Caitlin only has one bed.

"I can sleep on the couch," I say quickly.

"What?" Abby looks at me like I'm speaking total nonsense.

"That's ridiculous. It's a king-sized bed. It's literally the size of Lyon and Alicia's house."

"That's true."

And okay. I'm being ridiculous. Abby and I have shared floor space this small dozens of times, at Simon's house and Nick's house and every group sleepover. Even the car ride here forced us closer together. We could probably have three feet of empty space between us if we wanted to.

And anyway, it's just Abby.

But there's something about it being a bed.

She watches my face, brow wrinkling. "Or I could take the couch."

"No way. Caitlin's your friend."

"Well, she's my cousin's girlfriend's friend's sister."

"Right." I smile slightly. "Whatever. It's fine."

Of course it's fine.

19

I WAKE UP TO THE patter of rain on Caitlin's balcony. Abby's already awake. She's sitting cross-legged against the headboard, reading Harry Potter.

A wave of panic hits me. It's hard to explain, but the thought of Abby watching me sleep makes me want to throw up. Not that she was *watching* me. I mean, she's pretty absorbed in her book. But right now, my brain is dead set on reminding me how gross I look when I'm sleeping. My mouth was probably hanging open. I was probably snoring.

"Oh, you're up!" Abby says, folding down the corner of the page.

I gape at her. "Did you just dog-ear Harry Potter?"

"Oh boy." The edges of her lips curve up. "Should have known you were one of those people."

"One of those people? As in, I'm not a monster?" I shake my head slowly. Like, you look at Abby, and she's the picture of innocence: spiral curls, lavender pajama shorts. But no.

"Okay, this may blow your mind," I say, "but have you ever heard of—"

"Bookmarks. Yes. I know." She rolls her eyes. "Nick used to give me so much shit. I honestly think he bought me a hundred bookmarks while we were dating."

"So where are these hundred bookmarks now?"

"Well, obviously, I had to get rid of them."

"Because . . ."

"Because we broke up?" She shrugs. "I don't know. Nick stuff makes me sad. Is that weird?"

"Why would that be weird?"

She smiles wistfully. "I broke up with him. I'm not allowed to be sad."

"You can feel however you want."

"No, I know. But it's complicated."

And suddenly, she looks like she's going to burst into tears. Maybe Simon was right. Maybe Abby and Nick were never meant to break up.

"So, it's raining," Abby says.

"Yeah, I hear it."

"Do you think they'll cancel the tour?"

"I don't know."

"I mean, probably not, right? And maybe it will clear up by

this afternoon." She sighs, glancing at her phone. "Anyway, the boys are leaving Boston. I just heard from Simon. Apparently Nick just found out he got a scholarship to Tufts, and he really likes it there, so."

"Where are they going next?"

"Wesleyan—they're staying with Alice. And then tomorrow's NYU."

"That will be fun for Simon."

"Yeah." She stretches. "He's so funny. He's, like, so adamant that he doesn't mind doing long distance with Bram, and it's just a coincidence that he chose New York."

"Yeah," I say, and Abby smiles faintly.

I feel myself starting to calm down, heartbeat dialing back to normal. We make our way from the bed to the couch, and by noon, we're dressed and jacked up on Froot Loops. The rain has slowed to a drizzle, so I guess it could be worse. Of course, Abby brought wellies—bright green with polka dots.

"Did you know it was going to rain?"

"No. I just like them with this outfit. Is that weird?"

"It's pretty weird."

She pokes me in the arm.

But she doesn't look weird. She looks perfectly collegiate. I've always been so jealous of the way Abby layers clothes. She makes it look intentional. Case in point: today's skinny jeans and a navy plaid shirt, under a fitted gray sweater, rolled up at the elbows. And the wellies. When I try to layer, I just look like I'm hiding something.

I tuck my hair behind my ears. "Should we head to the admissions office?"

"Yes!" She pulls an umbrella out of her suitcase. Of course she brought an umbrella.

It's a quick drive to get there, and we sign in at a desk inside the admissions building. Then they direct us to an auditorium down the hall. We're a few minutes early, but the seats are already filling up.

Literally everyone is here with at least one of their parents. Everyone except Abby and me.

"We should make up fake identities," Abby whispers, settling in next to me in the back row.

"Why?"

"Because why not? We're totally anonymous right now."

"You do realize that these people are going to be our classmates in five months, right?"

She stares straight ahead, smiling. "So?"

"So, you're ridiculous."

She ignores me. "From now on, you have to call me Bubo Yass."

I laugh. "What?"

She gives me this smug little grin. "It's an anagram of my name."

"That's very Voldemorty of you."

"Oh, I just read that part like a week ago! All right. And your new name is Hue Barkle."

I look at her, stunned. "How did you do that so quickly?"

"I don't know."

"SAT Abby rides again." I shake my head. "Thank God you dog-ear pages."

"What?"

"Otherwise, you'd be too perfect. It's gross."

She scoffs. "Excuse me?"

"I'm just saying." I count it off on my fingers. "Cheerleading, dance, drama club, yearbook, student council. Perfect SAT scores—"

"Perfect *critical reading.*"

"Oh, okay, so you bombed math and writing."

"Well, no."

I grin. "Like I said. Perfect."

"Well, I have to be." Abby shrugs.

"Why?"

"Why do you think? Because that's my life. Because black girls have to work twice as hard. And even when we do—I mean, you heard what Morgan said."

"Ugh. I'm sorry." I rub my forehead. "Morgan's just—"

"But it's not just Morgan. Okay? What she said? That's not like a fringe point of view. I get that all. The. Time."

"That sucks."

"Yeah, it does." She tilts her head toward me. "I don't know. It just feels like I can't win sometimes."

I open my mouth to reply, but I have no clue what to say. For a minute, Abby and I just look at each other. I can't read her expression at all.

Finally, she smiles, almost wistfully. "It is what it is."

"I guess."

"Just don't call me perfect again. Deal?" She wrinkles her nose at me.

"Deal."

A man around my mom's age steps up to give a welcome speech. Then he introduces the tour guides—three girls and a guy, all UGA seniors. They split us into two groups, and we trail behind them into the parking lot, where there are actual buses waiting to be boarded.

"I kind of wish this was a double-decker bus tour."

"Or one of those duck tours."

I look at her. "What the fuck is a duck tour?"

"Say that ten times fast," says Abby.

"No way." We settle into a seat.

"Okay, so duck tours are those boats that go on land and water." Something about my expression makes her giggle. "No, seriously, Google it. This is a legit thing in DC."

I start to respond, but then I realize one of the student tour guides—Fatima—is saying something important right now. "You'll see it just to your left," she says, "and it *is* part of the meal plan."

Immediately, a dad jumps in with a slew of rapid-fire questions about his son's dietary restrictions. Fatima is unfazed. "The dining halls can absolutely accommodate students with food allergies," she begins.

"Well, my daughter is vegan," a mom chimes in, glaring up at Fatima like she's issuing a challenge.

"Totally fine. There are lots of vegan options—"

The mom cuts her off. "I'd appreciate something a little more specific than 'lots of vegan options.'" She makes air quotes as she says this. The vegan daughter in question shrinks into her seat, like she's trying to disappear.

"Now you know why I didn't want my parents here," Abby mutters.

"No kidding."

"I guarantee, right now my dad would be asking how they're going to gender segregate the dorms."

"Um . . . they're not?" I say, lips tugging upward. "Because it's college?"

"Yeah, he missed that memo."

I mean, that's the way to keep people from hooking up, Mr. Suso. Totally foolproof, except for the fact that gay people exist. How can Abby's dad not realize that? Seriously, how can a person with a lesbian sister not even consider that as a possibility?

Not that it *is* a possibility. Not for Abby anyway. Because Abby's as straight as a Popsicle stick.

Hours later, I'm in Caitlin's bathroom, attempting eyeliner. I've already given up on my hair. My hair is an asshole.

"Shit."

"You okay?" Abby asks, peeking in through the doorway.

"Eyeliner injury."

"Been there." She grimaces. "Hey, can I join you?"

"Sure." I step sideways, making room. She sets a bottle of goopy white stuff next to the sink and starts wetting her hair. "What's that?" I ask.

"Curl milk," she says. Then she squirts some into her hand. "Keeps the curls popping."

I really love your hair, I think.

"Good to know," I say.

"What do you think you're going to wear?" she asks, threading her hands through her hair.

"Um. This? And my combat boots? I didn't bring extra clothes."

"That works."

"Did you?"

I see her smiling in the mirror.

"Look at you, all prepared." I uncap my mascara.

She watches me for a moment. "Your eyes are so green."

I flush. "It's the lighting."

"Mmhmm. They're really pretty."

There's a hiccup in my stomach. I try to focus on my eyelashes. Which are nothing like Abby's eyelashes. Abby's eyelashes should have their own zip code.

She leaves, and then returns with a makeup bag. I wasn't sure she even wore makeup. As far as I can tell, she doesn't usually, at least not in school. But she knows what she's doing—dusting and blending until her skin glows and her eyes are wide and soft.

"This will be fun, right?" she says, glancing at me.

"If you say so."

She meets my eyes in the mirror and smiles before heading to the bedroom to change.

The party starts at eight thirty, but Abby won't let us head down until after nine. "We *really* don't want to be the first ones there," she says.

We take selfies while we wait—and it takes approximately a thousand tries before we get one that satisfies Abby. That's strangely reassuring. I always figured magical girls like Abby get their selfies right on the first try. She sends it to Simon, and he writes back immediately.

Wow.

With a period. And it's weird how the period makes it feel like he really means it. I stare at my knees.

Abby nudges me, grinning. "Should we head down there?"

"Sure."

We walk out to the elevators—and Abby grabs my hand, squeezing it quickly, before pressing the button for the fifth floor. It feels strange and surreal to be here, to be doing this. It's like a tiny trip through time. This could be us next year, wandering into Tuesday-night parties off campus.

I'm not 100 percent sure how I feel about that.

Or how I feel about the fact that she's still holding my hand. Why do straight girls do that? How do I interpret that?

She checks the room number one more time and then knocks on the door.

It swings open right away. "Abby!" says Caitlin. She's holding a drink—something pink in a clear plastic cup. "Guys, come meet Abby and Leah! They're friends with my brother."

"Just so you know, I've literally never met Caitlin's brother," Abby murmurs, a breath away from my ear. I follow her into the apartment, heart pounding in my chest.

The layout is identical to Caitlin's—same floor plan, same chrome appliances—but the décor is so different, it's almost disorienting. The room is lit only by dim floor lamps and a jumble of hanging Christmas lights. There's a giant red-and-purple batik tapestry draped across one wall and woven throw pillows on every surface. I'm pretty sure there's no TV.

There are only eight or nine people here besides us, packed onto the couch and around the kitchen table. A guy with a beard plays guitar while two girls sing along in harmony. We meet Eva, who is stop-you-in-your-tracks gorgeous—tall, sort of androgynous, with light brown skin and closely cropped hair. Caitlin rests a hand on each of our shoulders and asks if we want drinks.

Abby says yes, and I guess that sort of bugs me. Sometimes I think I'm the only person in the world who doesn't drink.

"Oh, Abby, I love your little boots!" Caitlin says, returning moments later with a plastic cup. We all settle in cross-legged on the floor.

Abby's wearing the ankle boots she bought yesterday and a short patterned skirt, and the effect is disarming. She's just so fucking wholesome. It almost pisses me off.

"Yo." Abby pokes me. "Why are you looking at me like that?"

"Like what?" *Holy. Fuck.* My cheeks are burning.

"Like you want to kill me."

For a moment, I'm speechless. I've never been so grateful for my resting bitch face. Ever.

Eva sinks down beside me. "So, Caitlin says you're a drummer."

"Kind of."

"Kind of?" Abby shoves me lightly. "She's an amazing drummer. Like, *amazing*."

"Huh," Eva says, turning to the guitarist on the couch. "Tom, Caitlin's friend is a drummer."

"No way," says the bearded guy.

"Way," Eva says. Then they turn back to me. "So, I don't know if Cait mentioned this, but they're going to need a new drummer after I graduate. You're going to be a freshman, right?"

I nod.

"Interesting," says Eva.

Meanwhile, Tom and the harmonizing girls have wandered over. The girls introduce themselves as Victoria and Nodoka, and they hug me like it's nothing. Like it's a handshake. They hug Abby, too.

It's as if someone unhooked my brain from my body. I'm here, but I'm not here. Smiling like it's a reflex. Nodding without knowing why.

"No pressure though," Nodoka says.

I look up with a start and realize everyone's looking at me.

"I'm . . ."

"Have you ever used an e-kit before?" asks Eva. "Took some getting used to, but now I'm a convert."

"Nick's kit is electric, right?" Abby says.

I nod slowly.

"Well, if you're up for it, we'd love to hear you play," Tom says.

"Right now?"

"Sure."

"Okay." I feel dazed. Like, holy shit. I'm at a college party full of gorgeous people, and I think I've just been invited to try out for a band.

"Let me dig out my headphones," says Eva.

Five minutes later, I'm perched on a drum stool in Eva's bedroom while Abby tucks into the desk chair, arms wrapped around her knees. Meanwhile, Eva, Nodoka, Tom, and Victoria sprawl out on the bed. My heart thuds against my rib cage. I don't know why I even bother drumming. I could just stick a microphone next to my chest.

I adjust Eva's headphones over my ears and give a few experimental taps on the snare. Electronic kits always throw me for a second. Not to mention the fact that I'm being watched by a bunch of actual musicians in an actual college band.

And Abby.

I'm just so *aware* of her sometimes.

But this is drumming, and I know drumming. If I could kick ass in the school talent show two years in a row, I can kick ass now. It's actually easier with headphones. They make me feel like my rhythms are a secret, like they live between my ears only. Even though I know that's not true. The sound's not deafening, like with an acoustic kit, but you can hear every thwack and tap on the pad. I just need to stop overthinking it.

I have to get in the zone. I have to find the pulse of the song and fall into it. I let my eyes drift shut as my sticks find the pads. I'll pretend I'm just messing around in Nick's basement. I don't even have to play a real song. Just wherever my hands take me.

When I open my eyes, Tom's nodding along, tapping the pads of his fingers together like guitar frets, the way Nick does. Nodoka's eyes are closed. And I catch Eva mouthing to Victoria: *wow.*

I grin, cheeks burning. And Abby's grinning, too.

I wouldn't say Abby's drunk, but she's bright-eyed and smiley. She leans against me all the way back to Caitlin's apartment.

"That was amazing," she says. "Aren't you glad we went?"

"Yeah," I admit.

"You did great. I was like, damn. This girl is drumming for these college kids like it's nothing."

I laugh. "Okay."

"You're going to call them, right? You're going to be their drummer, and I'm going to go to all your shows, and when you become famous, I'm going to tell everyone I know you." She sinks down on the couch and tugs off her boots. "Do you think you'll use a stage name?"

"I think we're getting a little ahead of ourselves."

I take my own boots off and tuck into the opposite corner of the couch. Funny how we've been here less than two days, but we've already claimed our couch territories. Me on the left, Abby on the right. An ocean of empty space in between us.

She leans back, sighing happily. "See, this is why I'm so glad to be single. Because I can just hang out with you and not have to run upstairs to call my boyfriend." She stretches her foot out to tap it against mine. "I can just be in the moment. I love this."

"Well, good."

She glances at me sidelong. "But you have to stop being so talented. I can't handle it."

"I'm sorry."

She smiles. "Don't apologize."

My heart thuds softly. She's barely a hand's width away from me.

"Actually, you should apologize."

I laugh nervously. "Why?"

"For making me question things."

I look at her. "Question what?"

"Things."

"I don't get it."

"Let's just say I really enjoyed watching you play." She gives the tiniest smile.

"Watching me play made you question things?"

"Yes." Her eyes flick downward. "So, can I ask you something?"

And just like that, my heart is racing. Something just shifted. I can't explain it, but I can feel it.

"Okay."

"I want to know who you like."

"Trick question. I hate everyone."

She laughs. "Okay, then who do you hate the least?"

"I don't want to answer that."

The corners of her mouth tug up. "Then you have to pick dare."

"I didn't realize we were playing Truth or Dare."

"Of course we are." She tucks her legs up and turns to face me, looking like she's about to burst out laughing. But she doesn't.

My breath hitches.

"I dare you to kiss me," she says.

20

MY WHOLE BRAIN SHORT-CIRCUITS. I just stare at her, speechless.

"If you want to," she adds, pressing her lips together.

"Do you want to?"

She nods, smiling faintly.

"Really?"

"Aren't you curious?"

"I don't know." My heart won't stop skittering. I've never kissed anyone before. I've spent so many hours worrying about that. Like, I'm going to mess this up. I know I will. I'll be sloppy or wet or too passive or too eager.

Abby laughs under her breath. "Leah, relax."

"I am. I'm just—"

All of a sudden, her lips are on mine. And I freeze.

Because.

Holy shit.

This is real. I'm kissing a person, and that person is Abby. It doesn't compute.

But her fingers graze my jawline, her thumb on my chin. A million details hit me at once. The way our knees touch. The way my lips move against hers. She tastes like fruit punch and vodka. I can't believe this is happening. My hands find her cheeks, and—

God. What the fuck am I doing? I don't like Abby. I can't like Abby, and I definitely can't kiss Abby. I don't even want to kiss her. Okay, maybe I used to want to. But that was barely anything. A month out of my life, ages and ages ago. It's buried. It's done. And I can't—

Wow. My heart won't stop pounding. Holy shit. Holy shit. Holy shit. Because maybe it wasn't ages ago. Maybe it's now. Maybe it's always.

It's like a lamp flickering on inside my chest. In my throat. Below my stomach. I don't know how to explain this. I don't think my brain's working.

Abby pulls back from the kiss, sinking into the couch cushions. She seems flustered, almost breathless. For a moment, we just stare at each other.

Then she laughs and says, "We're pretty good at this for two straight girls."

"I'm not straight."

She freezes. "Wait . . . really?"

The air leaks from my lungs.

"Leah." Abby reaches for my hand, but I jerk it away.

"Don't."

"Sorry," she says quietly, eyes sliding shut. "I—I had no idea."

"Yeah, well." I shrug. Like it's whatever. Like I could care less.

Except suddenly, I'm so angry, I'm shaking. "God, Abby, how dense are you? Seriously? I draw a picture where we're practically on top of each other, and it didn't occur to you that maybe, just maybe, I might actually like you?"

She shakes her head. "I didn't—"

"And then you're like, *oh, I have a secret, I'm so nervous.* How was I supposed to interpret that? But it's not like it matters, because ta-da! Here's Nick. And now you're flirting with him. And now you're dating him. And then the minute you're single, there you are, hardcore flirting with me again. But of course, it doesn't mean anything, because you're so fucking hetero. And then you kiss me?" My voice breaks. "That was my first kiss, Abby."

Her face crumples. "I'm sorry."

"I don't care." I squeeze my eyes shut. "I don't even care. Just don't fuck with my head. Please."

"I didn't mean to."

"Then why did you just kiss me?"

"Because I wanted to," she says. "And I wanted to at Morgan's house."

My lungs empty out in a single fierce whoosh. "What?"

"That's the secret. That's it. I wanted to kiss you, but I was scared." Her voice catches. "And I tried to tell you a million times, but I couldn't."

"Why not?"

"Because, Leah, you're terrifying. God. Half the time, I think you hate me."

I mean, I can't even look at her. It's like I've been put on lockdown.

Abby's close to tears. "I just feel *so*—I don't know what to do. My cousin Cassie was just talking about how shitty and selfish it is for straight girls to flirt with lesbians because they're curious or bored—"

"Or because they just broke up with their boyfriends."

"Or that." Abby winces. "But I thought you were straight. I swear to God."

"So you kissed me? That makes no sense."

"I mean, I thought we were two straight girls experimenting."

My heart twists. "Well, we're not."

"I know." She sniffs. "I'm so sorry. I just. I don't want to be this straight girl using you. But then it's like, maybe I'm not actually straight. I don't know. I've had crushes before, but I've never . . ."

"Crushes on girls?"

Abby shrugs.

"So what, now you think you're bi?"

"You make me think about it."

My heart skids to a stop.

Abby covers her face with both hands. "I don't know. It's just." She takes a deep breath. "You want to hear about my crushes? You want to know why I kept in touch with Caitlin?"

My heart sinks. "Not really."

"Leah, it's not—God. She's straight, okay? I had a boyfriend, and she has a boyfriend, and she's straight, and I'm fucking this up. I'm just." She exhales. "I don't like Caitlin, okay? I barely know her."

"Whatever. She's pretty."

"So are you," Abby whispers. I can't help but sneak a glance at her. She's hugging her knees, eyelashes thick with tears. "And I want to be friends. Or something. I don't know. I just hate this."

She swipes her fingers across her eyes, and my brain just unravels. I can't deal with this girl. I can't.

She makes me want to shove my hand into my chest and rip my own heart out.

* * *

Abby spends half the night trying to talk me out of sleeping on the couch. "I already feel like a jerk," she says. "Seriously, take the bed."

"Oh my God." I drag a pillow and blanket out to the living room. "It's fine, okay? Just stop."

"I'm going to sleep in the chair."

I roll my eyes. "That's your choice."

And I guess we're both that stubborn, because the bed stays empty all night. I wake up to find Abby in Caitlin's IKEA chair, head tilted slightly sideways, like she's sleeping on a plane. For a moment, I just watch her. Maybe that makes me a creepy little vampire, but I can't help it.

She's hugging a pillow, her hands clasped against it, and it rises and falls with her chest. Her lips are softly parted. I have this sudden mental image of her as a kid, which gives me this tug in my gut that I can't quite explain. It's not attraction, because obviously I'm not attracted to kids. It's more like wistfulness. Just this weird little wish that I could have known her then.

She wakes up pretty soon after that, and we pack our stuff in silence. I can barely breathe, I feel so tense and awkward. I have this feeling that my skin would crackle if you touched it. I don't know how we'll survive the trip home.

Caitlin comes over around ten to get her key and say good-bye, and when I look at her, all I can think about is what Abby said last night. *You want to know why I kept in touch with Caitlin?*

But I can't be jealous of Caitlin. I'm not that big of an asshole. This girl gave me an apartment and a parking pass and possibly a new *band*.

"I'm so excited we'll get to hang out next year," she says, hugging us both.

My stomach flips a little. It still catches me off guard that this isn't some random anomaly of a weekend. This is a preview of real life. These places, these people, this strange shot of freedom.

We arrive at Abby's car, and Caitlin hugs us each again. "Stay in touch, okay?"

She helps us load our bags and leaves, and I'm alone with Abby all over again. I hover nervously near the trunk. "Do you want me to drive?"

"Oh, don't worry about it." But then she hesitates. "Unless you want to, I mean."

"I don't care."

She looks at me.

"Abby, I really don't care."

She nods slowly. "Okay." She smiles slightly. "I'll drive. You relax."

I settle into the passenger seat and cue up my playlist while Abby merges onto the highway. Definitely the moody playlist this time: Nick Drake and Driftwood Scarecrow and Sufjan

Stevens. For almost twenty minutes, neither of us says a single word. Abby's clearly in agony. She keeps opening and closing her mouth, eyes flicking toward me. I don't think Abby Suso is capable of silence.

Sure enough, she breaks it before we're even out of Watkinsville. "So, do you think you'll try out for the band?"

"Probably not."

"Really?" Her brow furrows. "Why not?"

"Because I'm a mediocre drummer."

"Are you serious?"

I shrug. "I don't even own a drum kit."

"So you'll get one."

"I can't afford one."

Abby squeezes the steering wheel. "How much are they?"

"I don't know. A couple hundred dollars."

"Okay, so maybe you could get a job?" Immediately, she winces. "Ugh, that came out sounding really condescending. I don't mean it like that."

I shake my head. "It's fine. But yeah, I don't have a car, so . . ."

"But next year. We'll be so close to downtown Athens, or maybe there will be stuff on campus. I'm going to try to work next year."

"Maybe." I turn toward the window.

"Or," she says, and there's this shift in her voice. "Maybe you could make money with your drawings?"

"Mmm. I don't think so."

"I'm serious. Have you ever thought about putting some of them on the internet? Just to see what happens?"

"Abby, I'm on the internet."

"You have an art blog?"

"I'll text you the link if you want."

"I want." She grins. "Leah, this is perfect."

"Well, it's all fandom stuff. I don't make money off of it."

She pauses for a moment. "But what about taking commissions?"

It's funny—I've thought about it. Sometimes I even get private messages asking about it. But I've never taken the idea all that seriously. It's just hard to imagine someone could look at my shitty drawings and decide to give me real money.

"Or"—Abby glances at me—"you could set up an online store. Maybe you could upload some designs, and then people could order prints and phone cases and stuff."

"Mmhmm."

"I actually think you could make decent money, you know? And then you could spend it on a drum kit. It would be perfect."

"I'm not sure why you care."

Her face falls. "Because I do."

God. I'm such an asshole. I know I am. Abby's literally just trying to help. And her ideas aren't even that terrible. I mean, how cool would it be to make money from my art? To actually be able to buy shit for once. Maybe I could even help my mom out after I graduate. It's not like I'm opposed to what Abby is saying. I just feel like being bitchy to her.

Fucked up, I know. But that's where we are.

21

WHEN I GET HOME, THERE'S a Nordstrom bag on my bed. My yellow dress. I know before I even look inside. My stomach twists as soon as I see it.

I FaceTime Mom at work. "What the hell is this?"

"Wow. That's not the reaction I was expecting."

"We can't afford this." My cheeks feel warm. "I'm returning it."

"Leah."

"We're not spending two hundred and fifty dollars on a—"

She cuts me off. "Okay, first of all, it wasn't two hundred and fifty dollars. It was on sale."

"I don't believe you."

She flips her palms up. "Well, it's true. It was ten percent off, and then I got another fifteen percent for joining their email list."

"That's still almost two hundred dollars."

"Lee, this isn't for you to worry about."

"How can I not worry about it?" There's a lump forming in my throat. Yet again. This is ridiculous. I'm not even a crier, but now I'm spending half my life on the verge of a breakdown.

"Leah, we're fine. You know that, right?" She rubs the bridge of her nose. "I've got all that overtime from last month, and we've got another check coming in from your dad—"

"I don't want him paying for this."

"But you're okay with him paying for your cell phone? Your sketchpads? Lee, that's how child support works."

"Well, it's gross."

"Okay, you know what? He's only paying for another two months, and then you can be as financially independent as you want. But for now, can we just say, hey, it's done? It's paid for. He can afford it." She shakes her head. "Do you have to make everything hard?"

"Excuse me?" I say. And for a moment, we just stare at each other.

She exhales, shoulders sinking. "Look, can we talk about this when I get home?"

"Um. If you want."

"Okay. Good. Sweetie, please don't worry about the money, okay? We're fine, I promise."

I press my lips together.

"Leah, for real. We're good. I wouldn't have bought it if we couldn't afford it. You know that, right?"

"Okay." I feel myself softening.

"I love you, okay? I'll be home at six. I can't wait to hear about your trip."

"Love you, too," I mutter. "And thanks for the dress. I guess."

She snorts. "Keep playing it cool, Leah. And you're welcome."

But I'm not cool. Not even close. I practically rip the garment bag open as soon as we hang up. I stare at the dress.

It's as perfect as I remember. Maybe more perfect. I forgot how badass flowers can look.

I slip out of my jeans and wriggle into the gown, tugging the zipper up in back. The skirt trails on the floor all the way to the bathroom. We're talking *Beauty and the Beast*–level gliding. I fucking love it.

I flip on the bathroom light and peer at my reflection. And it's sort of a miracle: I don't look like shit. The yellow of the dress makes my skin look creamy, and my hair falls in loose waves past my shoulders. Even my cheeks look apple-round and flushed. Now I want to stare into the mirror until I memorize myself. I want to cast this version of me in every daydream. This is a Leah who could kick some solid ass. It's a Leah who could make out for *days.*

When I get back to my room, my phone screen lights up with a text. I sink onto the bed, still wearing the dress.

It's Anna. Are you back?

I want to say no. Maybe I could disappear. Just for the rest of spring break. I could hole up in my bedroom and not talk to anyone and spend the next four days cycling through my ever-expanding repertoire of daydreams. Like the one where I'm drumming under a strobe light, wearing my prom dress, totally nailing it, and then Abby catches my eye from the audience, and the music slows, and she's smiling that quiet half smile I can only assume she does because she's literally trying to wreck me.

I miss you! Anna adds. Want to do Starbucks on Friday?

Yeah. So now I feel like a dick, because I haven't even thought about Anna in days. I barely remembered she existed. And even though I'm mad at Morgan, Anna hasn't done anything wrong. I'm just a shitty, negligent friend.

Yes! Just us?

She writes back with a smiley emoji.

Luckily, Anna's an early bird, so I can head straight to Starbucks after dropping Mom off at work. But I forgot what a shitshow this place is on Friday mornings. The line for the drive-through is so long, I can barely get into the parking lot, and I end up having to park in the lot for the gentlemen's club next door. I'm five minutes early, but Anna's car is already here, and as soon as I step inside, I see her—dark hair in a neat ponytail, back to the door.

She's sitting across from Morgan.

I'm so angry, I could vomit. My stomach is actually lurching. Morgan catches my eye and murmurs something to Anna, who twists around to smile at me. She waves me over.

I just stand there, staring.

Anna turns back around, leans toward Morgan, presses her hand down on the table and stands. Then she walks straight toward me.

"Are you kidding me?" I ask her.

"Leah, no. Come on. You guys need to talk."

"I can't believe you lied to me."

Anna winces. "I didn't lie."

"You said it was just us."

"Technically, I replied with a very ambiguous emoji."

"It was a smiley! That's not ambiguous." I glance over her shoulder at Morgan, who gives me a tentative smile. Yeah, no. I turn away from her quickly. "You knew I didn't want to talk to her."

Anna rolls her eyes. "Okay, do you even realize how ridiculous you're being? It's senior year. There are two months left of school. Ever. And you guys have been friends since middle school. You're going to throw that away? Are you that fucking stubborn?"

"Don't you dare act like this is my fault."

"God, just stop." Anna sighs. "Leah, she knows she messed up. She was upset. She said something stupid. Can you please just let her apologize?"

"Abby's the one she should be apologizing to."

"Well, you're the one who's upset about this."

"You think Abby's not upset?" My cheeks are suddenly burning. I can't even say her name without blushing.

"Yeah, I've been wondering about that. How does Abby even know what Morgan said?" Anna asks, eyes narrowing.

"Are you asking if I told her?"

Anna shrugs.

"Oh my God. That's seriously what you're focusing on right now?"

"Leah, don't do this." She sighs. "Can you just talk to Morgan. Please?" Her voice softens. "I'm really sick of being in the middle."

"Then stop putting yourself in the middle."

"Can you just stop? Okay? I just want things to be normal. We don't have a lot of time left."

I look at her, and suddenly I'm eleven years old. A freckly mess of a sixth grader with no friends. Literally none. I'd go to school, come home, and watch TV with Mom. I'd spend lunch periods reading manga in the bathroom. It was right after my dad left, so my mom was always angry or weepy, and the thing about Morgan and Anna is that they were the first people here to give a shit about me. They were my friends even before I knew Simon and Nick existed. So maybe I'm an asshole. Maybe I'm overreacting.

I swear to God, someone tied a knot in my stomach.

Anna shakes her head slowly. "Like, what's next? Are you going to find a reason to hate me? And Nick? What about Simon? Are you going to shut us all out because you can't deal with saying good-bye?"

"Okay, that's bullshit, and you know it."

"Is it?"

"This isn't about me," I snap. "Morgan said something racist. And she didn't apologize to Abby. So, that's it. We're done here."

I turn on my heel and storm out of Starbucks, leaving Anna standing in front of the counter with her mouth hanging open.

22

SIMON TEXTS ME BEFORE I even get to my car. Can you come to Waffle House? Like right now?

I write back immediately. Eerily perfect timing. Just stepping out of Starbucks. I almost wonder if he knew. Waffle House is so close, I could actually walk there.

Oh awesome—we're in the back, come find us!

My stomach drops. Us?

Me and Nick, he replies.

Fuck. Fuckstravaganza.

God, the thought of facing Nick right now. I don't even know how I'll look him in the eye. What if he just knows? What if he can read it on my face? *Guess what, Nick! Guess what I did! With your ex-girlfriend! Who you're still in love with!*

Like, this isn't some minor fuckup. This is a straight-up friend felony.

I stare at the screen of my phone, wondering how I can possibly wriggle out of this. Maybe now's the time for one of those fictional diarrhea attacks Simon's so strangely fond of.

Or not. I don't know. I guess I'll have to face Nick eventually.

I can be there in five, I write back.

You're the best, Simon writes.

It's so warm and breezy out that I think I actually will walk. Might as well leave my car in the gentlemen's club parking lot. Wouldn't be the first time a car parked there for hours.

When I get there, they're slumped on opposite sides of a booth, picking at a single shared waffle. It's a sad fucking scene.

"Hey," I say, sliding in next to Simon.

Nick perks up. "Hey! Welcome back. How was your road trip?"

My heart twists when he says it. Maybe one day the phrase *road trip* won't remind me of Abby. I tuck my legs up, cross-legged on the seat, and press my lips together. "It was good."

"Good." He nods quickly. "Hey, so, I was wondering . . ."

"Here we go," Simon murmurs.

A waitress appears, and I order a waffle and a black coffee. All business. But as soon as she leaves, Nick launches right in. "How was Abby? Like, was she sort of okay, or—I mean, I don't know. Was she acting weird?"

Shit.

"She seemed . . ."

"Like, was she crying?"

"Um. A little bit?"

I mean, it's true. She cried a little bit. Right after I called her out. Which was right after she kissed me.

"Whoa. Okay." Nick's eyes widen. "That's . . . okay, good to know."

I leap frantically toward a subject change. "So, how was your trip?"

"It was great," Simon says. There's this catch in his voice.

But before I can ask him what's wrong, Nick's off and running again. "I just miss her, you know? Like, we haven't talked for a week. I keep almost calling her. It's completely automatic. I just. Ugh." He rubs his forehead. "This was a mistake, right? We shouldn't have broken up."

"Well," Simon says carefully. "She broke up with you."

It's like Nick doesn't even hear him. "I should have fought for her." His voice quivers. "She was the best thing that ever happened to me, and I just let her go. What was I thinking?"

Simon shoots me a glance.

"I mean, you didn't do anything wrong," I say finally.

"I just didn't fight hard enough." He shakes his head. "I should have applied to Georgia."

"But you love Tufts," Simon says uncertainly.

"I love Abby."

I feel almost dizzy. I can't quite line my thoughts up. All I know is this: Nick loves Abby. I kissed Abby. And if he knew, I don't think he'd ever be okay. He would never recover.

"Wait." He peers at me suddenly. "Did she hook up with someone?"

"What?"

"She did, didn't she?"

"Nick." Simon sighs.

"Just tell me." He leans forward. "Who was it—some frat bro?"

"Um."

"Fuck. I knew it." He leans back in the booth. "Shit. I can't believe this."

I swear to God, I might die. My stomach's twisting in twenty directions. I don't think I could speak if I tried.

"Come on." Simon turns to me. "Abby wouldn't do that. She didn't hook up with a frat boy. Right, Leah?"

I nod slowly.

"See? Everything's going to be fine." Simon leans his chin onto his hand. "It's just been a confusing week."

"Oh?" I say.

Simon sits there, nodding, while Nick stares vacantly into space.

"Simon?"

"Mmhmm?"

I don't know what to do with Simon when he gets like this.

Sometimes I get the vibe he wants me to read his mind. Like he's sitting there, trying to pour his thoughts directly into my brain, so he won't have to say them out loud.

I point my fork at him. "Hey."

"Yeah?"

"Spit it out."

He does this quiet laugh. "Okay." I hear him swallow. "I think I fell in love with a school," he says finally.

"Okay."

"And it's not NYU."

"Right. I got that." I pause, setting my fork down. "What school?"

"Haverford. It's really tiny."

"That's near Philly, right?"

He nods and bites his lip.

"But Bram's going to be in New York," Nick chimes in.

Simon sighs. "Yup."

"Ah."

Simon fidgets with the sugar packets.

"Have you talked to Bram?" I ask.

"Nope."

"You should do that."

"I know." He pauses. "Or not. I don't know. NYU was awesome, too. I'm being ridiculous, right?"

"What do you mean?"

"I'm needlessly complicating things."

"Yup," says Nick.

"Well, not necessarily." I shrug. "What's so great about Haverford?"

"Ugh. I don't know." Simon full-on grimaces. You'd think I'd asked him to speak fondly about calculus. "I just liked it."

"You just liked it."

"I'm going to pee," Nick says, standing abruptly. "Hold that thought."

But Simon turns to face me. "You wouldn't believe how many gay people go there. We kept running into them. Like, this one girl hosts a Pride bingo night every Thursday in her dorm room. I could literally go there and only be friends with gay people."

"Nice."

"I keep imagining what it would be like to have actual gay friends."

My heart twists when he says it. It's hard to explain. The guys think I'm straight, and I feel super weird about that. But also relieved. It's fucked up.

"I think I'd like that," he adds.

"But you know they have gay people in New York," I say. "Like, I'm pretty sure NYU is mega gay."

"I know, but those are hipster gay people. I need the nerdy gays."

"And Haverford has the nerdy gays?"

"It's like ninety-nine percent nerds there. That's an actual statistic."

I bite back a smile. "I think you found your people."

Simon groans softly and covers his face. "It's just . . . like I felt something when I was there. Like, I got to the campus and it just felt right. It felt like it chose me. You know what I mean?"

The question catches me off guard, and I let my mind drift back to the past few days. Funny how the campus tour already feels so hazy. I mostly just remember the look on Abby's face when she said *maybe I'm not actually straight.* I mean, she didn't seem so straight when she kissed me.

"I don't know," I say finally. "I think it's different. Like, I already knew I'd be going to Georgia. I wasn't looking for that kind of moment."

"I wasn't looking for it either," he mutters. "Like, what am I doing? Everything was perfect, and I just had to fuck it all up."

"You didn't fuck anything up, Simon." My coffee and waffle arrive all at once. I start in with the syrup—a tiny drop in each square. "Like, what's the worst-case scenario?"

He blinks. "We break up."

"Do you want to break up?"

He looks at me like I've smacked him in the face. "Are you kidding? No!"

"Does Bram?"

"No. Of course not. No."

"Then what am I missing?" I ask, taking a bite of waffle. "You guys will be fine."

"This is ridiculous. I should go to NYU. That's the plan. I don't know why this is even a question." Simon shakes his head quickly. "I should go to NYU, right?"

"Sure. Unless you like nerdy gay wonderland better."

He groans. "You're no help."

"I mean, how far is Philly from New York?"

"Like an hour and a half by train," he says immediately. Clearly, he's researched this. "A little shorter if I take the Acela."

"That's not that bad, Simon."

"I know. But." He frowns. "It's still long distance."

"And you don't want to be in a long-distance relationship."

"I mean, I don't mind it, in theory. I just don't know if they ever work."

"Tons of people make them work."

"Yeah, but look at Nick and Abby." He gestures vaguely toward the bathroom. "That's a freaking mess."

My heart almost stops. People need to warn me if they're going to mention her out of nowhere like that. Especially if they're going to talk about her and Nick being a freaking mess.

But Jesus Christ. I need to stop. I stab my waffle with my fork and shove it into my mouth. This is absurd. Literally absurd. As if Abby Suso, real-life Disney princess, is going to run straight into my arms. Even if she did, I couldn't do that to

Nick. Not that she would. I mean, she's not even really bi.

But she's questioning things. I *make* her question things.

"Are you . . . okay?" Simon asks, peering nervously through his glasses.

"What?" I whip my head up. "I'm fine. Why? Are *you* okay?"

"Okay, you're acting super weird."

"No, I'm not."

He raises his eyebrows. We stare each other down.

"*You're* acting weird," I mutter, looking away finally.

"I know." He covers his face. "I just need to think about this."

"I think you should talk to Bram. When are you seeing him?"

"Not until the game tomorrow."

"The soccer game?"

Simon nods.

"Then talk to him right afterward."

He sighs. "I don't know."

"Simon. You'll feel better, I swear."

That's right, Simon. Be totally open and tell him everything that's bothering you. Okay? You should definitely take my advice, because I'm just so fucking good at all this sharing and caring stuff myself. Feelings. I rule at them.

"Okay, I'll do it. But you have to come with me to the game and psych me up for it."

"You guys are coming to the game?" Nick says, reappearing at the end of the booth. "Sweet."

"Um." I glance at Simon. "I guess so."

"Yes. Good. That's good." Simon nods quickly. Then he stuffs a bunch of waffle into his mouth, cheeks puffing out like a hamster.

23

SATURDAY'S GAME IS IN THE soccer field behind the auxiliary gym. I spot Simon as soon as I get there, brooding in the stands.

I scoot up next to him. "How are you feeling?"

"I don't want to tell him," he blurts.

Okay, I seriously don't get couples. I'm sorry, but all this moping over an hour on the Acela? It's not ideal, I get that, but Simon's acting like it's apocalyptical.

He sighs. "It's just. I'm kind of freaking out. This is literally why Nick and Abby broke up, you know?"

"This is different."

"But how? How is it different?" He looks at me, almost beseechingly.

"It's so different." My thoughts are spinning in all directions. I need to cool my jets and focus. "It's not even close to the same situation, Simon. Nick's going to be in Boston."

"It just sucks," Simon says, staring straight ahead. I follow his gaze, taking in the freshly mowed fields and soccer goals and boys. So many boys. There are literally hundreds of boys at this school, and even more at the University of Georgia. It would be so easy to fall for one of them.

Easier—and much safer—than falling for Abby Suso.

"Is Nick okay?" I ask after a moment.

"Yeah, I guess," Simon says. And then he grabs my hand and squeezes it. And it's weird how perfect it feels, holding hands with Simon. Not a hint of romance. It just feels like home. "Now he's saying he wants to keep things normal," Simon says. "Like, he doesn't want us to change the plans for prom or anything."

"Oh God. Prom," I say. It's in a week. Literally one week from today. "I forgot about that."

"I know."

"They're not . . . still going together?"

Simon shakes his head. "They're both still going to dinner and the dance, but now they're going stag."

"Going stag. Do people still say that?"

He laughs. "I don't know."

I turn to watch the field in time to see Nick kick the shit out of the ball, so forcefully I almost wince. His face is bright red, eyes burning with an intensity I've never seen before. The coach nods from the sidelines, clapping slowly.

I turn to Simon, eyebrows raised. "Are we sure he's okay?"

"This is not good," Simon murmurs. But a minute later, the corners of his lips tug upward. His Bram face. And sure enough, Bram's on the field, grinning up at Simon as he runs.

"EYE ON THE BALL, GREENFELD," the coach yells. "AND LAUGHLIN. FOCUS. GODDAMMIT." I look up to see Garrett waving at me frantically with both arms.

"Hello, Garrett," I mutter, rolling my eyes. Simon laughs. I have to admit, I like the feeling of being pursued, even if it's only Garrett. It just feels nice. And maybe *nice* is kind of refreshing. Abby Suso makes me feel all kinds of things, but *nice* isn't one of them.

Stop. Thinking. About. Abby. *Jesus Christ.*

"This is just so weird." Simon sighs.

And it is.

I mean, here's a surprise: I have an actual date to prom, and Abby Suso's going alone.

I don't know if I should text her.

I mean, it's not like we're fighting. And it doesn't have to be weird. It was just a kiss. And I'm sure it only happened because she was tipsy. I should just send her something friendly and casual, because we're casual friends who send casual texts. It's just that every time I try to type something, my brain shuts down completely. I can't even type "hello" to this girl without bursting into flames.

I'm pretty sure this is the kind of crush you can die from.

I try to distract myself by stalking my own Tumblr, scrolling through my posts in reverse order. The further back I go, the shittier my drawings get—proportions all wrong, messed-up shading. I guess I should be glad I've improved, but I feel weirdly embarrassed about the older work. I wish I had the kind of talent that emerged fully formed. I don't like people seeing me in progress. It's like stepping off a stage and finding out your underwear was showing. Not that my metaphorical underwear is particularly well hidden now. I still see flaws in my work, everywhere I look. It's exhausting and mortifying and almost unbearable.

Except.

Okay.

I have yet another message from an anon, asking if I take commissions. **i like your art so much, im so in love with it**, it says.

So in love, they'd pay me for it. They're *asking* to pay me for it. I think of the drum kit I don't have. The car we couldn't afford to fix. I think of my two-hundred-and-fifty-dollar prom dress.

I think of Abby.

But I can't take commissions, because what if I draw the thing, and it's a steaming pile of shit? What if they ask for their money back? Or what if I post my commission rates and people just fall over laughing? What if no one ever contacts me? Maybe this anon is actually just trolling me. Maybe it's like the dudes in teen movies who pretend to ask the nerdy girl to prom.

My mouth goes dry. It's hard to explain. Maybe I should delete my whole Tumblr account. Except.

I don't know.

I'm curious.

Which doesn't mean I'm doing this. It doesn't mean anything at all.

24

I STEP OFF THE BUS on Monday, and Garrett pops out of the stairwell like a jack-in-the-box. "Burke!"

I jump. "Jesus, Garrett!"

"So, guess what," he says.

I narrow my eyes. "What?"

"I'm mad at you."

"Why?"

He smiles and ruffles his hair. "You disappeared before the game ended. Again. Why do you always do that?"

"Because." My mind goes blank. I mean, not *blank*, exactly. But it's definitely not giving me anything useful to work with.

Because.

Because Abby kissed me. Because she may not be straight. Which means I had to update every single one of my daydreams to reflect this. We're talking about a massive overhaul, Garrett. I don't think you realize how many Abby-related fantasies live in this brain.

"This was the most boring spring break ever," Garrett says. Now he's walking beside me, matching my pace. "You should have stayed home to entertain me."

"Entertain you?" I side-eye him.

"Well, Burke, I didn't mean it like that," he says, nudging me. "But now that you mention it . . ."

Then he winks at me, so—yeah. We're done here. "I'll see you at lunch, Garrett," I say, patting him once on the arm before veering down a side hall.

"I made dinner reservations!" he calls after me. "For prom!"

I give him a thumbs-up over my shoulder. What a fucking slightly adorable doofus.

I haven't talked to Abby since I stepped out of her car on Wednesday—and when I realize that, it throws me. It doesn't feel like it's been that long. But then again, I've thought about her approximately ten billion times a day.

All morning, I feel like I'm quietly buzzing. I don't have any classes with Abby until the afternoon. But there's lunch. At noon. In six and a half minutes. I can't stop staring at the clock.

Bram's already at the table when I get there, and I take a seat beside him, facing the door. It occurs to me that I have no idea whether Simon talked to him. So, that's awkward. *Hey,*

Bram—your boyfriend might move to Philly, and he told me first.

And then it actually hits me. Simon told me first. And if I'm being totally honest, I'm sort of gleeful about that. No one ever picks me first. But he did. I feel this sudden wave of affection for Simon. I think he might be the best friend I've ever had.

And maybe I should actually come out to him. Tell him I'm bi. I can picture it perfectly. I think he'll laugh when I tell him. Not in a douchey way. I just think he'll be happy.

"What are you smiling about?" Bram asks.

I shrug and look away.

And then I see her in the doorway. Understated Abby, goddess of restraint. Jeans and a long cardigan and glasses. I literally just spent two nights with her, and I had no idea she wore glasses. Of course she looks amazing in them.

Then she smiles at me slightly, and I can barely look at her. I literally can't remember if I'm supposed to be mad at her. She does a come-over-here gesture, and first I whip my head around to see who she's talking to. *Yes, you,* she mouths, grinning.

I get up from the table, just as Simon's sitting down. Abby's waiting in the hall, outside the doorway.

"Hi," she says, smiling tentatively.

"Hey."

"I can't sit there."

"Because of Nick?"

She shrugs. "It just seems mean."

For a moment, neither of us speaks. We just stand against the wall, watching the juniors stream into the cafeteria in clusters. Abby's foot taps on the molding, and there's this look in her eyes that I've never seen before. I can't decipher it.

"So, we really need to talk," Abby says finally.

"You and Nick?"

"No." She rolls her eyes, smiling. "You and me."

My heart flips. "Okay."

"Are you free after school this week?"

"What day?"

"Any day. Want to say Friday?" Abby pauses. "I just need to—"

But then she stops talking abruptly, leaning almost imperceptibly away from me. I look up, and there's Garrett.

"Hey, ladies."

The daily cringe, starring Garrett Laughlin. Today's episode: Garrett missed the memo about not calling women *ladies*.

"I was just filling everyone in on dinner plans for prom. We have a six o'clock reservation at the American Grill Bistro at North Point Mall. It's about twenty minutes from the nature center."

"I love that prom's at the nature center," says Abby. "It suits us."

"Because we're so naturally awesome?" Garrett asks.

"Because our classmates are literally wildlife," says Abby.

Garrett actually giggles, and I shake my head, smiling.

"Anyway, I should go," Abby says quickly, looking from Garrett to me. "But." She nudges my foot with her toe. "Friday afternoon. I'll find you." She flashes a quick smile and drifts back down the hallway. Then she turns a corner and disappears.

25

AND OF COURSE, I'M A hot mess for the rest of the day. I'm so far gone, it's not even funny. My head is just mush. Actual mush. And it would be one thing if it only happened in Abby's physical presence, but it's way beyond that. It's everything I do and everywhere I go. People try to talk to me, and I don't even hear them.

Simon intercepts me on my way to the buses. "Come on. I'm driving you home."

"You don't have to do that."

"It's not a question. Let's go." He hooks his arm around my shoulders and turns me toward the parking lot. Then he walks me the whole way there, like I'm a frail, stumbling great-grandmother.

"You're ridiculous," I inform him.

He opens the passenger door for me.

"Are you going to click my seat belt for me, too?" I add.

"Very funny."

"So, where's Nora?" I ask when he finally slides into the driver's seat.

"Funny you should ask."

"Funny how?"

"Well, by funny," he explains, "I mean not at all funny."

"Ah."

He backs slowly out of his parking spot, lips pressed together.

"Is everything okay?" I say after a moment.

"What? Oh yeah. I'm just." He shakes his head. "Did you know she's going to prom?"

"Nora?"

Simon nods.

"Oh. With Cal?"

He stops at a light, turning to me incredulously. "You knew about it?"

"No, but they were pretty flirty during the play."

"No they weren't! I would have noticed. I always notice this stuff." I snort out loud, and he narrows his eyes. "What?"

"Nothing."

"Hmph."

"So, are they dating?" I ask.

He sighs. "I don't know."

"Want me to ask her? I'll ask. I don't care."

"It's just weird, right?" he says, nodding earnestly. "He liked *me*."

"And you have a boyfriend. Which, speaking of—have you talked to Bram yet?"

"No. But I will. And, Leah, God. You know I'm not jealous, right? I'm just saying—it's weird."

"I don't think it's weird at all. You and Nora look a lot alike."

Simon smacks the steering wheel. "That's why it's weird."

"The dude has a type."

"I don't like it."

"I think you just don't like the idea of your little sister hooking up with someone."

"THEY'RE NOT HOOKING UP."

I shake my head, smiling.

"But she keeps staying after school with him for yearbook, and now he's giving her a ride home like every day."

"Aka, they're hooking up."

Simon huffs. "No they're not."

He turns onto Roswell Road, and for the next five minutes, we drive in silence. I don't say a single word until he pulls into my driveway.

"Seriously, are you okay?" I ask finally.

"What? Yeah."

"You need to talk to Bram."

"I know."

"Like now. Today."

He nods, slowly, jaw clenched. "This is stupid. I should just turn in my deposit for NYU, right?"

"Simon, I can't make this decision for you." I shake my head. Then I grab his hand and tug it. "All right. Come on."

"You want me to come in?" His brow furrows.

"Yup."

"Um. Yeah." Simon nods quickly. "Wow, I don't think I've actually been inside your house in years."

"I'm aware," I say, feeling stupidly self-conscious. It's not a secret that I'm not rich. And Simon's not going to judge me for having a small house, or clutter, or crappy secondhand IKEA furniture. But I'm just weird about having people over. It's like I can't help but be acutely aware of the stains on the carpet and my mismatched bedding. Or even just the fact that my whole room is the size of Simon's closet.

We walk in through the garage, and he follows me down the hall. "I can't even remember what your room looks like," he says.

"It's really small. Just warning you."

Then I open the door and step into my room. Simon lingers in the doorway. "This is amazing," he says softly.

I look at him to see if he's kidding.

"Did you draw all of these?" He walks toward the wall, peering closely at one of my sketches.

"Some of them. Some are from the internet."

My walls are covered with art—pencil sketches and carefully inked character portraits and chibis and yaoi. If I fall in love with something on DeviantArt, I print it. Or sometimes Morgan and Anna print them and give them to me. And I guess lately, more and more of them are mine. My Harry and Draco sketches, Haruka and Michiru, my original characters. And the picture I drew of Abby and me at Morgan's house. I hope to God Simon doesn't notice that.

"This room is so you," he says, smiling.

"I guess."

He flops backward onto my bed. That's the thing about Simon. He feels totally at home wherever he goes. I stretch out beside him, and we both stare at my ceiling fan.

Then Simon covers his face and sighs.

"Hey," I say.

"Hey."

"I know you're worried."

He sniffs and turns his head to look at me. There's a tear streaking down his cheek, sliding out from under his glasses. He wipes it away with the heel of his hand. "I just don't like good-byes."

"I know."

"I don't want to leave him or you or Abby or any of you guys." His voice catches. "I don't know anyone in Philly. I don't know how people do this."

I feel my throat start to tighten.

"I think I'm even going to miss Taylor."

"Okay, now you've lost me."

He laughs and sniffs again. "Come on. You know you'll miss her. How are we going to know if her metabolism is still rocking?"

"Probably from her daily Instagram updates."

"Okay, that's true."

"And that's a conservative estimate."

"I know." He scoots toward me, so close our heads are touching. Then he sighs quietly into my ear, ruffling my hair with his breath. I don't think I've ever loved him more. We just lie there like that, watching the fan move in circles.

I should tell him.

Right now. I don't think there's ever been a moment in history that was more perfect for coming out.

But I don't.

It's the weirdest thing. I'm lying in a room with my gay best friend, who's 100 percent likely to be completely fucking cool about this. Literally risk-free.

But it's like the words won't come.

26

AND THEN THERE'S THE ISSUE of Nick. Despite his Waffle House meltdown, he's totally normal on Monday and Tuesday—so normal, it's almost concerning. But on Wednesday afternoon, he skids straight off the edge.

I'm heading toward the buses when I hear—unmistakably—Nick's voice over the intercom. "Simon Spier and Leah Burke, please report to the atrium immediately."

I stop in my tracks, staring at the loudspeaker.

"I repeat: Simon and Leah, report to the atrium immediately."

I have no clue what he's playing at, but I head up there anyway. I catch Simon in the stairwell. "What's this about?" he asks.

I shake my head slowly. "No idea."

I follow Simon upstairs and into the atrium. It's teeming with people—laughing, jostling, and streaming out to the parking lot. But Nick isn't anywhere. I mean, I guess he must be somewhere. To be honest, he's probably suspended by now, because we definitely aren't allowed to use the intercom.

"Do you think he's pranking us?" asks Simon.

"I mean." I tilt my head. "If he is, I don't get it."

But moments later, he bursts out of the front office, looking wild-eyed and disheveled. "Hey, you're here. Cool, cool."

Simon peers at his face. "Are you okay?"

"What? Totally!" He nods quickly. "Totally."

For a moment, no one speaks.

"So, what's going on?" I ask finally.

Nick's eyes scan the room. And then he pauses. "Are you guys free right now?"

"I am." Simon nods.

"Okay, good. Because I need you"—he points at me—"and you"—he points at Simon—"and me to go to my house and eat shitty food and play video games. Just like old times. No Abby, no Bram, no Garrett."

"Okay, Garrett and I aren't—"

He cuts me off. "Just us. The original trio."

"Just us," Simon echoes. "Okay, let me text Nora. If you can give me a ride, I'll leave her the car."

"Excellent," says Nick, clamping a hand on each of our shoulders. Simon's eyes flick toward me nervously.

None of us speaks as we drift through the parking lot. The sky is dark and gloomy, with gray clouds hanging low. I swallow a prickle of dread as I slide into the passenger seat. It's only a short drive to Nick's house, and Simon fills the space with frantic chatter—about Nora and Cal, about tuxedo rentals. Nick doesn't say a word. He pulls straight into his garage and takes the spot where his mom usually parks. "They're both on call all night," he informs us. "And there's beer."

So, it's that kind of night.

Nick grabs a six-pack and his acoustic guitar and heads down to the basement. I curl into one of the video game chairs, and Simon sprawls out on the couch. But Nick bypasses everything comfortable, opting instead for the floor, where he crosses his legs and starts tuning his guitar. Then he takes a sip of beer and does a few experimental strums, his shoulders finally relaxing.

"Um, Nick?" Simon says after a moment. "Why are we here?"

"You mean evolutionarily or existentially?"

Simon's brow furrows. "I mean why are we in your basement?"

"Because we're friends, and that's what friends do. We hang out in basements." He strums a chord and takes a long swig of beer. "Also, everyone else suuuuuucks." He actually sings that last word instead of saying it.

Then he sets the beer down, repositions his guitar, and

starts playing a melody so intricate, my eyes can't keep up with his hands.

Simon slides off the couch and settles in next to Nick on the floor. "Okay, this sounds really great."

"It sounds like shit," Nick says, fingers still tearing across the frets. But he grins.

Simon pauses. "Seriously, are you okay?"

"Nope."

"Do you want to talk about it?"

"Nope."

"Okay," Simon says. He looks up at me desperately.

I lean forward in my chair. "Nick, you're freaking us out."

"Why?"

"Because you're acting super weird."

"No I'm not." He strums a loud chord. "I'm just." Chord. "Making music." Chord. "With my two best." Chord. "Friends." Then his hands fall suddenly still. "You know what's really awesome?"

Simon looks hopeful. "What?"

"The fact that from now on, for the *rest of my life*, I can tell people I got dumped two weeks before prom."

Yikes. I look at Simon. He puffs out his cheeks and then exhales loudly.

"Hilarious, right?"

I look at him. "Not really."

"I was in love with her," he says, his voice eerily calm. "And now she's totally over it. Like, whatever. Just like that."

"I don't think that's—" Simon starts to say.

"I'm just saying, do you even know what it's like to be in love with someone like that?"

I almost choke.

"Dude, I'm like seriously worried about you right now," Simon says. He glances at me again.

"Why? I'm fine." Nick smiles brightly. "I'm totally fine. You know what I need?"

"What?"

He sets the guitar down and chugs the rest of his beer. Then he grabs another beer and chugs that one, too. "That," he says, beaming. "God, I'm feeling so much better already."

"Okay," Simon says uncertainly. "Good."

Nick gasps. "I just had an idea."

"What?"

"We should play soccer!"

"Um."

"Yeah, okay. This is a great idea. We're totally doing this." Nick nods eagerly. "Let me get my balls. Ha. My ball."

Simon catches my eye and shakes his head wordlessly. For a minute, we just sit there, listening to Nick hum as he pokes around his storage closet. Already, he's working on a third beer. And it's not like I've never seen Nick drunk before, but I've never seen him this unhinged.

"Got it," he announces, emerging triumphantly with a

soccer ball. "This is going to be amazing."

"But it's raining," says Simon.

Nick smiles. "Even better." He slips through the basement door, out into the backyard, and starts kicking the ball gently from one foot to the other. It's not actually raining, but the air is thick and humid. "Come on," he says. "Leah, I'm passing to you."

"Remind me why we're doing this."

"Because we are," he says. Then, with a firm thud, he kicks the ball in my direction. I swing my foot halfheartedly, missing it by a mile.

"Okay, okay. Nice hustle," Nick says, clapping his hand against his fist.

I circle back to the ball, pick it up, and walk it back toward him.

Nick laughs. "You have to kick it."

"Yeah, I don't think that's a good idea."

He sets the ball down. "Did you know Abby and I used to do this all the time. She's, like, really good at soccer." He doesn't wait for us to react. "She is. She's really, really good. But guess what?"

Neither of us speaks.

He grins. "She broke up with me!" Then he kicks the ball so hard, it smacks against his neighbor's fence.

"Nick," Simon says, taking a step toward him. But Nick pulls away suddenly, jogging after the ball.

Then he dribbles it back. "You know, it's good, though. It's all good. Wasn't going to work, anyway, because long-distance relationships are the fucking worst. Am I right?"

Simon winces. "Right."

"No they're not," I say quickly.

"Yeah they are," Nick says. He kicks the ball to Simon. "They're doomed before they even start."

"Not necessarily." I look pointedly at Simon. "If you commit to making it work, it can work."

Simon frowns, staring straight ahead.

"Dude, you're supposed to kick it back."

"Oh." Simon's eyes cut to the soccer ball, and he gives it a halfhearted nudge with his foot. It rolls two feet and stops. "Have you talked to Abby at all?"

"Nope. Not interested." Nick grins. "Don't care enough."

"You don't care." Simon sounds dubious.

"Do you know how many girls there are at Tufts?" Nick asks calmly.

"A lot?"

"Millions. Millions and trillions." He taps the ball with his toe. "I mean, honestly, Abby did me a favor."

Simon's eyes flick toward mine.

"Anyway, I'm already over her," Nick adds.

Yeah, Nick, you *really* seem over her. Totally normal, and totally not having an epic fucking meltdown. God. I'm not an idiot, but wow: I'd love to believe him. Because if Nick were really over Abby, then maybe I'm not an asshole for hoping. Not for anything soon, obviously. Just. Maybe down the line—in a month or two—when things aren't quite so raw. I could kiss her for real.

Nick slams his foot back into the ball, sending it flying toward the house.

Maybe not.

This time Simon runs to fetch it.

"So, Leah, you're the one with all the romantic intrigue now," Nick says, and it's like someone smashing their fist on a piano. My heart sinks into my rib cage and drops out of my chest entirely.

"What are you talking about?" My voice comes out soft.

"Come on." He rubs the bridge of his nose. "You know Garrett has the biggest crush on you ever. But don't tell him I told you," he adds suddenly. "I'm not supposed to tell you that."

"That's—okay." My stomach wrenches, and I have this sudden sinking feeling that I might burst into tears. Which is crazy. I should be happy. Or flattered. Or something.

"You guys should hook up at prom. That's like the ultimate high school achievement, right?"

"You mean the ultimate high school cliché," I say flatly.

"Well, you should do it," Nick says.

"I don't want to."

"You don't want to what?" Simon asks, returning with the ball tucked under his arms.

"Guys. How many times do I have to say it? Stop carrying the fucking ball around."

Simon drops it.

"I don't want to hook up with Garrett," I say, louder than I mean to. It comes out like a declaration. And suddenly, I feel so certain about this, it almost takes my breath away. I press a hand to my cheek. "I don't want to kiss Garrett."

Simon laughs. "Okay, then don't."

Nick kicks, and the ball rolls quietly toward me. My thoughts are quietly rolling, too.

I don't want to kiss Garrett. I don't want to kiss anyone.

Except her.

Which would be the wildest, most reckless, worst idea ever. I might as well stomp all over Nick's heart, and then stomp all over my own. I can't actually fall for a straight girl. I can't fall for my best friend's ex-girlfriend.

I take a breath. And the ball—I crash into it. I kick it like banging a drum. I kick it so hard, it flies halfway to the moon.

27

"SIMON'S ACTING WEIRD," BRAM SAYS on Thursday, chin in hand. He and Garrett and I have claimed a table in the corner of the library. "It's like there's something he's not telling me."

"Maybe he's gay," Garrett whispers.

"Yeah, I've been wondering that." Bram's so deadpan when he says it that I can't help but smile. But God. I can't believe Simon hasn't told him. Does he really think the distance between New York and Philadelphia is a dealbreaker? We're not talking Paris or Tokyo. This is literally an hour and a half on the train.

"I don't know," Bram says finally. Garrett looks at me and shrugs. And it hits me, all of a sudden, how strange it is to be spending a morning in the library with these two. Not Simon and Nick, not Morgan and Anna. Just Bram, Garrett, and me.

That wouldn't have happened a year ago. I don't think it would have happened six months ago.

"Burke, I can't tell if you're staring into space or staring at Taylor's ass."

"Definitely Taylor's ass," I say automatically. I blink, and there she is, a couple of yards away from us. She's crouched down and appears to be helping a freshman sort through an array of scattered papers. Sometimes I forget what a Girl Scout she is.

"I think she's into Eisner," Garrett murmurs.

I nod. "Agreed."

"But what about Abby?" Bram asks.

Garrett shrugs. "I mean, she dumped him. He's a free agent."

"I guess so." Bram chews on his lip. "Prom's going to be interesting."

"Yeah, with Eisner and Suso in the same limo? Guaranteed shitshow."

"You think it will be bad?"

"For them? Yeah. But we'll have the best time, Burke, I promise." He smiles, and there's this softness in his eyes.

I freeze.

And then the bell rings. Thank God. "I should get to class." I stand quickly, almost upending my chair.

Because, wow. I can't do this. I can't deal with Garrett's mushy eyes and Nick's broken heart. And I really can't be this head over heels for a straight girl. The head and heels need to get back in line.

I need to fucking chill about this Abby situation.

There honestly can't *be* an Abby situation.

But I can't stop thinking about tomorrow afternoon. This mysterious after-school plan that Abby's concocting. She hasn't said a word about it all week, and I'm actually starting to wonder if she's forgotten about it entirely.

But just as we're leaving English, she tugs the sleeve of my cardigan. "Hey, are you taking the bus tomorrow?"

My stomach goes haywire.

Like, seriously? Fuck this. Fuck you, butterflies. Stop acting like this is a rom-com moment. *Am I taking the bus*. That's seriously a step above discussing the weather. But for some reason, my body's decided to treat this like a marriage proposal.

I blink and nod and exhale.

"Cool. I can drive you home." She grins. "I'm excited."

I can't even reply. I'm just a giant steaming mess.

The whole bus ride home, I'm like a blender on pulse. In one moment, I think I finally have my shit together, and then the anticipation hits me in one megawatt burst. Tomorrow, I get to be alone with Abby. Which doesn't mean anything will happen. I'm pretty sure I'm trash for even *wanting* anything to happen.

But I may actually be losing my mind. I'm in the weirdest

mood. I'm this close to flinging my arms out and running up a mountainside, *Sound of Music*–style.

I feel reckless.

And I want to *do* something.

I get online as soon as I get home and log into my art Tumblr. Because why shouldn't I? I don't even hesitate. I type some words and upload some pictures, and then I hold my breath and click *post*. Done. I link it to my sidebar.

And probably no one even gives a shit, and I'll never hear from anyone—but in this moment, I don't care. I really don't. Because I did the thing, and I posted it, and now I feel like Bigfoot. Like every step I take leaves an imprint.

It's right there on my Tumblr: I'm officially open for commissions.

28

BUT THE BIGFOOT FEELING VANISHES as soon as I get to school on Friday. Nick's at my locker, clearly waiting for me. He perks up as soon as I get there. "Hey, I heard you're hanging out with Abby today."

"Um." I hesitate. "Yeah. Is that okay?"

He nods. "Totally. Of course. I don't want to get in the way of your friendship." He does this weird, strained laugh. "It's so funny, because I didn't even know you guys were friends. But now you are! But, like, I'm totally cool with it."

"Are you sure?"

"Very sure. So sure." He nods like a Muppet. Holy shit.

I mean, he's falling apart—and this is over the idea of Abby and me as friends. Platonic, hetero, after-school friends. He would die if he knew. He would actually die. So, yeah.

"Hey. So." He stares at my forehead. "Will you let me know if she mentions me?"

"Sure."

"Cool. That's awesome. Oh man. I really appreciate that."

My stomach twists with guilt.

Of course, it's the longest day in the history of long days. Time is actually curdling.

Abby finds me at my locker, in the same exact spot where Nick stood this morning. "Are you ready?" she asks, smiling. For a moment, I just look at her.

Her hair is pulled back, and her cheeks are almost glowing. I think she might be wearing eyeliner, but it's actually hard to know. The eyelash situation is that intense. And she's wearing a dress—short-sleeved and belted, over tights and ankle boots.

"The boots are from Athens," she says, catching me staring, and I almost choke on my own spit.

"I know," I say finally.

"I really like your dress," she says.

It's the universe one, and I'm not going to lie. Other than my prom dress, it's the best thing I own.

"So the weather's really perfect. I know exactly where I want to take you."

Wow. Okay. Where she wants to take me? I don't want to lose my shit or anything, but she's really making this sound like a date.

"I'm good with whatever," I manage.

"Since when are you this agreeable?"

"I'm super agreeable. I don't know what you're talking about, Suso."

"Every time you call me Suso, I feel like you're actually Garrett wearing a Leah mask."

"Are there Leah masks?"

"There should be," Abby says. Then she turns down a side hall and down the back stairs. There's a set of double push doors at the end of the music hallway—and it's funny, because I'm here all the time, but I've never even noticed them. Abby pushes and holds one open with her hip, and I step out into the soft afternoon warmth. We're in a courtyard behind the school, where a path cuts toward the football stadium.

"Are you making me play football?" I ask. Because that's all I fucking need. Another weird, tense game of sportsball. Is this the universal post-breakup ritual?

"Obviously. You're a cornerback, right?"

"Okay. Can I ask you something?"

"Of course."

I step onto the path, matching her pace. "Are cornerback and quarterback actually two different things?"

"Is that a real question?" She seems amused.

"I figured it might just be lazy pronunciation."

"Okay. Wow. You are way too cute."

"No I'm not."

"Yes you are."

My cheeks are off-the-charts warm. I could grill steaks on them. I could break thermometers and straighten your hair and give you second-degree burns.

"Seriously, why are you taking me to the football field?"

"Because you've clearly never seen one before."

I bite back a smile. "False. I attended a single game at UGA five years ago."

"Let me guess—with Morgan?"

"Yeah." I roll my eyes.

"Did I tell you she apologized to me?"

"She did?"

"A few days ago. She seemed really messed up about it." She veers left, glancing over her shoulder to make sure I'm following. Then she leads me through a gap in the stands, onto the track that surrounds the football field.

"Well, she should be. She fucked up."

"She did." Abby nods. "But I'm glad she apologized."

Suddenly, Abby takes off, jogging to the center of the field and plopping onto the grass. By the time I catch up to her, she's lying supine, propped up on her elbows.

I settle in beside her. "So, are you cool with her now?"

"I guess so?" She shrugs. "I mean, I'm not going to lie. That comment sucked. It's just super hurtful. And I get it *all the time*. So then I get obsessed with the idea of proving people wrong and being, like, unimpeachably perfect, which probably isn't healthy, and it's just really exhausting. I hate it." She sighs. "But I also hate conflict, especially this close to graduation. So I don't know."

"Yeah."

"I guess it's like, I forgive her, but I don't really know if I can trust her again. Does that make sense?"

"Definitely." I nod. "No, that makes perfect sense."

Abby tilts her head toward me. "But I think it's cool that you stood up for me."

"I wasn't standing up for you. I was standing up for decency."

"I mean, decency is cool, too," she says, and the corners of her mouth tug up. I can't stop staring at her knees—the way the skirt of her dress drapes over them, fanning gently across the grass. "Anyway." She scrunches her nose at me.

Which makes me scrunch my nose back at her.

"Don't do that," she says, covering her eyes.

"Don't do what?"

"The thing." She waves her hand. "The thing with the nose and the freckles. Oh my God."

"I don't get it." I tap my finger to my nose.

She shakes her head, hands still over her face. But then she peeks through them. "You're just cute," she says softly.

"Oh."

"And now you're blushing."

"No I'm not."

"Yes you are," Abby says. "Which is also cute, so stop it."

I can't believe she's doing this. Either she's teasing me, which makes her an asshole, or she's not, which . . . I don't know.

I lie back on the grass, tucking my knees up into triangles. She looks at me for a moment, and then she scoots closer. Barely an inch of space between us. Just like September of junior year on Morgan's bedroom floor. There's a breeze now, cool and soft, and I watch it ruffle her bangs. She's so beautiful, it makes my stomach hurt. I turn my head away quickly, eyes fixed on the clouds.

"I'm still not getting why you wanted to bring me here," I say finally.

She laughs. "I know." Then she inhales. I think she's actually nervous. "I wanted to punch myself for picking Friday."

"Why?"

"Because I've been wanting to tell you something since last weekend, and it's been torture." I sneak a peek at her face. She's staring straight at the sky, a ghost of a smile on her lips.

"You wanted to tell me something?"

"Yes."

"Okay." I pause expectantly, but she just bites her lip without speaking. I look at her sidelong. "So, are you going to tell me?"

"Give me a second."

I nod, and my heart thuds wildly.

"Okay. So." She takes a deep breath. "I came out over the weekend."

"Came out, like . . . you came out?"

"Not to everyone," she says quickly. "Not to my parents or anyone here. Just my cousins. The twins." She turns toward me. "I was really nervous. Isn't that weird?"

"Why would that be weird?"

"I don't know. Because they're like the gayest family ever?" She shrugs. "They took it really well, obviously. They were psyched."

"That's awesome." I catch her eye. "Seriously, congrats."

She grins and doesn't reply, and for a moment, we just lie there.

"So, wait," I say finally. "Can I ask you something?"

"Mmhmm."

"What did you come out as?"

Abby laughs. "What do you mean?"

"Well, last I heard, you were straight, so."

"I don't think I'm straight," she says, and my heart almost stops.

"I don't know," she adds finally. "I guess I'm like lowkey bisexual?"

"I don't think that's a thing."

"What? It totally is." She pokes my arm. "Lowkey bi."

"You're either bi or you're not. That's like being a little bit pregnant."

"That's a thing, too. Why can't you be a little bit pregnant?"

"I think that's just called pregnant."

"Well, I'm a little bit bi, and I'm sticking with that."

I sit up. "I don't get you."

"What?"

I shake my head. "Lowkey bi, a little bit bi. Just be *bi*. Like, come on."

"What? No." She draws herself up. "You don't get to decide my label."

"It's not a real label!"

"Well, it's real for me." She exhales heavily. "God, sometimes, I don't even know . . ."

My jaw tightens. "Don't even know what?"

"What you want from me." She tilts her palms up. "Like, can you just . . . I don't know. This is weird for me, okay?"

"What I want from you?"

She nods, blinking quickly.

"Jesus Christ, Abby." I press my hands over my eyes. "I want you to stop messing with my head."

"I'm not—"

"Seriously? Lowkey bi?" I laugh flatly. "Otherwise known as what—you're bi, but you don't want to admit it? I'm not saying you have to march in a Pride parade. You don't have to come out. But *God*. At least admit it to yourself." I shrug. "Or don't. I don't care."

"Leah."

I can't even look at her. God. It's just all so pointless. It's not like we ever had a shot to begin with. What the hell kind of shitty friend would even think of kissing her best friend's ex-girlfriend? Two weeks after the breakup. *On the day before prom*. And poor, clueless Garrett, whom I haven't bothered to rebuff. I can't jump into this now. I'm not even out.

I stand abruptly, brushing my skirt down. "Okay, yeah. I'm not doing this. I'm going to go."

"What?" Abby blinks up at me.

"I'm going home."

"Let me drive you."

"I'll take the late bus."

She hugs her knees. "I'm trying, okay?" There's a quiver in her voice.

"Are you serious?" I clench my hands. "You're trying? Trying to do what?"

"I don't know."

"You know what? You want to be 'lowkey bi'? Good for you. Have a blast. But if you're not all in, leave me the fuck out of it. Don't you dare come knocking on my door with your post-breakup identity crisis." I look her straight in the eye. "You took my first kiss, Abby. You stole it."

"I am so—"

"And everyone thinks you have your shit together." I swallow thickly. "But you just do what you want and everyone gives you a free pass. And you don't even care who you hurt."

Abby's face falls. "You think I don't care?"

"I don't know what to think."

"I mean, yeah, I'm not perfect." A tear rolls down her cheek. "Okay? I'm completely fucking this up. I'm not like you. I don't have it all figured out. I have no clue what I'm doing, and I'm just really scared right now."

"Of what?"

"I don't know. That I'll get this wrong. That you'll hate me."

"I don't hate you."

"Or that I'll hurt you. I don't want to do that."

Time seems to freeze. For a moment, we just look at each other. I feel breathless and unsteady.

"Look, I'm fine," I say finally. "Okay? You'll figure this out. You've got this. I'm happy for you. You don't owe me anything." I exhale, shrugging.

"That's not—"

"Everything's fine. We're friends. I'll see you at prom."

"Okay," she says softly.

I don't bother replying. I leave without looking back.

29

"WE'RE GOING TO GET THIS. I swear to God." Mom stares at the screen of her phone and then catches my eye in the mirror. "I watched the tutorial like fifty times."

"I'm sure you did." I smile faintly.

"It's just not working. Why do I suck at this?"

"You don't suck." There's this little loop of hair hanging awkwardly over my ear, so I give it a tug. And now there's one straight chunk of hair stringing down like a massive sideburn. Welp.

Mom groans.

I've spent the last hour in her bedroom, letting her knock herself out with every hair appliance ever invented. I'm still in pajamas, and Garrett's not coming for another five hours. But Mom's obsessively checking the time on her phone, like he might bust in at any moment.

"Okay. Starting over." She combs her fingers through my hair, retrieving approximately ten thousand bobby pins. Then she spritzes it with water and brushes it straight again. "I swear to God . . ."

For my part, I'm numb. I just can't muster any fucks to give. I get that prom's supposed to be a huge deal—but for what? Why the effort? I honestly don't care about impressing my date. And maybe some stupid tiny part of me wants to impress *someone*—but if that someone is off-limits, then what's the point?

Mom licks her lips. "Let me blow-dry you again."

"Go for it."

She goes for it.

It's funny—I never even thought I'd go to prom, and here I am doing the whole routine that goes with it. We're taking pictures at Simon's house and then riding an actual limo to some fancy-pants restaurant in Alpharetta. It's just a real suburban high school wet dream.

Mom turns off the dryer. "I hate that you're fighting with Morgan and Anna," she says, out of nowhere.

"Why?"

"I just don't like that there's tension. I want you to have that perfect night."

"That's a myth."

"What's a myth?"

"The perfect prom night."

Mom laughs. "What do you mean?"

"It's like a teen movie cliché. You have the choreographed group dance number and the weird pining eye contact, and then the big smoochy kiss."

"That sounds like a great prom," Mom says.

"It's a joke."

"God, Leah." She trails her hands through my hair and loops a strand of it around her finger. "How did you get so cynical?"

"I can't help it. I'm a Slytherin."

And I'm the worst kind of Slytherin. I'm the kind who's so stupidly in love with a Gryffindor, she can't even function. I'm the Draco from some shitty Drarry fic that the author abandoned after four chapters.

"Well, my prom was beautiful," Mom says. "It was one of the most romantic nights of my life."

"Weren't you pregnant?"

"So? It was still wonderful." She smiles. "Did you know I had an ultrasound the day before my prom?"

"That's . . . cool?"

"It was cool! It was the big one, too. That's when I found out your gender."

"Gender is a social construction."

"I know, I know." She pokes my cheek. "I don't know. I was just so excited about it. I didn't even care what sex you were. I just wanted to know everything about you."

I snort. "That sounds about right."

"I just perfectly remember lying there on the table, seeing you on the little monitor. You were so . . ."

"Fetal?"

"Yes." She grins. "But also—I don't know. You were just such a little trouper in there. I remember being so moved by that. Here I was, with all this stuff going on—school and prom and your dad, but you just kept doing your thing. Growing and growing. You were unstoppable."

"I think that's, like, bare minimum fetus achievement."

"I don't know. I just found it so amazing. I still do. Look at you." I glance up in the mirror, meeting her eyes, and for a moment, we're both silent. When Mom finally speaks, it's almost a whisper. "Everyone was always telling me how fast it goes. It used to piss me off."

"Ha."

"Like, it was always some random lady in the grocery store. You'd be flailing around, pitching a fit, and *every single time,* some jerk would just have to come up and tell me I'd miss it one day. *Oh, she'll be off to college before you know it. Enjoy these moments now.* I was like, *cool story, fuck you.*" She twists a lock of my hair around the curling iron. "But they were so right."

"It happens."

"I just can't believe you're leaving." Mom blinks, a little too quickly.

"You realize I'll be an hour and a half away, right?"

"I know, I know." She smiles sadly. "But you know what I mean."

I wrinkle my nose at her. "Don't you dare cry."

"Why, because you'll cry?"

"No way. Never."

Mom laughs softly. "It's going to be so weird here without you, Leah."

"Mom."

"Okay, I'll stop. I don't want you sobbing over me and ruining your prom aesthetic."

"My prom aesthetic." I roll my eyes, smiling.

Mom smiles back. "You're going to have so much fun tonight, Lee."

"It's going to be weird."

"Even if it's weird. I loved my weird, messy prom night." She shrugs. "Just embrace it. That's what I did. I remember looking in the mirror and deciding my prom was going to be suck-free, even if it wasn't going to be how I imagined it."

"Well, mine's going to suck." I make a face at her in the mirror.

"But why? It doesn't have to." She leans forward, resting her chin on my head. "Just promise me you won't overthink this."

Then it hits me, like a kick in the crotch. *"Fuck."*

Mom meets my eyes in the mirror, brows raised. "You okay?"

"I am such an idiot."

"I highly doubt that."

"I don't have a bra."

"Mmm." Mom tucks a final strand of hair in place and smiles. "Not bad, right?"

I mean, yeah, Mom knocked it out of the park. I don't know how she did it, but my hair is smooth and wavy, swept back on the sides, with little soft pieces hanging down around my cheeks. Of course, the fact that I'm still in pajamas makes it seem like my head and body belong to two different people, but I guess it will look good with the dress.

Except for the fact that I don't have a fucking bra.

"I need something strapless."

"You don't have a strapless bra?"

"Why would I have a strapless bra?"

Mom's mouth quirks. "Because you have a strapless dress?"

"Okay, it's not funny. I'm kind of freaking out."

"Lee." She rests her hands on my shoulders. "We have a few hours until Garrett gets here. We can buy you a bra."

"From where?"

"From anywhere. How about Target? Go throw on some jeans." She grabs her purse. "Let's hit it."

Except the car won't start.

"Nope," Mom says as the key clicks uselessly. "Not today, Satan."

"Are you kidding me?"

"Hold on." She nudges the steering wheel and opens and closes her door. "I'm trying again."

Still nothing.

She looks vaguely panicked. "Should I blow on the key?"

"That's not a thing, Mom."

"Oh, come on," she mutters, smacking her hands down on the steering wheel. "Of all fuckin' days."

"Okay, please don't say *fuckin'*."

She shoots me a self-conscious glance. "I thought we liked cussing."

"We love cussing. But we say the fucking *g*. I don't want to hear that apostrophe, Mom."

"I can't believe this," she says.

I nod. "It's a sign."

"Of what?"

"That I should stay home."

Now Mom's rolling her eyes. "You want to miss prom because of a bra?"

"Because of the *lack* of a bra," I correct her. "And because I have no way of getting a bra."

Mom doesn't respond—she just digs into her purse for her phone. Then she taps into her favorite contacts.

"Who are you calling?"

She ignores me.

"Oh hell no." I make a grab for the phone, but she yanks it out of reach. "Are you calling Wells?"

No response. She presses send.

"Please tell me you're not asking Wells to buy me a fucking bra."

"Why not?" The phone starts ringing.

"Because it's a bra."

"So?"

"So, that's disgusting."

"What, a bra? You're grossed out by bras?" I open my mouth, but she just keeps talking. "Man, if you can't handle bras, wait till you learn about boobs—hi, honey." She cuts herself off, and her whole demeanor changes. I picture Wells on the other end of the call, phone mashed up to his tiny ear.

I smack her in the arm, and she turns to me and winks. "Leah and I need a favor."

I shake my head frantically, but Mom turns away, ignoring me. "So, the car just died, and we *just* realized that Leah doesn't have . . ."

I hug my arms across my chest.

". . . something she needs," Mom continues. Then she pauses. I can just barely hear Wells's voice through her speaker. "Right. Not till five." She pauses again, and then laughs. "Yeah, totally dead." Then she nods and flicks her eyes toward me, smiling. "Thanks, hon. Love you."

Okay, first of all: ick. Second of all: oh, fudge. So, Mom and Wells are at the *love you* stage. That's pretty fucking vomity.

She ends the call and turns toward me. "He'll be here in

fifteen minutes to jump the car."

"Great."

"Uh, you're welcome." She raises her eyebrows.

I blush. "Thanks."

And it's weird. We don't move from the car. We don't even unbuckle our seat belts. It's like someone paused the universe. Everything smells like hair spray, and I have that key-change, offbeat feeling again. That little itch in my gut. Mom drums on the steering wheel, humming.

"So are you and Wells secretly engaged or something?"

Her hands freeze. "What? Where did that come from?"

"It's just a question."

Mom sighs. "Leah, no. I'm not secretly engaged."

"Are you getting engaged?"

"Um." She smiles. "Not that I know of."

"Would you say yes if he asked you?"

"Leah, back up a minute. Where are you getting this?"

"It's just a hypothetical question." I tuck my feet onto the seat and turn toward the window. Everything's sun-soaked and green. Stupid perfect April day.

"If he asked me today? I don't know," Mom says. "Marriage is a big thing. I know I love him a lot."

I look at her. "Why?"

"Why do I love Wells?"

"I get the money thing, obviously."

"Um, excuse me?" Mom's eyes flash. "You know what?

That's really hurtful, and it's not true."

"Then I don't get it."

"Don't get what?"

"I mean, you're not marrying him for looks," I say, and before the words are even out of my mouth, I regret it. I feel heat rise in my cheeks. I don't know why I'm so mean.

"Okay, seriously?"

"I'm sorry," I mutter.

"You know, I happen to think he's really handsome."

"I know. I get it. I'm a jerk."

"You don't think he looks a little like Prince William?"

"Uh, isn't Wells like fifty?"

"He's forty-two."

"Still."

"Like a slightly older, balder Prince William. I'm just talking about his face." She pokes my knee. "You totally see it."

Fuck. I totally do. And even his name is so on point.

"So this whole relationship is literally a thing because of your lifelong Prince William fetish?"

"Okay, it's not a *fetish*. I just think he's sexy."

"You did not just call Prince William sexy."

"I did. It had to be said." She smiles, almost sadly. "You know, you'd probably really like him if you gave him half a chance."

"I don't have to like him. I'm graduating, remember?"

"Oh man. Do I remember."

And something about the way she says it makes my heart catch in my throat. I stare at the glove compartment, hugging my knees. "Sorry," I mutter.

"Sweetie, it's fine, you know? It's just—"

She cuts herself off as Wells pulls up next to us in his Beemer. He looks extra golfy today, in a tucked-in polo shirt, and now I can't unsee the Prince William thing. So, that's a little disturbing. He pops open the hood of his car, and Mom pops ours open beside it. Car foreplay for this car booty call. Mom slides out of the driver's seat and fishes a set of jumper cables out of the trunk.

I watch from the passenger seat as they clip their little alligator mouths somewhere in that mess of engine and battery parts. A moment later, Wells starts his car, and Mom leans in through the driver side door.

"Lee, try twisting the ignition."

I do, and it roars to life immediately.

"So, that's it?" I ask. "You fixed it?"

"Well, it started, which is good, but we'll need to keep the battery running for a while. Why don't you hop to the back?"

"Why?"

"Because Wells is going to drive us to Target, so he can keep the car running while we run in."

"Oh. Okay." God. Prom errands with Wells. But I guess he technically did just come to rescue us, and technically, I should be grateful. Or something.

Mom fills Wells in on prom gossip the whole way to Target. She remembers every detail I've ever mentioned. "Okay, Abby dumped Nick, so that's the main thing, but there's also Morgan creating issues," Mom explains. "And Garrett has a crush on Leah."

I lean forward. "That's hearsay."

"But," Mom plows on, twisting around to smile at me. "I think Leah likes someone else."

"Mom."

Holy shit. Like, she better not be implying what I think she's implying.

"I'm just saying." She grins. "It's going to be an interesting night."

As soon as we pull into the parking lot, Mom's phone rings.

"Oh, crap. I need to get that." She answers it, scrunching her face at me apologetically, and mouthing, *work*.

Awesome fucking timing.

For a minute, Wells and I just sit there, while Mom nods and says, "Uh-huh. Okay. Right. Uh-huh." She gropes in her purse for a pen and scribbles a few things down on the back of a receipt. "Well, I really—oh. *Oh.* Okay. No, no." She shoots me a look that's half guilty, half frantic. "Mmhmm," she murmurs. Then she unbuckles her seat belt and twists back to meet my eyes.

I look back at her and raise my eyebrows.

"Yes. Okay. Absolutely," she says into the phone. But she nods her head pointedly at me. Then she passes me her credit card.

"I'm supposed to do this myself?" I ask quietly.

She shrugs, gestures at her phone, and then points at the clock on the car's dashboard. Which has been broken for years, but I get what she's saying. Garrett will be at our house in two hours, and I'm wearing jeans and not a trace of makeup.

"I'll go with you," says Wells.

"Um. That's not necessary."

"It's actually perfect. I need to pick up a birthday card anyway."

I shoot Mom a look that says *are you fucking kidding me.* She shrugs and tips her hands up, eyes twinkling.

So isn't this magical. I'm bra shopping with Wells.

He shoves his hands in his pockets as we walk through the parking lot. "So, what is it that you need?"

"An item of clothing."

"An item of clothing?" He shoots me a confused smile. "Am I supposed to guess?"

"No," I say quickly. Fuck my life. "Just. It's a bra." For my boobs, Wells.

"Ah."

Now I can't even think straight. Maybe my brain is boiling. Maybe that's a thing that happens when you achieve peak mortification.

We step through the automatic doors, and the first thing I see is a bag display: giant canvas zipper totes and faux-leather purses and, already, a summery display of woven beach bags.

"Oh no." I smack my forehead.

"Everything okay?" Wells asks.

"I don't have a purse."

I mean, technically, I do. But the only purse I own is a ratty canvas thing I bought three years ago from Old Navy. I can't bring that piece of shit to prom.

"Okay. We've got this." He nods eagerly. "Would any of these purses work?"

"And shoes. I don't have shoes."

Okay, I'm honestly starting to freak out, because this really feels like a sign now. No bra, no shoes, no purse, car battery dead, Mom occupied. Universe, I hear you loud and clear. I shouldn't have even considered going to prom. I should go back home and watch HGTV, and return the dress as soon as the mall opens tomorrow.

I just wish. I don't know. I wish I were the kind of girl who remembered things like bras and shoes and purses. It's like there's a prom gene, and I'm missing it. And I guess it makes sense. I can barely be trusted to dress myself, normally. No surprise I'm a hot mess and a half when it comes to this crap.

"This is cool," Wells says, holding up a little clutch. It's made of gold fake leather, and it's shaped like a cat's face, and even I have to admit it's adorable.

I bite my lip. "How much is it?"

He checks the tag. "Oh, it's just twenty dollars."

"Welp. Never mind."

"Leah, I can cover that."

I laugh. "Yeah, no."

"I mean it. Seriously, don't worry about it."

God, I really hate this. Literally, the last person I want buying me shit is Wells. He's not my stepdad. He's definitely not my dad. And it's just weird and uncomfortable, and I feel like a sellout.

But. I don't know. I also don't want to carry a canvas bag to prom.

"I'm going to go find a bra," I say quickly, eyes starting to prickle. This is all so ridiculous. And honestly, I don't even know how I'm supposed to do this without Mom. I don't know anything about strapless bras. I don't know how they're supposed to fit. I don't even know if I'm allowed to try them on. I end up circling the racks in the lingerie area, probably looking like a little lost turtle. Finally, I grab the cheapest one in my size, but even the cheapest one is almost twenty-five dollars. For a bra I'm probably going to wear one time. And if I'm paying twenty-five dollars for a bra, there's no way I can buy shoes. I'll have to wear my sneakers. Just some giant ugly-ass sneakers. Now I'll really have a prom aesthetic.

I may be feeling slightly hysterical. Slightly.

Wells is already holding a Target bag when I find him at the self-checkout. He smiles and rubs the back of his neck. "Okay, I know you didn't want me to, but I got the cat purse."

"Seriously?"

"It's just, I thought you'd probably try to push back, and then I'd insist, and we'd go back and forth, and I know we don't have a lot of time. So." He bites his lip. "If you don't want to use it, that's totally fine."

"Oh. Um." I stare at the bag.

"I would have grabbed some shoes, too, but I didn't know what size."

"That's . . . fine. That's really cool of you, Wells."

It's weird. I'm used to saying his name with a sarcastic kind of emphasis, a tiny vocal eye roll. Saying *Wells* without that little bite feels strange and incomplete.

I pay for the bra with Mom's card, and we head back to the car. But when we get there, Mom's still on the phone, so Wells and I lean against the trunk, side by side.

"So, are you excited?" he asks.

"For prom?"

"Yeah." He shrugs. "I never went to mine."

"I never thought I would."

"Just don't forget to bring a camera. Your mom's going to want pictures."

"My camera?" I mean, of course Wells would suggest that. As if I'm going to roll into prom with a giant old-timey camera and a tripod. Maybe I should skip the camera altogether. I'll just bring some oil paints and a fucking easel.

"I guess you'll have your phone for that, huh?"

"Uh, yeah." I smile.

He smiles back. And for a minute, we just stand there.

"Thanks for the purse, by the way," I say finally. I scuff my shoe on the asphalt. "You didn't have to do that."

"I was happy to."

"Well, I appreciate it," I say, blushing faintly. Because apparently I'm not capable of thanking people without making it awkward. Wells probably thinks I'm ridiculous, getting so flustered over a twenty-dollar purse. Twenty dollars is probably nothing to him. He probably uses twenties as toilet paper.

But Wells just shakes his head. "I know this kind of thing can be really uncomfortable. I used to hate receiving gifts."

"Me too."

"Even if I knew the person could afford it. I just didn't like feeling like I was getting a handout." He looks at me, and it's as if he's reading my mind. "I didn't have a lot of money growing up."

"Really?"

He nods. "Yeah. I was kind of the poor kid in the rich neighborhood. My friends all had houses, and we were in this tiny little apartment. I don't think some people even realize there are apartments in the suburbs."

"Wow."

"Wow?"

"I just. I don't know. I totally figured you were kind of a country club kid."

"Well, I was, in a way." He smiles. "I was a caddy."

"That is . . . a golf thing, isn't it?"

"Nailed it," he says. And it's strange. I feel lighter. Like maybe this nerdy dude can stick around if he wants. Maybe Mom could use a bootleg Prince William to distract her. I guess it's either that or haunting the aisles of Publix, warning the baby moms how fast it all flies by.

Here's the thing, though: no one ever warns the babies.

30

GARRETT'S EXACTLY ON TIME, AND I step out onto the front stoop to meet him. He looks at me, opens his mouth, and shuts it. I think it's the first time I've ever seen him speechless.

"Holy shit, Burke," he says finally.

"Holy shit, Laughlin." I tug the end of my hair.

I guess I do feel kind of pretty. Now that I'm dressed, the hair totally works, and I've got the rosy cheeks thing and the smoky eye thing and the freckled shoulder thing all happening at once. And as it turns out, my boots are the exact same shade of gold as my cat purse. So, that's a thing that's happening. I'm wearing combat boots to prom.

Garrett just stares at my mouth. I guess I'm glad he's not staring at my boobs.

He gives me a bone-white corsage for my wrist, and Mom

helps me pin a boutonniere to the lapel of his tux. Then she herds us outside the house for the photo shoot from hell. It doesn't help that Garrett has no clue where his hands go. First he hooks his arm around my waist—then my shoulders—then back around my waist. I half expect him to whip out his phone to consult Google on the issue.

When it's finally time to go, he opens the car door for me—and it's honestly super weird to be wearing a prom dress in Garrett's mom's minivan. Garrett's as quiet tonight as I've ever seen him. I can't help but steal a few glances at his profile.

"You clean up nicely, Garrett," I say finally. And it's true. Garrett's so annoying half the time that it's hard to remember he's handsome. But he is. He's got a nice jawline and thick hair, and those bright blue eyes.

"So do you," he says. "Really." For a moment, he's quiet. "Are you excited for prom?"

"I guess?"

"You guess? I love your enthusiasm, Burke."

"Wait, let me try again." I clear my throat. "I guess, exclamation point."

He laughs. "Much better."

I look at him and smile, but I feel this quiet smack of guilt. Because Garrett really is so funny and decent. He'd probably be a great boyfriend. He's just not for me.

And I should probably tell him that. *Hey, Garrett. Just a heads-up! All that movie prom stuff you're picturing? Isn't happening. There will be no choreographed dance. No longing eye contact. Definitely no smoochy prom kiss.*

Hey, Garrett. I'm sort of painfully in love with someone else.

At least I finally get the point of tuxedos. They make boys 75 percent cuter. And it's not just Garrett—it's all of them. I almost die when I see Nick, Simon, and Bram.

Currently, Simon, Bram, Nora, and Cal are enduring an epic photo shoot with the parents. Nick's sitting alone on the stoop, tapping his fingers on the edge of the bricks. But Anna runs straight toward me, Morgan trailing behind. And because I've turned into an actual cliché, I jump straight into the whole routine. *Oh my God, I love your dress! Oh my God, are you so excited?*

Anna looks too cute. She really does. She's wearing a two-piece gown with just a hint of tummy showing, and her hair is pinned up and braided. Anna and Morgan are both really tiny, and sometimes when I'm around them, I feel like the Hulk.

But no.

Because my brain can shut up, for fucking once. Hello, brain: please let me feel beautiful.

I think I actually do. Feel beautiful.

Morgan shoots me a cautious smile. "You look so gorgeous, Leah."

I freeze. I should have prepared for this. I knew I'd have to be around her. But I kept putting that out of my mind. She *did* apologize. And Abby forgives her. I mean, that's something.

"Thanks," I say. "So do you."

"Can we talk?" she asks softly.

It's strange. I keep going back to what Anna said—that maybe I've blown this situation up to make the good-bye feel smaller. I'm pretty sure that's bullshit. Morgan fucked up all on her own. It's not like I asked her to be racist so I'd miss her less.

"Okay," I say finally. I glance back at the dogwood, where Simon's dad is zooming in for awkward close-ups of Nora's and Cal's faces. I gesture vaguely at the road. "Over there?"

"That works."

There's this weird, taut silence as we walk down the driveway. I tug my skirt forward and settle onto the curb. Morgan's eyes keep flicking toward me, like she's waiting for me to speak. But I don't know what to say. I don't even know what to feel.

She leans back on her hands and sighs. "So, I apologized to Abby."

"I heard."

For a minute, we both sit there, looking anywhere but at each other.

"I fucked up," she says finally. "I can't believe I said what I said. I feel so shitty about it."

"You should."

"I know." She shuts her eyes. "I know. Like, yeah, I was upset. I was so—God, I can't even explain what that felt like. Getting rejected."

"But that's not an excuse, Morgan."

"Oh, I know. It's not. It's not okay. Like, I call myself an ally." She exhales. "But then the second it gets personal, it all flies out the window. I'll never forget that I said that."

"Yeah."

"And you don't have to forgive me. I get that. I just wanted you to know I'm so fucking sorry. I'm going to do better."

I glance at her sidelong. Her lips are pressed together, and her brows are knitted tightly. She's so painfully sincere. It's written all over her face.

But secondhand forgiveness is so messy. I never know where to land. If Abby's over it, should I be? If Simon forgives Martin, should I forgive him, too?

I open my mouth to speak. I don't even know what I'm about to say.

Before I can say anything, Garrett appears. "Hey, so the limo guy's around the corner. Has anyone heard from Abby?"

"Oh, she's not here yet?" I cringe as soon as I say it. I'm even worse than Taylor. *Abby's not here yet? Wow, I totally didn't notice! It's not like I've been obsessively scanning the road for her car!*

God. What if she skips prom? What if she can't handle the awkwardness? I should text her. Just to check in. I even start to pull my phone out of my purse. But just the thought of it makes my heart sink. What would I even say?

Eventually, Simon drifts over, hooking an arm around my shoulders. "Okay, Abby's almost here—she's stuck in traffic. We should go ahead and do group pictures, though. We'll just do the guys first." Then he leans in and whispers straight in my ear. "You look amazing."

"Pshh."

"I'm just saying."

"So do you."

He grins and tugs my hair, and then he collects Garrett for pictures. Cal's already left with Nora, but Simon's dad lines the rest of the guys up under the dogwood tree. They're quite a squad—I'm not going to lie. They look like a boy band. Garrett's easily the tallest, so Mr. Spier puts him in the middle, with Bram and Simon on one side and Nick on the other. They're all doing the prom dude pose with their hands clasped near their crotches while Simon's mom frantically snaps pictures. It's pretty amazing.

But I've got one eye on the road, and every time a car approaches, my heart starts pounding. I know she's almost here, but it feels like that moment won't ever arrive. Time is dragging so slowly, and everything's blurry and dreamlike. I try to focus on the warmth of the sun on my shoulders. Anything to keep me centered. I feel like I've swallowed a helium balloon.

Then Abby's car pulls up, and my whole brain clicks into

place. Her mom turns into Simon's driveway, and Abby slides out of the passenger seat, gripping her skirt in one hand and holding a clutch in the other.

She lets her skirt fall.

And fuck my life forever.

She looks like a cloud. Or a ballerina. Her whole dress is pale blue tulle, light as air, with straps crossed neatly between her shoulder blades. Her hair is pinned up loosely, her bangs swept to the side, and her lips and cheeks are soft and pink. It's too much. I swear to God. This girl is too much, and I'm way too far gone.

She looks at me, and her eyes flare wide. *Wow,* she mouths.

For a moment, I just stare at her. Twenty-four hours ago, I was yelling at her on a football field, and now she's grinning at me like it's the easiest thing in the world. I can't decide if I'm relieved or gutted. Like, come on: you're not even going to be awkward about that? Not even a little?

I'm jolted back to earth by Simon's mom, who sidles between Abby and me, clapping her hands together. "Your paparazzi awaits." She's wearing an oversized red T-shirt that says, in giant black letters, *FEAR THE SQUIRREL.*

"Why should we fear the squirrel?" I ask.

"Because," she says. And then she turns around to show off the back of her shirt. Which has a picture of a squirrel and the words *HAVERFORD MOM.*

"Their mascot is a squirrel?" asks Abby.

I catch Simon's eye across the driveway. *Bram knows?* I mouth.

He tilts his head, looking confused.

I take out my phone and text him. Bram knows about Haverford?

Simon pulls his phone out of his back pocket, glances at the screen, and grins. He writes back, He knows. Smiley emoji.

We head over to the dogwood, and Simon's dad arranges us for pictures. Peak awkwardness. I don't know if Simon's parents are clueless or if they're messing with me, but they seem determined to place me between Abby and Garrett in every. Fucking. Picture. Except the ones where I'm supposed to stand by Morgan. "Huddle up close, guys. Act like you like each other."

How do parents do this? How do they always manage to say true things without knowing they're true?

Mr. Spier is *just* about to step in it by demanding a couples' shot of Nick and Abby—but Simon heads it off at the pass, and then the limo pulls up. I slide in between Garrett and Nick while Simon's mom pokes her head in to snap more pictures.

The inside of the limo is essentially a strip club. Not that I've actually been inside a strip club. But there are seats on both sides, and a thin, fluorescent stripe along the wall, like a color-changing glow stick. And there's a minibar—with bottles of water instead of booze. But *still.* I feel like I've stepped into someone else's life. Like a Kardashian, or Beyoncé. I don't want to look out the windows, or I'll remember we're in Shady Creek.

"I bet people think we're famous," says Simon.

"I mean, that's what I'd assume, seeing a limo full of high school kids rolling through the suburbs in April," Abby says. "*Definitely* a film premiere."

"Or the Oscars," chimes Bram.

"Couldn't be prom."

"Shut up." Simon grins and elbows both of them at once.

Then Garrett stretches and—honest to God—slips his arm behind my shoulders. Master of subtlety. I scoot forward, just an inch. Far enough to put a little space between us, but not far enough for anyone to notice.

Except Abby notices. She raises her eyebrows, almost imperceptibly, and shoots me a tiny, secret smile.

And yeah.

Holy shit.

This is going to be quite a night.

31

THE DRIVER CAN'T FIND THE restaurant. He rolls down the divider, peering at us in the rearview mirror. "The American Grill?"

"The American Grill Bistro," Garrett says.

"And you're sure this is the mall?"

"Positive." Garrett extracts his arm from behind my back, leaning forward in his seat. "North Point Mall, the American Grill Bistro."

We circle for a few minutes, until the driver gives up and lets us off at Macy's. Walking through the mall in formal wear is surreal. There are old ladies smiling at us and little kids staring, and one dude even snaps a picture.

"Creeper," says Morgan.

Garrett takes the lead, guiding us past Forever 21, the

Apple store, and Francesca's. But we get all the way to Sears, and there aren't any restaurants. Garrett looks perplexed. "It was definitely down this way. Definitely."

"Should I check the map?" Anna asks.

"It should be right here."

We all stand there for a minute in our dresses and tuxes. It's a little disorienting. Like, I'm a suburban girl—I know malls. But this isn't my usual mall, which means it's like stepping into a parallel universe. I watch Simon chew on his lip while Garrett stares at the directory. "Maybe we should eat at the food court," Anna suggests.

"No, wait," Abby says, hand flying to her mouth.

"Are you okay?"

She nods slowly. "Let me just . . . I'll be right back," she says, furrowing her brow—and then, a moment later, she disappears around a corner.

Garrett drifts back toward me, looking distraught. "I swear, I made a reservation. I talked to someone. On the *phone*," he adds.

"Garrett, it's fine."

"I did, though. I promise."

"I believe you," I say, scanning the floor for Abby. There's a Starbucks and a set of escalators and dozens and dozens of people. But she's nowhere.

"I want a massage chair," says Simon, staring into Brookstone.

"I'll be your massage chair," says Bram.

"You did not just say that." I scrunch my nose at him. But he just squeezes Simon's shoulders, and then tugs him closer. Simon smiles and leans back.

"Hey," Abby says breathlessly. I look up with a start. And she's a sunbeam. She has her smile cranked up to a million, and her eyes are bright and crinkly. "So, Garrett," she says.

"Suso."

She takes both his hands. "We have a reservation."

"We do?" He looks hopeful. "Where did the restaurant go?"

"It's not a restaurant," Abby says.

I look at her. "What?"

"I mean, it's sort of a restaurant . . ." She looks like she's ready to burst. "But it's in there." She points to a spot behind her shoulder.

"That's the American Girl store," says Simon.

"Yes."

"As in dolls."

"Yes." Abby's eyes are twinkling.

"I don't get it." Simon looks baffled.

"Well," she says, "it appears that Garrett made our prom dinner reservations at the American Girl Bistro."

Garrett shakes his head. "No, it's the American *Grill* Bistro."

"Okay." Abby cocks her head. "But the American Girl Bistro has a reservation on file for a party of eight, and it's under your name, so . . ."

"Oh." Garrett's eyes go wide. "Fuck."

Simon face-plants into my shoulder, almost sobbing with laughter.

This whole place is pink. Blindingly bright pink. Everything—the walls, the tables, the fake flower centerpieces.

"I love it here," breathes Abby.

I grin at her. "You would."

There's an old-timey soda fountain up against one wall, underneath a twinkly lit ceiling, and light fixtures shaped like giant pink flowers. And everywhere I look, I see American Girl dolls. I think we're the only people here who didn't bring our sidekicks. It's the cutest thing in the world, though. The dolls sit in booster seats, clamped onto the tables, and the waiters bring them tiny cups of doll tea.

"I remember when this store opened," Morgan says. "I was *obsessed* with American Girls."

Anna raises her eyebrows. "You're still obsessed."

"Not with all of them." Morgan swipes her. "Just Rebecca. But, like, she's Jewish, so she's family."

"I think you can rent dolls," Bram points out. "For the meal."

"I'm renting a doll," says Simon.

"Guys, I'm so fucking sorry." Garrett covers his face.

Abby grins. "Are you kidding me? This is the greatest prom dinner ever."

"Agreed," Morgan says. She clasps her hands together.

The hostess seats us at a long table in front of the soda fountain counter, with pink polka-dot chairs and intricately folded white cloth napkins. The first thing Simon does is ask her about the rental dolls—and then he, Abby, and Bram end up following her back to the hostess stand. The boys return moments later with pink booster seats and a pair of blond dolls who look disturbingly like Taylor Metternich.

"Abby's still deciding," Simon explains. I glance back at the hostess stand, and Abby actually winks at me.

When she finally comes back, she's hugging a black doll with pigtails. "I'm naming her Hermione," she announces.

Simon gasps. "It's finally happening. Abby's becoming a Potterhead."

"Something like that." She looks straight at me.

I end up seated between Doll-Hermione and Garrett, across from Simon and Bram—while Nick stares dazedly at the menu, looking tense and miserable. My eyes drift back to Abby, who tucks her chin in her hand and smiles. "Let's talk about how Simon's new school mascot is a squirrel."

"A black squirrel."

"Still a squirrel."

"I love squirrels." Simon grins. "Oh, and guess what. Amtrak has a student discount."

"That'll come in handy," Abby says.

"I think we're going to shoot for visiting every other weekend," Bram says.

"And we're going to Skype," adds Simon. "And we're bringing back the Jacques and Blue emails."

"Aww, I love it. That's a great plan."

"Yeah, we've got this. Long distance can totally work—" Simon catches himself, glancing back and forth between Abby and Nick. "It can totally work for some people," he adds awkwardly.

"I heard it was a dealbreaker," Nick says loudly, and everyone falls silent. It's the first time he's spoken all night. I glance back at Abby, who's smiling brightly, but blinking fast.

Nick shrugs. "But maybe that's just a thing people say when they're dumping you right before prom."

Abby pushes her chair out and stands. "Excuse me."

Simon sighs. "Nick." The boys all shift in their seats, and Morgan and Anna exchange wide-eyed glances. A millennium passes, and no one says a word.

Finally, I stand and grip the back of my chair. "I'll talk to her."

Then I take a deep breath, and follow her into the bathroom.

Abby's sitting on the ledge by the sinks, toes turned out like a ballerina, jelly flats peeking out from under her dress. She looks up at me, startled. "What are you doing here?"

"Looking for you." I rub the back of my neck. "Just making sure you're okay."

She shrugs. "I'm fine."

"Okay."

For a moment, neither of us speak.

"Why are you in the bathroom?" I ask finally.

"Did you know they have doll holders in the stalls?" she asks.

I blink. "What?"

"Like, there's a little hook in there where you can set your doll. I'm serious. Go look."

"But why?"

"So the doll can experience this bathroom with you," Abby says.

"That's . . . strange."

"Right?" She laughs, but then it's swallowed by a sigh.

I peer into her face. "Seriously, are you okay?"

"You should probably be asking Nick that."

"Well, I'm not. I'm asking you."

She gives me a curious look—all eyebrows. I can't entirely decipher it. I feel my cheeks and my chest and the back of my neck go warm.

"Well," she says finally, cupping her chin. "I'm officially the worst."

"No you're not."

"I've made everything awkward."

"Trust me—the boys make themselves awkward."

She laughs. "It's not just the boys, though."

My heart pounds when she says that. I don't even know why. But I have this urge to hoist myself onto the ledge, into the tiny space beside her. I'd sit in the sink if I had to. I want to look into the mirror and see our reflections, side by side.

But I'm frozen in place. "I don't like this."

"Me neither." She tilts her head back and sighs. "Prom sucks."

"It sucks balls."

As soon as I say it, I think of Mom and her determination to have a suck-free prom night. But I think it must have been different for her. Because maybe she was the only pregnant girl at her prom, but at least she got to kiss whomever she wanted to kiss. If I kiss Abby Suso, I burn my friendships to the ground. If she kisses me back, we bring down the apocalypse.

So I just stand there and look at her until the edges of her lips tug upward. Which makes it even worse. Because every time Abby smiles at me, it feels like getting stabbed.

32

AS SOON WE'RE BACK IN the limo, Nick whips a flask out of some secret jacket pocket. I couldn't be less surprised.

He swigs it and passes it to Anna, and I just sit there, stiff-shouldered, thinking: here's why I don't do school dances. I know exactly how tonight will play out. Everyone will get sloppy drunk, and then they'll talk about how drunk they are, and then they'll beg me to drink, too. Because it's *proooom night.* Because I should *just try it, just a sip.* Drunk people are basically zombies. Once they're infected, they want to take you down with them. Seriously, even my friends are like that, and we're supposed to be the nerds. Fuck that.

"Leah?" Garrett nudges the flask toward me.

I pass it straight to Bram, who then passes it straight to

Simon, who passes it to Abby, and then Morgan, and I notice with a start that no one's actually drinking it. So maybe I'm wrong. Maybe this is just a Nick thing.

As soon as the flask returns to Nick, he tilts his head back and chugs it. Then he makes a huge scene out of smiling at everyone except Abby. Simon catches my eye and raises his eyebrows, and I shake my head slightly. I love Nick to pieces, but this is cringe central. And prom hasn't even started yet.

The sun's just starting to set as we pull into the Chattahoochee Nature Center, but people are already streaming across the parking lot in groups of two and three and ten. There's a whole line of limos parked at the curb, and it's just so Shady Creek. My side-eye is so intense, I should be walking sideways to compensate.

Of course, the first person I see is Martin Addison—in a powder blue tux, hair gelled like a helmet. He's walking next to Maddie, formerly of student council and currently known as the Nutcracker—ever since she punched David Silvera in the balls for beating her in the school election. I couldn't have picked a better date for Martin if I'd tried. I'm about to snark about it to Simon, but then I spot the pavilion—and my heart catches in my throat.

Okay, yes: prom is stupid.

But everything's lit with twinkle lights, and the hanging white curtains seem to glow against the sunset. There are giant rented speakers blasting a song I don't recognize, but it has the most perfect thudding bass, like a heartbeat. The effect is somehow otherworldly. It doesn't feel like this space could have anything to do with Creekwood High School, but Creekwood people are everywhere—on the paths, by the aviary, seated at picnic tables on the grass.

There are stairs that lead straight down to the pavilion, but I veer off onto the side path instead. It's still strange, walking in a gown. It swishes around my feet with every step I take. But at least I don't trip. Thank God for combat boots.

"Hey." I feel a nudge.

Of course, it's Abby, sidling up to me so closely, our arms almost touch. I feel a two-punch in my gut: flutter and *yoink*. I could easily grab her hand. I could lace my fingers through hers, and no one would think anything of it, because straight girls hold hands all the time. Especially at dances. They hold hands and take cheek-kissing selfies and sit sideways on benches with their feet in each other's laps. I could honestly just—

"This is really cool," Abby says, jolting me back to earth. She's peering around, wide-eyed, taking everything in. All along the path, there are screened-in enclosures—habitats for birds of prey, mostly. She pauses in front of one. "Is this an owl? Is there an owl at our prom?"

And yup. It's an actual owl, staring unblinking and motionless as we cut down the path. As if this wasn't already the weirdest prom ever.

"Insert Harry Potter reference here," I say.

She grins. "That's exactly what I was thinking."

We end up reaching the end of the path just as Simon and Bram step off the staircase. "Fancy meeting you here," Abby says.

I realize with a start that they're holding hands. Like the real kind of hand-holding, not the ready-to-spring-apart-at-any-moment kind. And they both look so sweetly self-conscious about it, even though you can tell they're trying to be super casual.

"So, do we just walk in?" Bram asks.

Abby shrugs. "I think so."

Already, there's a crowd of people milling around the dance floor, even though no one's really dancing yet. But there's an emcee working the crowd, pumping his fist up and bellowing, "ARE THERE ANY SENIORS IN THE HOUSE?"

"This is literally junior and senior prom," says Simon.

"I can't hear you. ARE THERE ANY SEEEEEEEEEEE-NIORS IN THA HOUUUUSE?"

"Does he realize he's white?" Abby asks.

But everyone screams and howls in response, and it's completely surreal. Under the pavilion, the lights are dim and tinted orange in a way that makes people's skin seem to glow. I catch a glimpse of white in my periphery, which turns out to be Taylor in a full-on glide. Evidently, she's decided to wear Kate Middleton's wedding dress to prom.

"Is she . . . ?" Abby asks.

"Yup."

"Wow."

We exchange grins.

"Taylor, don't ever change," I say.

Then Garrett appears at my side. "There you are! I've been looking for you, Burke."

Right. My date.

"Want to dance? I'm ready to dance."

"Right now?"

"Yes, right now." He takes my hand. "Come on, I love this song."

"Um. Really?" The deejay's playing some wordless techno song that sounds exactly like robots having sex.

"I mean, the lyrics are genius."

I peek at his face, and all at once, I realize: he's nervous. I don't know if that's really clicked for me until now. But he's smiling too widely and scratching the back of his neck, and a part of me just wants to hug the poor kid. Or hand him a beer. He just needs to relax.

I let him take my hand and tug me to the dance floor, right up front, near the emcee. "YO YO YO. ARE THERE ANY SENIORS IN THA HOUUUUUUUUUUSE?" Suddenly, there's a microphone in my face.

"Yes," I say flatly.

"Say it louder for my peeps in the back! ONE MORE TIME. ARE THERE ANY SENIORS IN THE HOUSE?!"

"Yes, we've established that there are seniors in the house," I say into the mic. Out of the corner of my eye, I catch Abby giggling.

"Come on. We're dancing." Garrett tugs me closer, his hands finding my waist.

"Are we really slow dancing to this random techno song?"

"Yes."

I shake my head and roll my eyes a little, but my hands settle onto his shoulders. And then we sway. There's barely anyone dancing—people are mostly just hovering around the dance floor—and it's hard to shake the feeling that everyone's watching me. I think self-consciousness is in my bones.

But then the song changes to Nicki Minaj, which seems to flip the switch. People storm the dance floor. I disentangle from Garrett and end up pressed up between Simon and Bram. And—okay—other than the musicals, I don't think I've ever seen Simon dance. But he's pure Muppet. He's basically bobbing up and down and shuffling his feet—and as stiff as he is, Bram's even worse. I grin up at both of them, and Simon takes my hands and twirls me. I feel almost breathless.

I guess all the teen movies were right: prom is slightly, *slightly* magical. There's just something about being crammed onto a dance floor with all your friends, surrounded by twinkle lights and dressed up like movie stars. Simon grins down at me and bumps his hip against mine. Then he grabs Abby's hands and they spin together in circles. Bram and Garrett are attempting some kind of shoulder swerve, and I'm pretty sure Martin Addison's reeling in the Nutcracker like a fish.

"ARE THERE ANY SEEEEEEEEEEEEEEEEEENIORS IN THE HOWOWOWOWOWSE?"

"YES, WE'RE SENIORS!" Abby yells. Then she catches me looking and shoots me a bashful grin.

The song changes again, the beat thumping softly, and everyone crowds in a little closer. Simon grabs my hand and lifts it, and suddenly, I'm stretching both arms skyward, smiling with my eyes closed. And it's exactly the feeling I get when I'm drumming. I'm caught up in the music—just totally lost to it. I can't remember the last time I've felt so weightless.

Until it smacks me like a cannonball: all of this is ending.

Holy shit. We're graduating. We have—what—five weeks of normalcy, and then the whole world resets. Intellectually, I've always known things would be different after graduation. That's just life.

But I guess it's finally hitting me—the magnitude of this change. I don't think I've looked it in the eye until this moment.

"I miss you," I say to Simon.

"WHAT?"

"I MISS YOU!"

I mean. Fuck everything. I already miss them. I miss Simon and Bram and Nick and Garrett and Nora and Anna and even Morgan. It already hurts.

"GOD, I MISS YOU, TOO," Simon yells, smiling—and

just when I think he doesn't get it at all, he flings his arms around me tightly and leans close to my ear. "You know I'm going to lose my mind without you, right?"

"Me too," I say softly, leaning into his chest.

33

BUT HERE'S THE WEIRD THING: I've barely seen Nick all night. And normally, I wouldn't think twice about it, but this isn't regular Nick—this is Sad Drunk Nick. So, I have to assume he's either vomiting in the butterfly house or passed out next to the vulture enclosure.

Or he's fine. He's probably fine. Even though he's not replying to any of my texts. Maybe he's fine, and he just hates me. In his position, I'd hate me. Maybe Abby said something to him. Or maybe my stupid Abby crush is written plainly all over my face.

I try to shake the thought from my mind, but I can't help peering around the edges of the space. For the record, finding a particular boy in a dimly lit, crowded pavilion is pretty near fucking impossible. The kid is wearing a black tuxedo in a sea of black tuxedos. For a moment, Martin Addison's wardrobe choices make a twisted kind of sense.

Except then Nick whirls in out of nowhere, flushed and beaming. "Hey!" I start to say—but he cuts me off with a quick, tight hug and a wet smacking kiss on the cheek.

"Um. Are you—"

He pokes me in the nose. "Leah Burke, you're about to have your mind blown."

Okay, so now I'm slightly terrified.

Nick crosses the dance floor with actual swagger. This is something I've never before witnessed in my years of friendship with Nick Eisner. He reaches the deejay table and leans forward to say something, and then the deejay nods, and they bump fists.

"Are you watching this?" Simon asks, leaning in close.

"You mean Nick?"

Simon nods. "What do you think he's scheming?"

"No idea." But as soon as I say it, I catch a glimpse of Abby, her blue skirt flaring as she spins around with Nora. "Unless . . ."

Simon follows my gaze. "Oh God. Do you think he's planning some big gesture to win her back?"

"Maybe. I don't know." I press my lips together. "Or it could be a revenge thing."

"Like Nick taking revenge on Abby?" Simon laughs incredulously.

"Maybe something to embarrass her."

Simon shakes his head. "Nick wouldn't do that."

"I don't know. He's acting really weird."

"Yeah, but this is *Nick*," Simon insists, though I catch a flicker of uncertainty in his eyes. "He wouldn't."

For a moment, we just look at each other.

"I think we should talk to him," I say finally.

"Yeah. Okay." Simon nods. "Let's just . . . see what he's thinking."

Simon grabs my hand, and we weave through the crowd on the dance floor. Nick is in a crowd of soccer guys at the very edge of the pavilion, his arms flung around Garrett's and Bram's shoulders. Which is reassuring, I think. If Bram's involved—even if Garrett's involved—there's no way Nick is planning anything cruel. I mean, unless Bram and Garrett don't know about the plan.

God, how do I even word this? *Hey, Nick. I think you're amazing and I totally adore you, and I just wanted to quickly confirm that you're not a giant living, breathing human phallus.*

Simon squeezes my hand and tugs me forward, inhaling sharply. "Hey, guys," he says in his patented I'm-Simon-Spier-and-I'm-so-casual-I'm-hardly-even-squeaking voice. "Uh, Nick, can we talk to you for a sec?"

"Yeah, what's up?" Nick smiles expectantly. But when I look over his shoulder, I see a dozen other soccer guys, also smiling expectantly.

"In private," I add.

"Uh-oh, Eisner." A random soccer bro ruffles Nick's hair. "She looks pissed."

I roll my eyes—but Nick extracts himself from the guys and follows Simon and me onto the porch. I feel instantly calmer—even though the porch is attached to the pavilion, and the music's still loud, and there are still people everywhere. But it's nice that the porch is totally uncovered, except for a few strings of twinkle lights. There's a railing all around it, and beyond that, a clear, tree-lined lake. I hang my arms over the railing's edge and take a deep breath.

"Nick, what's going on?"

"What do you mean?" He grins.

"You're acting weird."

"Why did you talk to the deejay?" asks Simon.

"Aha." Nick's smile widens. "All will be revealed."

Simon glances at me nervously.

I look Nick dead on. "Just tell me this. Is it Abby-related?"

He opens his mouth to reply—but then the song switches, and his whole demeanor changes. He pats us each on the shoulder before jogging back to the soccer boys as Simon and I watch, agape.

"Fuck," Simon mutters, but it just sort of hangs there.

Because I'm staring at the boys as they assemble themselves into a triangle formation. Nick's at the front, flanked by Bram and Garrett, with the rest of the soccer boys fanning out behind them. Music blasts from the speakers.

CH-ch-ch-ch, ch-ch-CH-ch-ch ERM. CH-ch-ch-ch, ch-ch-CH-ch-ch ERM.

Moving in unison, they sway rhythmically from side to side, and then suddenly freeze. Then Nick thrusts his hips out, and the other guys follow—and then they all kick their legs out, and they're off.

Holy shit.

It's the choreographed prom moment, straight out of a teen movie.

Suddenly, we're surrounded by people, cheering and singing along to a song I've never heard before, about a girl being poison.

I lean toward Simon. "Is this . . . about Abby?"

"I mean, it's a real song . . . ," Simon starts to say, but he trails off, staring at Bram. I can't even blame him. There is so much gyration happening right before our eyes. I didn't even think boys knew about hips. I definitely didn't think Bram and Nick knew about them.

"ARE THERE ANY SENIORS IN THE HOUSE?" the emcee yells.

Nick falls to his knees, head thrust backward for the grand finale. I turn to gape at Simon—but he's disappeared, and all of a sudden, I find myself standing next to Abby. She smiles faintly.

"So, this is awkward," I murmur.

She nods. "Yup."

"I guess he's making a statement."

"Well, it's funny." She leans toward me. "They've been working on the choreography for months. I actually knew they were planning this."

"Are you serious? With that song choice?"

Abby laughs flatly. "Just a coincidence. They didn't know I was poison yet."

"You're not . . . ," I start to say, but my eyes drift back to the dance floor. "Oh shit."

It's the theater boys—Simon, Martin, Cal, and a few others—and they're doing what appears to be a country western line dance. To the poison song.

Abby shakes her head slowly. "Okay, that's definitely one of their dances from the play."

"Jesus Christ."

"And they're doing it to 'Poison.'"

"Yes. Yes they are." I murmur while Simon and Martin do-si-do in their tuxes. "I'm just."

"Yeah."

"I'm so confused."

Abby takes my hand, and leans in closer. "I think we're witnessing a dance battle," she whispers, threading her fingers through mine.

My heart slams in my chest. This can't actually be happening. I'm next to Abby, who's dressed like Cinderella, and we're literally just standing here holding hands. Watching a dance battle, like it's the most normal thing in the world. I think I've forgotten how to breathe.

"You okay?" she asks, peering at me.

I nod quickly.

She keeps peering. I rack my brain for something to say. Don't mention the hands. Don't mention the kiss. Don't mention Nick—

"Nick should be dancing with them. He's a theater boy now," I say.

Awesome. My brain actually hates me.

But Abby just grins. "Well, his character's dead in this song. Kind of."

"Oh, so it's a *fuck you, Nick* song."

"Basically, yeah."

But Nick's laughing so hard, he can't even stand up straight. He's literally leaning into Bram's shoulder, head buried in the folds of his jacket. Meanwhile, the theater guys have assembled into their final pose, complete with jazz hands.

Someone starts a slow clap, and Abby untangles our hands to join in. I feel a tiny punch of disappointment. My hand feels so useless now.

"That was amazing," Abby says as soon as Simon wanders back to us. "Ten out of ten, would recommend."

Simon beams. "Obviously, I had to defend your honor."

"Because I'm the poison girl."

"No way," he says. "I mean, kind of. But you're *not*."

Abby raises her eyebrows.

"Do you want to dance?" Simon blurts.

There's a slow song playing—I think it's Ed Sheeran. Simon tugs my hair, and then takes Abby's hand. She smiles at me over her shoulder as he leads her to the dance floor.

For a minute, I stand there, watching them. Simon's actually a decent slow dancer. Somehow, he knows to hold Abby's hand up, like grandparents do. I bet he practiced with his mom. It's funny how ten seconds ago, he was tiny Simon Spier in a wolf shirt—and suddenly, out of nowhere, he's this dapper guy in a tux. How did we get so old?

"Why, hello, Burke." I look up, and it's Garrett, hands clasped behind his back.

"Hey." I tear my eyes away from Abby and Simon. "So, who knew you were this amazing dancer?"

He smiles, just a little. "You thought I was amazing?"

"I mean, you weren't terrible."

"Oh my God. You loved it. What did you love most? Was it this move?" He thrusts his pelvis three times, in rapid succession.

"Definitely that one."

"Or was it this one?" He shoots his hands up, like he's holding on to monkey bars. Then he swivels his hips in circles.

"Yes. All of the above."

"Damn." He grins. "So that's what it takes to impress you, huh?"

I shrug and smile vaguely. God, I'm such a shitty person. I should shut this down. Right now. I'm just going to spit it out, really nicely, so we're all on the same page and no one gets their hopes up. I shut my eyes and take a deep breath, and then we both speak at once.

It comes out in a jumble. "You go first," I say quickly.

"Okay." Garrett inhales. "Do you want to dance?"

And . . . fuck.

I just stand there. "Sure," I say finally.

I mean. He's my date. We should dance. It's not even a question.

We walk hand in hand to the dance floor, and then Garrett pauses, facing me. "So, should we just . . ."

His hands fall to my waist, and I wrap mine around his shoulders. And we sway. He tugs me closer—so close that our chests are mashed together, which is actually pretty unnerving. I think I'm radiating awkwardness—like it's some sort of gaseous substance, rolling off me in waves.

And the thing that freaks me out most is that Garrett hasn't said a word. He's just looking at me with this sweetly dopey expression, and I feel like the biggest asshole on earth.

I am very much not in love with Garrett Laughlin. And he probably deserves to know that. But when I open my mouth, all that comes out is "What happens when they're seventy?"

"What?"

"In the song. He says he'll love this girl until they're seventy. But then what? He's just like, *peace, I'm out*?"

"Wow," Garrett says, laughing. "You are the actual least romantic person on earth."

Not true, I think. Case in point: at this very moment, it's taking every ounce of self-control not to stare wistfully at Abby.

Instead, I peer over Garrett's shoulder and gasp. "Are you kidding me?"

Garrett furrows his brow.

"Turn around sideways."

Because, holy shit. It's Nick. Dancing with Taylor Metternich. But not just dancing. Their hands are everywhere. Nick's fingers trail down the back of Taylor's Kate Middleton wedding bodice, *way* too close to her ass, and there isn't an inch of space between them anywhere.

Except their mouths. There's *just* about an inch there.

My eyes fall immediately to Abby, who's six feet away, watching this shitshow unfold. I mean, *of course* she's watching. Simon is, too. They're both frozen in place, eyebrows raised to the moon.

"He just kissed her. They're kissing," Garrett murmurs. "Daaaamn."

Holy mother of God. What's even happening right now? Nick is kissing a girl on the dance floor, right in front of Abby, and the girl is Taylor Metternich. And yes, if they have babies one day, those babies will have awesome singing voices, but in the meantime: WHAT?

I glance back at Abby, and this time, she's looking straight at me, her expression unreadable. I catch her gaze, and she shoots me this sad half smile.

God. She's so. I don't even know what.

I shouldn't stare.

And I *definitely* shouldn't gaze longingly. Like, holy shit, Leah. Cool your jets. This is not a fucking teen movie.

I turn away quickly, tuning back in to the soft-core porn channel that is Taylor and Nick. And wow. That is some sloppy kissing. Are all the chaperones high right now? Are they dead? Because I'm pretty sure I'm about to watch Nick get Taylor pregnant, right here on the dance floor.

Right in front of Nick's ex-girlfriend.

Except.

When my eyes flick back just a minute or two later, Simon's standing beneath the edge of the pavilion, alone. And Abby's gone.

34

I HEAD STRAIGHT FOR SIMON as soon as the song ends. By then, he's found a table with Bram, and they've both draped their tux jackets over their chairs.

"Did Abby leave?" I ask, settling in beside Bram.

Simon nods, leaning forward. "Yeah, right in the middle of the dance. She said she wanted to be alone."

"Really?"

"Okay, that's weird, right? I mean, it's weird for Abby?"

"Is she upset?"

"I don't know." Simon looks slightly distraught. "I guess so. I mean, I wouldn't blame her."

"God." I close my eyes. "Yeah."

Bram bites his lip and nods.

"I should have gone with her," Simon says, rubbing his forehead. "Ugh. Now she probably thinks she's kicked out of our squad. Like, we're going to replace her with Taylor."

"Okay, there's no way she thinks that," Bram says.

"Maybe I'll text her," I say, and I promptly start blushing. Way to be mega obvious, Leah. I might as well whip out my heart and set it on the table for the boys to examine.

But Simon just nods eagerly. "Yeah, that's a good idea."

And it is. It's a great idea, and I should totally text her. Nothing weird about that. I'm a friend. I'm checking in.

Hey, are you okay?

I stare at my phone for a moment, but there's nothing. No dots. She's not typing.

Nick's an asshole, I add.

"Did she write back?" Simon asks.

I shake my head slowly. God. I don't know why this is making me so antsy. She's probably not even looking at her phone. Or maybe she just wants some space, for once. I should leave her alone. And I shouldn't even care. Really, I shouldn't.

But—okay. I guess it kind of bothers me. Just the thought of her off crying somewhere over Nick. Like, I get it. Believe me. I know exactly how it feels to be out-of-your-mind in love with someone. And I know exactly how it feels to watch them kiss someone else.

My heart flips in my chest. There's this awful part of me

that thinks she deserves this. Just a little taste of what last year was like for me. But another part of me wants to punch Nick in the face.

And then, as if I've conjured him myself, Nick appears at our table. He's alone—Taylor seems to have disappeared. But he's not looking for Taylor.

"Abby's gone." He slides into the seat next to Simon. His lips are puffy, and his eyes are like glass. "Shit. I fucked up. I shouldn't have—"

"Made out with Taylor right in front of her?" I raise my eyebrows.

"Am I the biggest asshole?" He buries his head in his hands and groans. "She probably hates me. Fuck. I have to find her."

"I don't think you should do that."

"Do you know which way she went?" Nick stares past my shoulder, into the distance.

Simon frowns. "I'm not sure. It looked like she turned left."

"Toward the aviary?"

"Other left," says Simon.

"Okay." He nods resolutely. "I'm going to just . . ." He starts to stand.

"Nope. That's a really bad idea." I tug him back by the sleeve.

"I have to make sure she's okay."

"I guarantee she doesn't want to talk to you right now."

Nick presses his hands down on the table. "Well, someone needs to go check on her."

"Fine," I say quickly. The boys all turn to face me, and I feel my face burning. "I'll go check on her, okay?"

Then I push out my chair.

There are trails veering away from the pavilion in every direction, and for a moment, I stand, frozen. I have no clue where to begin. Simon said she went left, but *left* could mean the picnic tables, or back through the trees, or she could have circled back behind the aviary. I have to put myself in her brain. If I'd just watched my ex-boyfriend kiss Taylor Metternich, which path would I take?

Probably the one leading straight to the bathroom, so I could spend the rest of my life vomiting.

But okay.

I need to not overthink this.

I pick the path through the trees, and it's like stepping into a fairy tale. Girl in a gown walks into a forest. It's strange how secluded this feels, even with the pavilion directly behind me. The trees are so thick, they're practically a curtain, and the music sounds like it's beaming in from another galaxy.

A twig cracks beneath my shoe, and I shriek like it's a bone.

Then, out of nowhere. "Who's there?"

I freeze.

Abby's voice, slightly nervous. "Hello?"

How nice: my body's decided to mutiny. My feet are like barbells, my voice is nonexistent, and my lungs are totally checked out. But my heart's beating like a hummingbird. I just stand there, staring into the foliage.

"Okay, I know someone's there."

"Abby?" I manage.

"Oh, thank God."

"Why can't I see you?" I'm peering all around.

"I'm behind you."

I whirl around, and now I don't know how I missed it: a wooden observation deck, up a short ramp, overlooking the lake. There's a bench in the middle, and Abby's sitting on it sideways with her legs tucked up. She waves when she catches my eye. I head up the ramp to meet her.

"Way to scare the crap out of me," she says, scooting down the bench to make room. But I walk straight to the railing and lean against that instead, my back to the lake.

I peer down at her face. "What are you doing here?"

"I don't know."

"You don't know?" I picture her on the ledge in the American Girl store bathroom. I can't believe that was tonight. It feels like centuries have passed. "You keep running away."

"You keep finding me."

For a moment, I'm speechless.

"Did you get my texts?" I ask finally.

"You texted me?"

"I was worried."

She pulls her phone out of her clutch and taps into her messages. Then she glances back up at me. "I mean, yeah, Nick's an asshole." She pauses. "But Nick isn't the problem."

My heart flips. "What's the problem?"

"I swear to God, Leah." She shakes her head, smiling faintly. "And you think I'm the dense one."

"What's that supposed to mean?"

She just stares at me with an expression I can't begin to decipher. Then she looks away, tapping back into her phone.

I feel weird watching her type, so I turn to face the lake, resting my arms on the railing. It's a quiet spot, with trees overhanging so thickly, you can only see a tiny pool of inky black water. But the effect makes it look like a wild, untamed lagoon. Distantly, in the pavilion, the song changes tempo. Something different but familiar. I shut my eyes and try to place it.

"Check your Tumblr," Abby says suddenly.

My eyes flutter open. "What?"

"Just check it." Then she tucks her face into the crook of her elbow.

I tap into my phone, staring into the brightness of my screen. My app is still logged into my art page, and I can see right away that I have a new ask. I don't know how Abby knew that. Unless—

I tap into the message, feeling like the ground just tilted. I have to read it three times before the words sink in.

Commission request: two girls kissing on prom night.

The whole world seems to freeze, and my lungs empty like a balloon. *Two girls kissing. On prom night.* I look at Abby, but her face is still buried.

"Is this . . ." My voice shakes. "Are you joking?"

She lifts her head to peek up at me. "Why would you even think that?"

"Because. I don't know."

"Leah, I'm just. I've been losing my mind." Her whole body is tense and still, skirt trailing to the floor of the platform. And I swear, I've stopped breathing. Abby Suso wants to kiss me. At prom. Right now. My whole body feels electric: chest and stomach and everywhere below. It feels like having to pee, except it's not actually pee. It's lightning.

She laughs nervously. "Please say something."

My hands fall to my sides. "I mean, obviously." I swallow. "Obviously, I like you."

Her face falls. "But."

"It's just the timing," I say.

"I know."

"Like, you don't even." I shut my eyes. "I just. I *really* like you."

"Me too. God. I think I'm . . ."

"Me too."

We just stare at each other. My heart is pounding out of my chest.

"I mean, the good news is that we'll be at the same school," I say finally.

"We'll be roommates." She sniffs, and then smiles.

"Yeah. That's probably not a good idea."

"I don't care." She stands, suddenly, brushing her skirt down. Then she walks over to the railing beside me, hanging her arms over the side.

I tilt my head toward her. "I just think we should let some time pass."

She sucks in a breath. "Okay."

"I'm sorry."

"I mean, you're right. You're very practical, Leah."

"I know." I swallow. "This will be good, though. Nick will have moved on—"

"Wait, are you talking about Taylor Metternich's face barnacle?" Abby asks. "Because I'm pretty sure *that* Nick has moved on."

I smile sadly. "See, I don't think he has. Not even close."

I turn to look at her, but she's staring out at the lake.

I keep talking. "It's just that everything's a mess, you know? With prom and graduation—and you're right, we don't want drama. Nick would be so—"

"I know," Abby says quickly. "Yeah. Nick would lose it. He's already losing it. And Garrett too, probably."

"God." *Garrett.* "Yeah."

"It just sucks." She sighs. "I mean, I get it. I totally get it. And I shouldn't have even—it's not." She covers her face. "I don't know. I'm an idiot."

"No you're not."

She laughs flatly. "Yeah, but I am. This is so—just. I mean, I screwed this up a long time ago. We could have been—" But she cuts herself off.

For a moment, we're silent. I feel my eyes start to prickle.

"We could have been what?" I ask finally.

"We could have been like Simon and Bram," she says, her voice quivering faintly. "I was so—like, this whole time, this could have been us, you know? Being the cutest girlfriends and kissing and grossing everyone out with how in love we are."

And there it is: that runaway tear. I wipe it away quickly, but it regenerates. I hate crying. I hate it more than anything in the world.

Abby sniffs. "We need a Time-Turner."

I laugh, and it sounds like a hiccup. "God. Are you like the biggest Potterhead ever now?"

"Not really," she says, smiling tearfully. Then she sighs. "I'm literally just trying to impress a girl."

"Oh." My heart thumps.

"So, yeah. This sucks."

"Yeah."

"And obviously I don't want to hurt anyone."

"Me neither. I mean, we just can't. We can't do this to Nick."

"I know." Her voice cracks. "I *know*."

It actually hurts to look at her. "Abby, I'm so—"

"Just don't. Okay? It's fine. We're fine." And even though her eyes are wet, her smile lights up her face. "This is totally my fault, and I get that, and just . . ." She turns around, leaning her back against the railing. "I don't know, Leah. Maybe you should get back to your date."

"Abby."

"It's fine! We're good. I just need a minute." She presses the corners of her eyes. "I'll be right behind you, I promise."

I nod quickly. And holy fuck. I am dangerously close to sobbing. I can't even form words. I just cut down the ramp and flee back down the path, without a backward glance.

Of course, I'm back at the pavilion approximately ten seconds later, but I'm nowhere near ready. I can barely breathe, much less speak. It's weird, but all I want to do is lie on the ground. Sleep in the dirt. I don't even care about the dress.

It just sucks, and it sucks harder because it was so painfully close to being wonderful. Imagine if the kiss in Athens wasn't an awkward mistake. If I were a little less stubborn. If Abby were a little less clueless. What if she'd never dated Nick at all?

What if we were out and happy and as famously in love as every other obnoxious Creekwood couple?

Maybe Abby would have talked me into trying out for the play. Maybe I'd have spent a little less time watching the action from the back of the auditorium. Maybe I'd have spent more time making out in the back of the auditorium.

Instead, I'm standing here watching prom happen from twenty feet away.

My eyes land on Simon and Bram at the edge of the pavilion, in their jacketless tuxedos, leaning against the railing. They're not dancing—just standing—and I can only see their backs. Simon's arm is hooked around Bram's waist, their bodies so close they practically blur together. And Bram's hand sweeps smoothly over the nape of Simon's neck.

Sometimes watching them makes my throat hurt.

The song changes again, and I instantly recognize the opening bars. Stevie Wonder. Mom's song. Awesome, because what I really need right now is to feel Mom peering over my shoulder.

Except. I don't know. It kind of feels like a sign. Like a whispered secret message: *don't overthink this.*

Stop obsessing. Don't overanalyze. And don't cry.

But it's hopeless.

My hands fly to my face, but these are full-body sobs. I can barely catch my breath. Because here are Simon and Bram, with their arms around each other, and they're so fucking brave in ways I'll never understand. And now we're about to graduate, and all I have to show for it is the saddest crush of the century.

And *God*. It would be so sensible to wait until college. To let Nick bounce back to normal. To let Garrett down gently. Let the dust settle. Let our friends know. Dip our toes in first, and let everything evolve slowly. We could ease into dating in a couple of months, if we wanted.

But I don't want to wait for months. And I don't feel like being sensible.

Don't overthink this.

Suddenly, I'm running, almost tripping over my dress, hair falling in my face. And it's reckless and stupid, and probably pointless, too—because I doubt she's even where I left her. I bet she disappeared entirely. I bet she—

"Leah?" Abby says.

And then I barrel straight into her.

"Oof."

"Wow." She grabs my shoulders to steady me. "Are you—" She stops short. "Leah, you're crying."

"No I'm not."

"So, you're going to stand here gushing tears, telling me you're not crying."

"Yes," I say. Then I take a deep breath. "No."

"Okay—"

"Because I'm not just going to stand here."

The whole world stops, and I can hardly hear the music. All I hear is my heartbeat. I cup my hands around her cheeks.

"I'm going to do this," I say softly.

And then I kiss her.

Really fast.

And now she's gaping at me, her eyes huge and startled.

My hands fall. "Oh God. You were—"

"No." She cuts me off. "Don't you dare freak out."

"I'm not."

"Good." She smiles, and then takes a deep breath. "Let's try this again."

When I nod, she pulls me closer, threading her fingers through my hair.

My heart thumps wildly. "My hair's a mess."

"Yup. And it's about to get worse." Her thumb grazes my ear. "So much worse."

And suddenly, her lips are on mine, and my hands are on her waist, and I'm kissing her back so fiercely, I forget how to breathe. I feel like a campfire, like I could burn for days. Because the thing about Abby is that she kisses like she dances. Like she's totally there. Like she's handing you her heart.

She pulls back, resting her forehead on mine. "So, this is happening," she says.

"I think so."

She exhales. "Wow."

"Is that a happy wow or a holy shit wow?"

"It's both. It's holy shit, I'm so happy." Then she kisses me again, and my eyes flutter shut. I feel everything at once: her thumb tracing my cheekbones, the quiet pressure of her lips. My knees are jelly. I don't even know how I'm standing. I slide my hands up over her shoulder blades and pull her even closer.

I am just. Holy fuck. I am kissing the girl.

"You're giggling," she says, lips still flush with mine.

"No way. I don't giggle."

I feel her smile. "That's such a lie."

"Maybe I only giggle around you."

"Oh, really?" She grins and draws back, hands falling to my shoulders. "God, Leah. Just look at you."

"Hot mess?"

"Beautiful," she says. "I hope you know that."

The way she's looking at me makes me lose my breath. I press my fingertips to my mouth. I swear, my lips have a pulse.

"What are you thinking about?" she asks.

"You." I don't even pause. God. I'm never this unfiltered. But I feel giddy and wild and twenty times braver than usual. I kiss her again softly. "It's like you give off light."

She shakes her head, smiling. "You are out of your mind."

"I seriously am." I feel breathless, almost loopy. I press my hand to my cheek.

And then suddenly, my eyes are drawn to Garrett's corsage on my wrist.

"Oh, hell no," Abby says, following my gaze. "Don't you start questioning things." She takes both my hands, clasping them between us.

"I'm not," I say quickly, but I feel my stomach lurching. I just kissed a person who isn't my prom date. I just—holy shit. I kissed Nick's ex-girlfriend.

"Leah," Abby says warningly.

"Okay, but—"

"Nope. Just. Kiss me, right now."

"Just right now? On command?"

"*Leah,*" she says again, rolling her eyes. Then she kisses me so hard that I practically unravel.

Time stops.

And something in me unlocks.

"Okay?" she says finally, her voice cracking slightly. "Stop thinking about Nick, stop thinking about Garrett, and *definitely* stop thinking about if it's a cliché to kiss on prom night."

I sniff. "It is a cliché."

"Whatever. Clichés rule."

I just look at her. I can't believe I'm allowed to do this. I can just stare at her face without it being creepy. I want to memorize every single inch of this Abby—the shine of her cheekbones and the brightness of her eyes. There are tears in her lashes, and her lips are sort of puffy. I don't know how this girl can go from laughing to crying to kissing and back, and still come out of it looking like an actual moonbeam.

I am done for. Totally, utterly, irreversibly done for.

"So, I think I'm going to like having a drummer girlfriend," she says.

"Girlfriend." My heart flips.

She looks suddenly nervous. "Or not."

"Just give me, like, a second to process this." I squeeze her hands. "Girlfriend, huh?"

"And roommate."

I laugh. "That's literally the worst idea ever."

"Like I care." She smiles.

"You are trouble, Suso."

"You have no idea."

I can't even form words, so I shut up and kiss her. I swear to God, I could make a career out of this. Professional kisser of Abby Suso. She tugs me closer, hands falling to my waist, and I still can't believe it. I'm wearing a prom dress on a dirt trail on a starlit April night, kissing the nerdiest fucking cheerleader in the whole entire world. This can't actually be real.

But then I hear it: the crunch of twigs beneath shoes, and the quietest gasp. Abby stiffens, and we quickly disentangle.

Someone's standing right behind me, watching. I slowly turn around, my stomach clenched with dread. I mean, what the fuck kind of day is this? What does the universe even have to say for itself? I forgot to buy a bra. Our car broke down. Our restaurant was bright pink. Martin Addison showed up in a powder blue tux, so now that's forever burned into my brain. Everything's a mess. Abby and I are the biggest hot mess of all. I don't even know what we were thinking, kissing so close to the pavilion. Literally any Creekwood asshole could have stumbled up the trail and found us. Anyone.

Except.

Maybe the universe doesn't hate me after all.

Because when I look up, there are only two people staring at Abby and me with their mouths hanging open.

Simon's hand flies to his face. "Wait," he says faintly. He opens his mouth like he's going to say more, but then he just snaps it shut. Bram doesn't say a word.

Abby laughs nervously. "Surprise."

Simon glances back and forth between us like he's waiting for the punch line.

"Well." Deep breath. "I guess you thought I was straight."

He tilts his head to one side, but I don't wait for him to respond.

"So, yeah. I'm not. Like *really* not. I am really, really bi."

"So am I," Abby chimes in.

"Holy crap. I'm just." Simon blinks. "Really?"

"Really."

"Wow. Oh my God. I have so many questions right now." He shakes his head slowly. "Does Nick know?"

"Nick will be fine." Bram smiles. "I am *so* happy for you guys."

"Oh, God, me too!" Simon smacks himself on the forehead. "But you knew that, right? Holy shit. Yeah. Nick is going to . . . I mean, whatever, right? I'm so fucking thrilled. Okay. Okay," he keeps saying, like a tiny broken robot. "Okay. Wow. How long have you been . . . ?"

"Bi?"

"No. I mean." He gestures vaguely between Abby and me. "How long has this been a thing?"

"Fifteen minutes," I say.

Abby grins. "Give or take two weeks."

"Or a year and a half."

"Just. Holy shit," says Simon.

Abby takes my hand and threads our fingers together.

"Like, you have no idea how happy this makes me. No idea. I just wanted you guys to be friends, even, but *this*." Simon stares at our hands, his eyes like saucers.

"That's right," Abby says. "We went above and beyond for you, Simon."

"So, you're welcome," I add.

"I'm shook," Simon says, and Bram pats him on the arm.

So now I'm walking down a tree-lined path, holding hands with Abby Suso.

Holding hands with my girlfriend. My girlfriend who is Abby Suso. My brain is totally obsessed with this fact. Like, I'm pretty sure my academic career is over, and God help me on the AP exams, because how are you supposed to think about calculus WHEN ABBY SUSO IS YOUR GIRLFRIEND?

Now we're practically at the pavilion, and my heart's in my throat.

Because inside the pavilion is my prom date. And my possibly racist friend. And Abby's ex-boyfriend. And the girl he's making out with. And probably a slew of casual homophobes.

This is not my perfect prom night, and it's not the happy ending I pictured. It's not an ending at all.

But it's mine.

This whole moment is mine. This electric-bright pavilion, with music so loud I can feel it. It's mine.

And maybe everything's a mess. Maybe everything's changing. I'm sure my face is a swollen splotchfest, and my boots are muddy, and my hair's completely undone. I don't even know if my voice works. But I keep following Simon and Bram back down the trail. I keep holding Abby's hand.

Until we're close enough to the pavilion that I can practically smell it. Corsages and sweat. This night. My prom.

And even though I'm looking in from the outside, I get closer with every step.

35

FROM: leahontheoffbeat@gmail.com

TO: simonirvinspier@gmail.com

DATE: Sep 21 at 1:34 AM

SUBJECT: Re: You were born!!!

Okay, I can't even tell you how much I love the fact that you sent me an actual birthday email. In Garamond. That's like peak Simon. If you ever change, I swear to God I'll kill you.

But the birthday was good! Abby's such a fucking nerd. She made me breakfast in bed, and by *breakfast*, I mean *cookies*, and by *made* I mean wore a *cargo jacket with cookie-sized pockets to the dining hall*. And, make no mistake, we live five minutes from a cookie delivery bakery (let that sink in. Cookie. Delivery. Bakery). But of course, some sacrifices are necessary, especially when a person and her girlfriend are saving every dollar for the April New York trip that is DEFINITELY HAPPENING. So tell your boy to clear out some Leah and Abby-sized floor space in his dorm room (like Bram would ever have clutter on his floor, God, what am I even saying?).

So I'm ignoring your first question, because I know you don't actually want to know about Intro to Sociology (it fucking rules, though, just fyi). I'm not ignoring your second question, but I've been sitting here staring at Abby's laptop screen for ten minutes trying to find the exact words to explain what it's like, and apparently those words don't exist, so. Yeah. It's good. Like, really, really good. She's just Abby. You know? Like today. It was one of those perfect sunny days, so we just spread a blanket out on the North Campus quad and she was reading and I was drawing and she kept pushing her sock against mine, like our feet were kissing and NOW I'M BLUSHING, ARE YOU HAPPY?

Because I am. Happy. Honestly. It's kind of weird.

And yes I did talk to Nick, but he did NOT mention the Taylor development! Are you serious? God, I think he's going to wake up one day and discover he's married to her. She'll make it happen. But good for her, I guess? I mean, good for . . . them? Not going to lie, I'm a little freaked out that I'm dating someone who was dating someone who is dating Taylor Metternich.

Yikes.

Okay, but Garrett and Morgan—WHAT? Bram needs to get us all the details (hi, Bram!). Are you still heading up to New York this weekend? You better text me lots of pictures. I love you a lot, Simon Spier. You know that, right?

Love,

Leah (your platonic soul mate forever and ever and ever) (and I don't care if I'm being corny right now, because corny is the new me, I'm turning into my mom, YEAH I SAID IT) (I love you)

Acknowledgments

This book wouldn't be a book without the combined powers of so many incredible people. Infinite thanks to:

Donna Bray, aka Leah's mom, aka rock star editor, aka I'm the luckiest author in the world.

Brooks Sherman, my fiercest advocate, and the best and most badass agent in the business.

My brilliant, passionate teams at HarperCollins, Janklow & Nesbit, the Bent Agency, Penguin UK, and my other incredible international publishers: Caroline Sun, Alessandra Balzer, Patty Rosati, Nellie Kurtzman, Viana Siniscalchi, Tiara Kittrell, Molly Motch, Stephanie Macy, Bess Braswell, Audrey Diestelkamp, Jane Lee, Tyler Breitfeller, Alison Donalty, David Curtis, Chris Bilheimer, Margot Wood, Bethany Reis, Ronnie Ambrose, Andrew Eliopulos, Kate Morgan Jackson, Suzanne

Murphy, Andrea Pappenheimer, Kerry Moynagh, Kathleen Faber, Suman Seewat, Maeve O'Regan, Kaiti Vincent, Cory Beatty, Molly Ker Hawn, Anthea Townsend, Ben Horslen, Vicky Photiou, Clare Kelly, Tina Gumnior, and so many more.

My *Simon* film team, who brought Creekwood High School to life: Greg Berlanti, Isaac Klausner, Wyck Godfrey, Marty Bowen, Elizabeth Gabler, Erin Siminoff, Fox 2000 Studios, Mary Pender, David Mortimer, Pouya Shahbazian, Chris McEwan, Tim Bourne, Elizabeth Berger, Isaac Aptaker, Aaron Osborne, John Guleserian, Harry Jierjian, Denise Chamian, Jimmy Gibbons, Nick Robinson, and the rest of the cast—especially my Leah, Katherine Langford. I'm so grateful to the hundreds of people in front of and behind the cameras who made miracles happen.

My friend and hero, Shannon Purser, who made all my audiobook dreams come true.

My earliest readers, who made this book a million times better: David Arnold, Nic Stone, Weezie Wood, Mason Deaver, Cody Roecker, Camryn Garrett, Ava Mortier, Alex Davison, Kevin Savoie, Angie Thomas, Adam Silvera, and Matthew Eppard.

The librarians, booksellers, bloggers, publishing professionals, teachers, fanfiction writers, artists, Discord members, group chatters, and readers who make this job so off-the-charts wonderful.

To the friends who carried me through the hard stuff:

Adam Silvera, David Arnold, Angie Thomas, Aisha Saeed, Jasmine Warga, Nic Stone, Laura Silverman, Julie Murphy, Kimberly Ito, Raquel Dominguez, Jaime Hensel, Diane Blumenfeld, Lauren Starks, Jaime Semensohn, Amy Austin, Emily Carpenter, Manda Turetsky (who gave Garrett the idea for his epic prom dinner), Chris Negron, George Weinstein, Jen Gaska, Emily Townsend, Nicola Yoon, Heidi Schulz, Lianne Oelke, Stefani Sloma, Mark O'Brien, Shelumiel Delos Santos, Kevin Savoie, Matthew Eppard, Katy-Lynn Cook, Brandie Rendon, Kate Goud, Anderson Rothwell, Tom-Erik Fure, Sarah Cannon, Jenn Dugan, Arvin Ahmadi, Mackenzi Lee, and a gazillion more.

To Caroline Goldstein, Sam Goldstein, Eileen Thomas, Jim and Candy Goldstein, Cameron Klein, William Cotton, Curt and Gini Albertalli, Jim Albertalli, Cyris and Lulu Albertalli, Gail McLaurin, Adele Thomas, and the rest of the Albertalli/Goldstein/Thomas/Berman/Overholts/Wechsler/Levine/Witchel crew.

To Brian, Owen, and Henry, my forever favorites.

And for you. Keep resisting.

Turn the page for a sneak peek at Becky Albertalli's collaboration with *New York Times* bestselling author Adam Silvera:

WHAT IF IT'S US

CHAPTER ONE

ARTHUR

Monday, July 9

I AM NOT A NEW YORKER, and I want to go home.

There are so many unspoken rules when you live here, like the way you're never supposed to stop in the middle of the sidewalk or stare dreamily up at tall buildings or pause to read graffiti. No giant folding maps, no fanny packs, no eye contact. No humming songs from *Dear Evan Hansen* in public. And you're definitely not supposed to take selfies at street corners, even if there's a hot dog stand and a whole line of yellow taxis in the background, which is eerily how you always pictured New York. You're allowed to silently appreciate it, but you have to be cool. From what I can tell, that's the whole point of New York: being cool.

I'm not cool.

Take this morning. I made the mistake of glancing up at the sky, just for a moment, and now I can't unstick my eyes. Looking up from this angle, it's like the world's tipping inward: dizzyingly tall buildings and a bright fireball sun.

It's beautiful. I'll give New York credit for that. It's beautiful and surreal, and absolutely nothing like Georgia. I tilt my phone to snap a picture. Not an Instagram Story, no filters. Nothing drawn-out.

One tiny, quick picture.

Instantaneous pedestrian rage: *Jesus. Come on. MOVE. Fucking tourists.* Literally, I take a two-second photograph, and now I'm obstruction personified. I'm responsible for every subway delay, every road closure, the very phenomenon of wind resistance.

Fucking tourists.

I'm not even a tourist. I somewhat live here, at least for the summer. It's not like I'm taking a joyful sightseeing stroll at noon on a Monday. I'm at work. I mean, I'm on a Starbucks run, but it counts.

And maybe I'm taking the long way. Maybe I need a few extra minutes away from Mom's office. Normally, being an intern is more boring than terrible, but today's uniquely shitty. You know that kind of day where the printer runs out of paper, and there's none in the supply room, so you try to steal some from the copier, but you can't get the drawer open, and then you push some wrong button and the copier starts beeping? And you're standing there thinking that whoever invented copy machines is *this* close to getting their ass kicked? By you? By a five-foot-six Jewish kid with ADHD and the rage of a tornado? That kind of day? Yeah.

And all I want to do is vent to Ethan and Jessie, but I still haven't figured out how to text while walking.

I step off the sidewalk, near the entrance to a post office—and wow. They don't make post offices like this in Milton, Georgia. It's got a white stone exterior with pillars and brass accents, and it's so painfully classy, I almost feel underdressed. And I'm wearing a tie.

I text the sunny street picture to Ethan and Jessie. Rough day at the office!

Jessie writes back immediately. I hate you and I want to be you.

Here's the thing: Jessie and Ethan have been my best friends since the dawn of time, and I've always been Real Arthur with them. Lonely Messy Arthur, as opposed to Upbeat Instagram Arthur. But for some reason, I need them to think my New York life is awesome. I just do. So I've been sending them Upbeat Instagram Arthur texts for weeks. I don't know if I'm really selling it, though.

Also I miss you, Jessie writes, throwing down a whole line

of kissy emojis. She's like my bubbe in a sixteen-year-old body. She'd text a lipstick smudge onto my cheek if she could. The weird thing is that we've never had one of those ooey-gooey friendships—at least not until prom night. Which happens to be the night I told Jessie and Ethan I'm gay.

I miss you guys, too, I admit.

COME HOME, ARTHUR.

Four more weeks. Not that I'm counting.

Ethan finally chimes in with the most ambiguous of all emojis: the grimace. Like, come on. The *grimace*? If post-prom Jessie texts like my bubbe, post-prom Ethan texts like a mime. He's actually not so bad in the group text most of the time, but one-on-one? I'll just say my phone stopped blowing up with his texts approximately five seconds after I came out. I'm not going to lie: it's the crappiest feeling ever. One of these days, I'm going to call him out, and it's going to be soon. Maybe even today. Maybe—

But then the post office door swings open, revealing—no joke—a pair of identical twin men in matching rompers. With handlebar mustaches. Ethan would *love* this. Which pisses me off. This happens constantly with Ethan. A minute ago, I was ready to friend-dump his emojily ambiguous ass. Now I just want to hear him laugh. A full emotional one-eighty in a span of sixty seconds.

The twins amble past me, and I see they both have man buns. Of course they have man buns. New York must be its own planet, I swear, because no one even blinks.

Except.

There's a boy walking toward the entrance, holding a cardboard box, and he literally stops in his tracks when the twins walk by. He looks so confused, I laugh out loud.

And then he catches my eye.

And then he smiles.

And holy shit.

I mean it. Holy mother of shit. Cutest boy ever. Maybe it's the hair or the freckles or the pinkness of his cheeks. And I say this as someone who's never noticed another person's cheeks in my life. But his cheeks are worth noticing. Everything about him is worth noticing. Perfectly rumpled light brown hair. Fitted jeans, scuffed shoes, gray shirt—with the words *Dream and Bean Coffee* barely visible above the box he's holding. He's taller than me—which, okay, most guys are.

He's still looking at me.

But twenty points to Gryffindor, because I manage to smile up at him. "Do you think they parked their tandem bicycle at the mustache-wax parlor?"

His startled laugh is so cute, it makes me light-headed. "Definitely the mustache-wax parlor slash art gallery slash microbrewery," he says.

For a minute, we grin at each other without speaking.

"Um, are you going in?" he asks finally.

I glance up at the door. "Yeah."

And I do it. I follow him into the post office. It's not even a decision. Or if it is, my body's already decided. There's something about him. It's this tug in my chest. It's this feeling like I *have* to know him, like it's inevitable.

Okay, I'm about to admit something, and you're probably going to cringe. You're probably already cringing, but whatever. Hear me out.

I believe in love at first sight. Fate, the universe, all of it. But not how you're thinking. I don't mean it in the *our souls were split and you're my other half forever and ever* sort of way. I just think you're meant to meet some people. I think the universe nudges them into your path.

Even on random Monday afternoons in July. Even at the post office.

But let's be real—this is no normal post office. It's big enough to be a ballroom, with gleaming floors and rows of numbered PO boxes and actual sculptures, like a museum. Box Boy walks over to a short counter near the entrance, props the package beside him, and starts filling out a mailing label.

So I swipe a Priority Mail envelope from a nearby rack and drift toward his counter. Super casual. This doesn't have to be weird. I just need to find the perfect words to keep this conversation going. To be honest, I'm normally really good at talking to strangers. I don't know if it's a Georgia thing or only an Arthur thing, but if there's an elderly man in a grocery store, I'm there price-checking prune juices for him. If there's a pregnant lady on an airplane, she's named her unborn kid after me by the time the plane lands. It's the one thing I have going for me.

Or I did, until today. I don't even think I can form sounds. It's like my throat's caving in on itself. But I have to channel my inner New Yorker—cool and nonchalant. I shoot him a tentative grin. Deep breath. "That's a big package."

And . . . shit.

The words tumble out. "I don't mean *package*. Just. Your box. Is big." I hold my hands apart to demonstrate. Because apparently that's the way to prove it's not an innuendo. By spreading my hands out dick-measuringly.

Box Boy furrows his brow.

"Sorry. I don't . . . I swear I don't usually comment on the size of other guys' boxes."

He meets my eyes and smiles, just a little. "Nice tie," he says.

I look down at it, blushing. Of course I couldn't have worn a normal tie today. Of course I'm wearing one from the Dad collection. Navy blue, printed with hundreds of tiny hot dogs.

"At least it's not a romper?" I say.

"Good point." He smiles again—so of course I notice his lips. Which are shaped exactly like Emma Watson's lips. *Emma Watson's lips.* Right there on his face.

"So you're not from here," Box Boy says.

I look up at him, startled. "How did you know?"

"Well, you keep talking to me." Then he blushes. "That

came out wrong. I just mean it's usually only tourists who strike up conversations."

"Oh."

"I don't mind, though," he says.

"I'm not a tourist."

"You're not?"

"Okay, I'm not *technically* from here, but I live here now. For the summer. I'm from Milton, Georgia."

"Milton, Georgia." He smiles.

I feel inexplicably frantic. Like, my limbs are weird and loose, and my head's full of cotton. I'm probably electric bright red now. I don't even want to know. I just need to keep talking. "I know, right? *Milton.* It sounds like a Jewish great-uncle."

"I wasn't—"

"I actually do have a Jewish great-uncle Milton. That's whose apartment we're staying in."

"Who's we?"

"You mean who do I live with in my great-uncle Milton's apartment?"

He nods, and I just look at him. Like, who does he think I live with? My boyfriend? My twenty-eight-year-old smoldering-hot boyfriend who has big gaping holes in his earlobes and maybe a tongue piercing and a tattoo of my name on his pec? On *both* pecs?

"With my parents," I say quickly. "My mom's a lawyer, and her firm has an office here, so she came up at the end of April for this case she's working on, and I totally would have come up then, but my mom was like, *Nice try, Arthur, you have a month of school left*. But it ended up being for the best, because I guess I thought New York was going to be one thing, and it's really another thing, and now I'm kind of stuck here, and I miss my friends, and I miss my car, and I miss Waffle House."

"In that order?"

"Well, mostly the car." I grin. "We left it at my bubbe's house in New Haven. She lives right by Yale, which is hopefully, *hopefully* my future school. Fingers crossed." It's like I can't stop talking. "I guess you probably don't need my life story."

"I don't mind." Box Boy pauses, balancing the box on his hip. "Want to get on line?"

I nod, falling into step behind him. He shifts sideways to face me, but the box looms between us. He hasn't stuck the shipping label on yet. It's sitting on top of the package. I try to sneak a peek at the address, but his handwriting sucks, and I can't read upside down.

He catches me looking. "Are you really nosy or something?" He's watching me through narrowed eyes.

"Oh." I swallow. "Kind of. Yeah."

That makes him smile. "It's not that interesting. It's left-overs from a breakup."

"Leftovers?"

"Books, gifts, Harry Potter wand. Everything I don't want to look at anymore."

"You don't want to look at a Harry Potter wand?"

"Not when it's from my ex-boyfriend."

Ex-boyfriend.

Which means Box Boy dates guys.

And okay. Wow. This doesn't happen to me. It just doesn't. But maybe the universe works differently in New York.

Box Boy dates guys.

I'M A GUY.

"That's really cool," I say. Perfectly casual. But then he looks at me funny, and my hand flies to my mouth. "Not cool. God. No. Breakups aren't cool. I'm just—I'm so sorry for your loss."

"He's not dead."

"Oh, right. Yeah. I'm gonna . . ." I exhale, hand resting for a moment on the retractable line barrier.

Box Boy smiles tightly. "Right. So you're one of those guys who gets weird around gay dudes."

"What?" I yelp. "No. Not at all."

"Yeah." He rolls his eyes, glancing over my shoulder.

"I'm not," I say quickly. "Listen. I'm gay."

And the whole world stops. My tongue feels thick and heavy.

I guess I don't say those words out loud all that often. *I'm gay.* My parents know, Ethan and Jessie know, and I kind of randomly told the summer associates at Mom's firm. But I'm not a person who goes around announcing it at the post office.

Except apparently, I kind of am.

"Are you for real?" Box Boy asks. "Or are you just being an asshole?"

"I'm for real." It comes out breathless. It's weird—now I want to prove it. I want some gay ID card to whip out like a cop badge. Or I could demonstrate in other ways. God. I would happily demonstrate.

Box Boy smiles, his shoulders relaxing. "Cool."

And holy shit. This is actually happening. I can hardly catch my breath. It's like the universe willed this moment into existence.

A voice booms from behind the counter. "You on line or not?" I look up to see a woman with a lip ring raining down the stink-eye. No fucks given by this postal employee. "Yo, Freckles. Let's go."

Box Boy shoots me a halting glance before stepping up to the counter. Already, there's a line stretching out behind me. And okay—I'm not *eavesdropping* on Box Boy. Not exactly. It's more like my ears are drawn to his voice. His arms are crossed, shoulders tense.

"Twenty-six fifty for Priority," says Lip Ring.

"Twenty-six fifty? Like twenty-six dollars?"

"No. Like twenty-six fifty."

Box Boy shakes his head. "That's a lot."

"That's what we got. Take it or leave it."

For a moment, Box Boy just stands there. Then he takes the box back, hugging it to his chest. "Sorry."

"Next," says Lip Ring. She beckons to me, but I swerve out of line.

Box Boy blinks. "How is it twenty-six fifty to send a package?"

"I don't know. That's messed up."

"Guess that's the universe saying I should hold on to it."

The *universe.*

Holy shit.

He's a believer. He believes in the universe. And I don't want to jump to conclusions or anything, but Box Boy believing in the universe is definitely a sign from the universe.

"Okay." My heartbeat quickens. "But what if the universe is actually telling you to throw his stuff away?"

"That's not how it works."

"Oh really?"

"Think about it. Getting rid of the box is plan A, right? The universe isn't going to thwart plan A just so I'll go with another version of plan A. This is clearly the universe calling for plan B."

"And plan B is . . ."

"Accepting that the universe is an asshole—"

"The universe isn't an asshole!"

"It is. Trust me."

"How could you possibly know that?"

"I know the universe has some fucked-up plan for this box."

"But that's the thing!" I stare him down. "You don't actually know. You have no idea where the universe is going with this. Maybe the whole reason you're here is because the universe wanted you to meet me, so I could tell you to throw the box away."

He smiles. "You think the universe wanted us to meet?"

"What? No! I mean, I don't know. That's the point. We have no way of knowing."

"Well, I guess we'll see how it plays out." He peers at the shipping label for a moment and then rips it in half, wadding it and tossing it into the trash. At least he aims for the trash, but it lands on the floor. "Anyway," he says. "Um, are you—"

"Excuse me." A man's voice reverberates through an intercom. "Can I have your attention?"

I glance sidelong at Box Boy. "Is this—"

There's a sudden squeal of feedback and a rising piano intro.

And then a literal fucking marching band walks in.

A marching band.

People flood into the post office, carrying giant drums and flutes and tubas, blasting a somewhat off-key rendition of that Bruno Mars song "Marry You." And now dozens of people—old people, people I thought were on line to buy stamps—have launched into a choreographed dance number, with high kicks and hip thrusts and shimmying arms. Basically everyone who's not dancing is filming this, but I'm too stunned to even grab my phone. I mean, I don't want to read too much into things, but wow: I meet a cute boy, and five seconds later, I'm in the middle of a flash mob wedding proposal? Could this message from the universe be any clearer?

The crowd parts, and a tattooed guy rolls in on a skateboard, skidding to a stop in front of the service desk. He's holding a jewelry box, but instead of taking a knee, he plants his elbows on the counter and beams up at Lip Ring. "Kelsey. Babe. Will you marry me?"

Kelsey's black mascara tracks all the way down to her lip ring. "Yes!" She grabs his face for a tear-soaked kiss, and the crowd erupts into cheers.

It hits me deep in my chest. It's that New York feeling, like they talk about in musicals—that wide-open, top-volume, Technicolor joy. Here I've spent the whole summer moping around and missing Georgia, but it's like someone flipped a light switch inside of me.

I wonder if Box Boy feels it, too. I turn toward him, already smiling, and my hand's pressed to my heart—

But he's gone.

My hand falls limply. The boy is nowhere. His box is nowhere. I peer around, scanning every single face in the post office. Maybe he got pushed aside by the flash mob. Maybe he was part of the flash mob. Maybe he had some kind of urgent appointment—so urgent he couldn't stop to get my number. He couldn't even say good-bye.

I can't believe he didn't say good-bye.

I thought—I don't know, it's stupid, but I thought we had

some kind of moment. I mean, the universe basically scooped us up and delivered us to each other. That's what just happened, right? I don't even know how else you could interpret it.

Except he vanished. He's Cinderella at midnight. It's like he never even existed. And now I'll never know his name, or how my name sounds when he says it. I'll never get to show him that the universe isn't an asshole.

Gone. Totally gone. And the disappointment hits me so hard, I almost double over.

Until my eyes land on the trash can.

Okay. I'm not saying I'm going to dig through the trash. Obviously not. I'm a mess, but I'm not *that* messy.

But maybe Box Boy is right. Maybe the universe is calling for plan B.

Here's my question: if a piece of trash never makes it into a trash can, can you even call it trash? Because let's just imagine—and this is totally hypothetical—let's say there's a crumpled shipping label on the floor. Is that trash?

What if it's a glass slipper?